I0676866

Readers love
JAIME SAMMS

Off Stage: Beyond the Footlights

"This was such an amazing read…. I am now hooked on this group of men and the trials and tribulations that they are all going through."
—Gay Book Reviews

"I loved every book in this series and this one no less than the first two. It's been my genuine pleasure to read Lenny, Trevor and Kilmer's stories."
—Jessie G Books

Like Heaven On Earth

"You definitely don't want to miss out on this series as each one will leave you wanting more and leave you with a sense of joy and warmth."
—Diverse Reader

"This was a brilliantly written story that stole my heart."
—Two Chicks Obsessed

Like You've Never Been Hurt

"This is an intriguing story about passion, broken dreams, and the wonders of family and friendship."
—Three Books Over the Rainbow

"*Like You've Never Been Hurt* is a worthy second installment in a series that I feel gets stronger with each new story."
—The Novel Approach

By JAIME SAMMS

Better
Bound to Fall
Eugene and the Box of Nails
The Foster Family
My Rugby-playing Twink
New Linen
Not As Easy As It Looks
Patchwork Heaven
Paying the Piper
Permanent Ink
Renegade
Scars on His Heart
Stained Glass
Still Life
Sunshine in the Dragon's Heart
Wishing on a Blue Star Anthology

DANCE, LOVE, LIVE
Like No One is Watching
Like You've Never Been Hurt
Like Heaven on Earth
Dance, Love, Live Anthology

OFF STAGE
Off Stage: Right
Off Stage: In the Wings
Off Stage: Beyond the Footlights
Off Stage Anthology

WINGS OF FAITH
Angel Elegy
Angel Requiem

Published by DREAMSPINNER PRESS
www.dreamspinnerpress.com

Sunshine
in the
DRAGON'S
HEART

JAIME SAMMS

Published by

DREAMSPINNER PRESS

5032 Capital Circle SW, Suite 2, PMB# 279, Tallahassee, FL 32305-7886 USA
www.dreamspinnerpress.com

Sunshine in the Dragon's Heart
© 2018 Jaime Samms.

Cover Art
© 2018 Tiferet Design.
http://www.tiferetdesign.com/
Cover content is for illustrative purposes only and any person depicted on the cover is a model.

Trade Paperback ISBN: 978-1-64080-974-1
Digital ISBN: 978-1-64080-973-4
Library of Congress Control Number: 2018951848
Trade Paperback published December 2018
v. 1.0

Printed in the United States of America

This paper meets the requirements of
ANSI/NISO Z39.48-1992 (Permanence of Paper).

For every dragon lover out there who always knew there was one more way to see them besides fire-breathing monsters.

Acknowledgments

THANKS, MARY. Just thanks.

Thanks, Mr. Blackwell, for reading us *The Hobbit* in grade six. My mom freaked out, but that door you opened into the world of fantasy and magic helped to make my life what it is. You'll never know how much I appreciate that.

Thanks, Lynn, for giving me another chance to get this right.

And thanks, Gin, because this is a stronger book because you took the time to help me make it that way.

CHAPTER 1

THIS WAS all his.

More to the point, it was *only* his.

Sunny hopped out of his old Land Rover and surveyed his domain. He'd driven forty-five minutes to get here and appreciated that the spring thaw—and the resultant muddy mess—had dried to summer grasses. Once winter-bare branches now sprouted rustling leaves of early June, adding dancing shadows to the display. A grin spread slowly over his face. The front yard sloping gently away from the covered porch of the compact cottage would be ideal for his planned gardens. Behind that, various outbuildings waited under the eaves of towering pines.

Besides the city being almost an hour away, the nearest town, a small hamlet with a general store, an LCBO, and a mobile library, was a thirty-minute drive in the opposite direction. His nearest neighbour was ten minutes away. One hundred fifty-six acres all to himself. No one dropping by to borrow a cup of sugar. No media. No awkward questions about his parents or how he was feeling.

Isolated? Hell yes. Just the way he liked it.

He pulled the deed from his back pocket and unfolded it to take another look. Yep. There was his full name in all its hippie glory, right there, neatly typed on the line marked "Buyer:"

Sunshine Rainbow Barklay.

That had gotten him a skeptical look from the realtor, but his ID bore it out. He couldn't help what his free-spirited parents had thought was a good name. At least he'd fared better than his little sister, Moonpetal Daisyleaf.

As of today, Sunny had everything he wanted or needed: his small spread, his tiny home, and the dog—Fernforest, because his mother could never resist, could she?

"Shit." The familiar burn of anger and loss caught at his throat, stung his eyes, and he ground his teeth, blinked it away. After turning back to the Land Rover, he opened the passenger door and motioned to the dog. "Let's go, Ferny. Time to check out our new place."

The dog, a knee-high mutt with wiry tan-coloured hair and a skinny but deadly tail, yipped at him and, as was his way, tumbled out onto the grass.

"You're an idiot," Sunny chided, affection spilling into his voice. Ferny grinned at him, wagged his back half, and then his nose took over. He whipped his head around, gaze and nose trained on the bottom of the yard. When Sunny said his name again, Ferny's ears pricked distractedly, but then he was off.

"Hey!" Sunny hurried after him to a trail that led along a short, crooked fence struggling to hold back a raspberry bramble. The path jogged over an arched wooden bridge, then disappeared quickly under the canopy of poplar leaves, taking his curious dog with it.

"Ferny!"

Not even a yip in response.

"Dammit. *Asshole* dog!" Sunny hadn't brought the dog out here yet. If he took off into the woods with no previous introduction to the area, Sunny might never get him back. "Fernforest!"

He dug his hands into his hair, curls turning around his fingers and gripping them in their wild tangles. Why was today the day Ferny chose for a display of independence he'd never shown any inclination towards before?

"*Shit*head dog. Fernforest!" Sunny ignored the rickety creak of the bridge as he crossed it into the trees.

"BLAST." EMIKKU—HE was going to have to come up with a more human-sounding name—ducked behind a clump of foliage. He didn't have the energy to run, and if he didn't act fast, that dog was going to sniff out his hiding place.

Closing his eyes, he focused and managed to mask his scent as the dog plunged into the forest. The crackling of leaves and twigs gentled to snuffling as the animal discovered a chipmunk's den. Emikku let out a breath, soft as the summer breeze around him.

Just don't come any closer. Please.

The house had seemed like it would be perfect. For days he'd watched to make sure it was abandoned, and no one had come anywhere near. He hadn't heard any activity or smelled any hint of recent human presence. He'd been so sure, he'd almost blundered out into the clearing around it—and then the noisy, smelly metal crate had roared up.

The auto, he thought it was called—his research hadn't been terribly up-to-date—looked different from the spindly one he'd seen images of. When one of the panels on the side swung open and a man stepped out, well. Emikku had mixed emotions about that.

Now that he had a better view through the trees, he wished the man would turn his head to show his face hidden behind that thatch of curls. And like the wind and the wish were one and the same, a gust lifted the curls away.

"Oh!" He covered his mouth, the slip of sound causing his heart to race. He had to be careful. No one could know he was here. But oh! This was a pretty thing. Sun sank sweet, warm fingers into blond coils of hair and caressed high-boned cheeks it had already blessed with its touch many times over. Though his shoulders were broad, this human wasn't so much bigger than what Emikku was used to at home. His eyes, though. They glowed gold as he tilted his head and the sun slid through them from the side.

"Oh my." Emikku's grasp on his magic slipped for a bare instant when his heart skipped. This was probably not a good thing.

Careful to make no sound, he backed deeper into the shadows cast by the broad leaves overhead. The pretty human's lips curved down as he approached his dog. He said something Emikku would have had to draw on his magic again to hear, but masking his scent had been about as strenuous as he could manage.

The human gripped the collar around the dog's neck and led him back over the bridge to the clearing around the house. The dog kept glancing back, though, his interest fixed on the spot where Emikku crouched.

It was time to go.

CHAPTER 2

SUNNY WASN'T going to get any rest or peace of mind until he took Fernforest out, he could tell. The dog kept whining at the front door, letting out the occasional sharp, ear-ringing bark, then glaring at Sunny with reproach. He was glad now that Daisy had helped by hiring a moving company to do most of the work for him. His furniture was in place, right down to the bed made and the dishes and food in the cupboards and fridge.

Daisy had recommended her best friend's moving company—and probably overseen the work through Skype, knowing her. His baby sister was the big sister he never had. Now he was overjoyed he'd let her have her way because all he had left to move in were his personal trinkets and clothes, and his gardening tools. Still, every time Sunny tried to bring in another box, Ferny made a dash for the outside.

"Fine." Sunny kicked the door shut with one flip-flopped foot and made a face at his dog. "Fine. This is how it's going to be?" He rooted in the box he'd just brought inside and found the leash he hardly ever used. "You play by my rules, mutt." He snapped the leash to Ferny's collar, receiving another sullen glare for his efforts.

"Hey. Don't pout. You're lucky I'm doing this at all. I have human things to do, ingrate."

Fernforest licked his fingers, and Sunny smiled.

"I do love you. So first we take a look around on leash, and when I can trust you not to take off on me again, I'll let you off." With a flourish, he opened the door, and, true to the contrary beast he was, Fernforest sat at the threshold, politely waiting for Sunny to invite him out.

"Seriously?" The grin that stole over Sunny's face couldn't be helped. "You're an asshole. Come on." He gave a tiny wave of his hand, and Fernforest rose to trot out and stand by his side while he closed the door.

On the other side of the adorable arched bridge spanning the creek at the bottom of the yard, pleasant shade soon shrouded the trail. Fernforest led the way, nose to the ground, every inch of the fifteen-foot leash stretched out between them. Sunny wasn't worried. Bears lived in the area, but if there was one around, the particular stench they gave off would alert even Sunny long before they crossed paths.

Just a few minutes into the bush, tall grass and ferns that reached Sunny's chest overgrew their path. The dog wandered easily around their stems, casting this way and that for whatever had his attention. Sunny had to swim through the undergrowth, following the winding slash between the trees where no saplings had yet grown up.

Around them, the summer afternoon slept, but for the distinctive calls of a killdeer circling overhead.

"Weird." Killdeer didn't live in forests, and he'd been very young the last time he'd heard one in the region. But there was no mistaking that call. He stopped to look up, but the canopy, though broken, wasn't open enough to let him find the bird.

He held his breath, trying to discern from which direction the call had come. He couldn't see Fernforest anymore, only the thin tether of nylon that connected them, so maybe the dog had found a clearing and disturbed the bird. Nothing else in the bush around him stirred. The squirrels and chickadees, the crows and robins, all were quiet. A breeze stirred up the soft rustle of aspen leaves overhead, and Sunny took a few steps along the path, past the Balm-of-Gilead poplars and into the lighter, greener light of the aspens.

The sun was warm and the soft wind perfect. Goosebumps skidded down his back. A twig cracked in the silence, and he whipped his head around in the direction of the sound. "Ferny?"

Of course not, because the leash led off in a different direction. If the dog heard him, he ignored the call.

Slowly, Sunny wended through the ferns. He wasn't trying to be quiet. That was impossible. But he sniffed every few feet and prayed there were no cougars in the area. He didn't think so. Foxes, yes. Probably coyotes. Unlikely, there might be wolves, but it had been decades since anyone had reported such. The silence unnerved him, but the only logical conclusion was that his dog and his own presence had disturbed wildlife grown accustomed to not having humans around.

That was a good sign, because he'd come out here for precisely that reason. No humans. Not for miles. Just the way he liked it. He'd learned the hard way he was better off on his own.

Without warning, the stand of unusually tall ferns opened out into a clearing. Another creek, this one more boisterous than the lazy one near his house, laughed its way along the south side of the small meadow.

It flowed over the feet of some impressive cedar trees—tall for living this far north. The darkness under those trees differed from the pretty, sun-dappled shadow he'd emerged from. Under the cedars, it was moist, deep green, and old. In the corner of the clearing, a weeping willow trailed its delicate filigree leaves in the babbling water. Slanting rays of late-afternoon sun burnished the western edge of the clearing behind the willow to a golden glow.

"Oh wow."

Fernforest stood on the bank of the creek, peering intently across the water. The light dashed off the fur the breeze tossed up, giving the dog an ever-undulating gilded halo.

"Ferny!" he called, though not very loud, reluctant to disturb the magical quiet of the space.

The dog's tail waved in the air and one ear pricked in his direction.

"Ferny. Come here." Sunny took a step into the short grass of the clearing. The ground gave like a sponge under his feet, and he glanced down. Green-on-green moss peeked between the short stems of emerald grass. He could lie down on this ground and sink into it like a bed.

The thought made him shiver again, and he called a little louder to the dog.

This time Fernforest glanced at him, barked once, and turned back to the darker forest under the cedars. He cocked his head, then whined and yipped, jump-hopping along the bank, tail flipping more energetically side to side.

"Ferny! Come!" A sudden fear that despite the leash, and Sunny's death grip on it, the dog might jump the water and disappear into that strange wood turned Sunny's heart over. Not his dog too. "Ferny!" The command was sharp, and Fernforest looked at him, completely unruffled.

"Come," Sunny said, calmer now he had the dog's attention. "Come on."

With a last glance into the woods, the dog finally abandoned his vigil and dashed across the little lawn to Sunny's side.

For about the millionth time even though they'd been out here for less than an hour, Sunny revelled in knowing everywhere he walked was his. No one else could walk these trails. No other person had the right to invade this space, and the thought made him practically giddy. He was so done with the demands other people made on him and the emotional strain of putting on a good face for Daisy. Moving out here had been the exact right thing to do.

He ran a hand along the foliage next to the path and smiled to himself. Just Ferny, wilderness, and the magical, quiet isolation of his forest.

No one could take that from him.

"Come on, Ferny. Let's check out the stream." He wandered across the spongy ground to the foot of the willow, where he stopped to stare into the tumbling water. Colourful rounded stones carpeted the bottom of the stream. "Wow. That's awesome."

Kneeling, he peered through the glitter of water where the stones tumbled over one another. "It's like a mosaic." The stones clinked and clacked over one another, reminding him of how pictures formed and reformed in the clouds on breezy days just like this.

"Check it out." He pointed, and Fernforest tipped his head at the water, ears propped far forward, eyes bright, head cocking this way and that. Sunny could imagine he saw a crude moving picture of a dragon in flight. Pink and purple stones shimmered along the edges of its legs. A golden ball gamboled along below the dragon, and Sunny couldn't look away.

As he leaned closer, the brook's laughter got louder and the water more tumultuous. He reached for a stone, but Fernforest yelped and snatched at his arm.

"Hey! Ferny!"

Fernforest barked and backed away from the stream.

Confused at his odd behavior, Sunny turned to him. A splash of water hit Sunny in the face, and he whipped back around to the brook. It tumbled along, almost placid in its course over the bed of stones that lay shimmering and still at the bottom of the little stream.

"Maybe you're right." He crawled away from the bank. He didn't remember kneeling or getting so close to the edge where he'd been gripping the overhanging sod. "Let's cross and see what's past the cedars. I want to have a look at my land."

He made a motion for Fernforest to heel, and the dog came to him, sticking close to his side now as he followed the stream to a spot narrow enough to hop across. An eddy of water swirled below him as he jumped.

He decided it was a natural formation of the banks causing the flow, and not the stream laughing at him. Because *that* was crazy.

On the far side of the stream, he found a narrow path, probably a game trail, but he followed it under the cedar boughs. It wound along next to the little brook where the air felt cool and still, heavy compared to the open spaces. "What do you think, Ferny? How far you want to go?"

The dog seemed to be over his fright at the water's edge and was casting about, sniffing and snorting like normal. For a few minutes, Sunny watched him, content to be walking his land, enjoying the warm June day. The cedars by the creekside gave way to more common spruce, pine, and poplar. Birches edged the open spaces, saplings fighting back from some scourge that had reduced their numbers in the area over the past decade. He was pleased to see the bright splashes of their white bark among the other trees.

A bend in the path snaked around a rise of ground to their left. With a yip, Fernforest jolted forwards, yanking the leash from Sunny's inattentive grasp. In a heartbeat, the dog was out of sight around the corner.

"Ferny!" As Sunny rounded the curve, the woods opened up. Trees fell away to an opening of goldenrod, yarrow, and pearly everlasting. Moss covered the spaces between, and tufts of clubrush poked through the stony sections. At the far side of this new clearing, a small shack leaned slightly to one side, propped against the trunk of an impressive red pine.

"Huh." Sunny approached the hut, where Fernforest was sniffing around the partially open door. His tail was up, though it waved reservedly, and his ears pricked forward. He smelled something that had him intrigued but not frightened or overly excited. So not a rodent. He'd be frantically hunting that down. Nor was it anything threatening, or he'd be much less relaxed.

"What do you smell, Ferny?" Sunny eased the shack door open, expecting to find the ramshackle building empty. Not so, and he stopped in his tracks. His gut twisted, accompanied by a leap in his heart rate and a flash of anger.

Lying on a cot in the far corner, illuminated by a spray of sunshine through a grubby window, sprawled a man. Long wavy hair of the darkest auburn, almost black, but with enough red as to appear almost burgundy, spread over his shoulders and chest. Old, moth-eaten afghans covered him from hips to knees, but his chest and legs were utterly bare and smudged with dirt. The soft rumble of snores accompanied the steady rise and fall of his chest.

His face made Sunny's breath catch in his throat, a bubble of shocked awe.

Dark-as-night lashes made perfect, luxurious crescents on translucently pale skin. The pinkest of freckles dashed across his impossibly high cheekbones, nothing at all like the sprays of copper spots splashed over just about every scrap of Sunny's own skin. His lips, drawn down in the slightest of frowns, were plump and perfect, the colour of sun-kissed wild roses. He was lean but not skinny. Yet. It was clear he hadn't been eating well.

That detail curbed Sunny's initial irritation at finding an interloper on his land.

Defined muscles didn't quite fill out his skin as they should, and his ribs and collarbones stuck out more than looked healthy. One long, delicately boned arm dangled off the side of the cot, fingers trailing close to the floor.

The sunlight dawdled over him, making him seem fantastical and otherworldly. Sunny didn't think he'd ever seen anything or anyone as perfectly lovely as the man sleeping in a shoddy hut on the edge of his new acreage. He couldn't quite catch his breath. If he believed in such things, he might think an angel had landed in his forgotten little hunter's hut.

Which was a ridiculous thought to have, and he was aware he should be a lot angrier at the trespass. For some reason he couldn't put his finger on, the sleeping man, far from raising his ire, tugged at his sympathies instead.

"Hello?" Sunny whispered, reluctant in case any disturbance might cause the vision to fade.

Fernforest had no such compunction. He walked right over, sniffed the sleeping man's face, and proceeded to lick his fingers until he stirred.

THE DREAM, as patchy as it was, didn't hold the trepidation so many of his dreams had since Emikku had come here. It consisted mostly of the water sprites teasing and playing at fortune telling, splashing their mirth at the intended recipient of their message, who didn't have a clue what the sprites were showing.

To be fair, water sprites were notorious for being imprecise with their messages even before they infused them with riddles and vague images.

Sunshine played about the edges of the dream, bouncing this way and that, flashing off golden skin and shining teeth, curly hair, and the flying, feathery coat of… the dog. Something wet flicked over his finger. The water sprites teasing again, splashing at him because they knew how he dreaded getting wet.

He waved them off, muttering, then started when something chilled dug into his ribs.

"Ah!" He jumped, shuffling to the back of his little nest and covering the spot. "No!"

He blinked into dusty sunlight.

Next to his cot, the dog watched him, head cocked.

"What are you doing here?" Emikku asked, staring back.

The dog's tail whipped from side to side. His ears perked up and forward. He lolled his tongue out and *smiled*.

"I think, more to the point, what are *you* doing here?"

"Oh!" He pressed his back against the wall. There was no place else to go. Belatedly he realised the blankets he'd been using had slipped to the floor and he was crouched, naked, staring at the pretty blond man with the halo of curls and shards of sun in his eyes. "You," he whispered.

"Me," he agreed, expression wary. "Sunny. Who are you? Where are your clothes?" He glanced around the hut, but it was obviously empty but for the cot, the blankets, and him. The cupboard hung open, empty, and there was no place else to stash anything, including his dignity.

"Em…."

"Um?" Sunny cocked his head, much like his dog had done.

"Em-Emile," he corrected, dredging up the one name he could remember from his research, thankful it was close enough to his own he would—probably—remember to respond to it. He glanced out the door past Sunny to see the creek flash on its merry way along the foot of the little rise just outside. "Côté. Emile Côté." He held out a hand, dismayed when it shook and he couldn't stop it.

Sunny stepped inside, picked up a blanket, and handed it to him. Once Emile had covered his lap, Sunny held out a hand. "Sunny Barklay. Why are you sleeping rough in my hunt shack? How did you get here?"

"Thiees iees yours?" He shook his head, knowing the words came out too stretched out and slippery. He had to get that under control or Sunny would know he wasn't from here.

"Wow. You are really French." Sunny let his hand drop.

French? He blinked. "Pardon?"

"You're not from around here."

Oh dear. "Erm. No. I guees no."

Sunny drew in a deep breath. "Well. That's…. Come on. You can't stay here." He shoved a hand into his curls, where it caught, making him wince and mutter something Emikku—Emile—wasn't supposed to hear. He figured it was a curse, because Sunny scrubbed at his scalp a moment, then sighed and dropped his hand. "Yeah. You can't stay here."

"I… no?" His gut tightened. He didn't have any place else to go. He had nothing and knew no one.

"Of course not." Sunny frowned at the rickety walls. "I mean, it's fine for now. It's warm, but it won't stay that way. And when it rains, I'm not so sure this place will keep you dry. And—" Sunny wiggled a hand at him. "No clothes. I mean…."

"Dry. Warm." Emile glanced around the darkening hut. The sun was lowering enough it no longer streamed inside. "No." He'd been very cold some nights, but the weather had warmed since he'd first arrived, so that wasn't as much of a problem.

"Do you need a hand?"

"A… hand?" He tugged at the blankets. "To…?"

"A hand up." Once more, Sunny held out his hand, and this time Emile remembered what that gesture meant, and he took it in his, shaking it up and down vigorously.

Sunny laughed, a lapis and shimmering sound, so bright and full of colour Emile had to close his eyes. The touch of skin on skin was quicksilver and lightning in his veins, intensified in the dark behind his lids. His heart skipped, and his skin came alive with need. His cock, horrifyingly, stiffened where it hid beneath the scratchy blankets.

It was like Sunny was magic personified. Emile snatched his hand back. "I sorry! I should—"

"No!" Sunny moved closer to the cot, crouched, and picked up the second blanket. "Here." He draped the cover over Emile's shoulders. His fingers brushed sensitised skin, sending a flutter of rose-and-periwinkle-hued shards up around them. Emile's breath caught. Surely that little spurt of magic escaping had been obvious.

He studied Sunny's face, but the human seemed oblivious.

The dog, however, was hopping up on his hind legs, snapping at the dissipating sparks like he hoped to catch one.

"Ferny," Sunny admonished softly. "Settle down." He sighed, his face going still, almost blank. "You can see he's fragile. Let's just get him back to the house and we'll figure out what's next." He turned to Emile. "Can you get up?"

"I—yees. Of course." He unfolded his legs, pushed to the edge of the cot, stifling the uncertain twinge. It wasn't uncommon that humans wouldn't see the magic sparking. That much had been oft-reported in his research. It was disappointing, for reasons he didn't have time right now to think about. He wobbled to his feet, steadying himself on the wall and offering a stiff smile.

"I can carry you," Sunny offered. "You don't look like you weigh that much."

Emile was hunched, bringing his head close to the same height as Sunny's, but if he straightened, he'd be easily a head taller. Still, he knew he was thin, and his shifter nature meant his bones were less dense—if stronger—than the average human's. He'd found many studies on human physiology. He mostly didn't want to know why, when the rest of human culture had been recorded so sparingly, it was easy to find information on the inner workings of the human body.

He knew his kind were not exactly known for being benevolent in human history and stories, but he didn't like to think that maybe there was good reason for that. Though many scholars claimed human stories were exaggerated, Emile had seen plenty of evidence pointing to a past his people probably shouldn't be proud of. That idea was enough to take care of his burgeoning erection.

"Is fine," he assured Sunny. "I can walk. Just slow."

"Slow it is." Sunny beamed at him. "We have all afternoon. Come on."

He motioned for Emile to precede him out the door, and Emile obliged, shivering with the warmth of Sunny's hand at the small of his back.

Everything about this human called to him. His magic, his body, his essence. Surely that couldn't end well. For either of them.

CHAPTER 3

EMILE. SUCH an old-fashioned name. Sunny watched his unexpected guest as he made his way down the narrow path. The blankets hid most of him, but spindly legs and a knobby arm still showed. Sunny's fingers slipped through holes in the shifting afghan draped over Emil's shoulders, and smooth, cool skin greeted his touch.

He caught his breath, his mouth going dry. The undulating protrusion of Emile's spine seemed to heat as he grazed his fingers over it. A trickle of Emile's long locks teased his wrist. Another breath caught in Sunny's throat as a ripple of fire coursed over his skin. He almost yanked his hand back.

Emile stumbled, grunting and cursing softly as he pitched forward.

"Easy." Sunny moved closer, flung an arm across Emile's chest to stop his fall. "You okay?" He was so thin. *I need to bring him into town. He needs a doctor. And clothes. Why doesn't he have clothes?* Sunny tangled the fingers of his free hand into his curls and tugged. The sharp pull focused him. *Get him back to the house, clothed, fed. Find out what's going on, then decide. Just help him first and worry about if I'm nuts later.*

"Forgot how hard these is," Emile grumbled, almost to himself.

Sunny barely heard the words. "I'm sorry, what? What's hard?" he asked.

"Walk—that is…." Emile grunted and gripped the afghan tighter.

Sunny rounded in front of him, concerned. "Emile?"

"I…." Emile's brow knit, but that was all of him Sunny could see, his head hung so low. His shoulders were rounded, his back bent. He projected a forlorn sadness that eclipsed the irritation Sunny might otherwise have felt at a stranger's presence on his land.

Gently, Sunny lifted his chin. "What is it? How can I help? I have a phone at the house. We can call someone if you want?"

Emile blinked at him, and Sunny gasped. Out here in the sunlight, Emile's eyes were an impossible colour; the deepest azure of a summer sky, but sharper, shining with inner flames of blue heat.

Then Emile blinked again, and Sunny saw past the glamour and sparkle to a distress that made it so hard for Sunny to breathe. He smoothed a thumb over Emile's chin, drawing his attention.

"My feet," Emile said at last. He pulled in a sharp breath and let it out with a huff. He straightened his shoulders, pulling himself up to reveal height Sunny hadn't expected. "I'm fine. It's nothing." He dragged his face from Sunny's light grip and took a few halting steps, face set against a grimace.

"Here." Sunny kicked off his flip-flops and nudged them closer to Emile's feet. "Put those on." It was the least he could do, though he was sure that soul-deep hurt went a lot further than stone-bruised feet.

"No. I cannot." Emile turned his brilliant eyes on Sunny again.

What little saliva Sunny had left vanished. Pinned by Emile's bright, confused stare, he found it impossible to speak. Energy arched between them, and Sunny was possessed with an urge to kiss Emile so strong he'd leaned in for it before he caught himself.

Emile's eyes flew wide, and he took a stumbling step away.

"I—" Heat flashed into Sunny's cheeks. Fernforest whined and pressed against his legs. When Sunny glanced down, he found his dog in near contortions trying to stick to him and go to Emile at the same time. The poor animal was beside himself.

"Ferny likes you," Sunny blurted, desperate for anything that might draw attention away from his inappropriate gesture.

It worked, because Emile looked down.

Fernforest calmed as they made eye contact. His tail beat a painful whipping tattoo against the back of Sunny's calf, vulnerable where his cargo shorts didn't cover. "It's okay," Sunny told the dog. "Relax."

Emile smiled, his attention all on the dog now. "Be still, little one," he said, bending to hold a hand out.

Fernforest calmed instantly, stretching his nose to touch Emile's fingertips. He licked them, whined again, and leaned on Sunny. He plopped his butt in the dirt next to Sunny's bare feet, tail sweeping the dry leaves aside on its slowed swing.

"He *really* likes you." Sunny had to bend slightly to put his hand on the dog's head, but the contact calmed his own heavy-beating heart, and he swallowed, relieved. The fierce protectiveness he'd felt for his new land since the moment he'd signed the papers eased in his chest. In a weird way, finding Emile here on his very first day made it feel like Emile was *part* of the land. Certainly, the twigs caught in his hair and the dirt smudged over most of his body indicated he'd been out here more than a few days already. Odd as it was when Sunny thought about finding a naked man in his old hut, Emile felt a part of the place.

"Fernforest is a notoriously good judge of character."

"And I like him." Emile knelt, already grubby knees picking up more dust. He scratched around the base of one of Fernforest's ears. "Very much," he said, directly to the dog. "You bring so much light."

Fernforest cocked his head.

"He belonged to my mother." Sunny furrowed his brow. Ferny was his dog now. He didn't normally talk about his parents. Discomfited, he patted the dog's head, energy sparking along his skin as his fingers came into contact with Emile's. He gasped and stilled, hoping. The lightning sizzle came again as Emile caressed the backs of his fingers. For a moment—the space of a breath—their fingertips connected, held. Then Emile rose again. The touch trailed away. The sizzle faded, leaving behind a memory of heat and jumbled sensation.

"I am rested," Emile announced. Carefully, he slipped his feet, oddly long and narrow, into Sunny's shoes. His heels hung off the backs, but he smiled at Sunny anyway. "Thank you."

"Oh." Sunny's heart faltered. He gulped. "It's nothing." He managed to get the words out, but it was a near thing before his breath deserted him. Emile's smile had the flutter of butterfly wings and flitting sunlight through the tree leaves around the edges. Like he was as nervous as Sunny felt.

Sunny echoed his expression as best he could, curling a smile past his nerves. "Let's get you inside. Showered. Fed, maybe?"

Emile's smile solidified into light itself. "Food would be…." He drew in a breath through his nose. "Yes. Wonderful. Thank you."

"Then you can call whoever—"

"There is no one." The flat finality of that twisted Sunny's heart.

"I'm sorry."

Emile pursed his lips, flared his nostrils, but twisted a forced smile back onto his face. "Don't be. The choice has been made." He turned to carefully pick his way along the uneven ground.

Unable to resist the desire to help, Sunny returned his hand to Emile's back, low on his spine. He didn't imagine the shudder that went through his strange guest as his fingers once more brushed cool, silky skin, and bit his lip. Perhaps he'd found the source of that eternally sad look in Emile's gaze.

CHAPTER 4

AFTERNOON SUNSHINE, finally overcoming the ever-more-sparse cloud cover, sparkled down through the leaves overhead. It soaked into Sunny's tanned skin only to shine out again whenever he smiled. Emile wanted more of those smiles, but it might seem awkward—not to mention obvious—twisting around to get a look at Sunny's face every three steps. Instead, he followed the direction of the gentle pressure at his back. The heat of the touch sparked constantly, pricking at his magic until his skin rippled with the power.

He was a moth to Sunny's irresistible glow. Sometimes the surges coming off Sunny clashed with his own magic, sometimes coupled with it in a strange push-me-pull-me dance of energy he found difficult to ignore. It pulled at his own magic in a way nothing and no one ever had before.

The floppy shoes on his feet, more trouble than they were worth, tripped him up at every bump in the path, but he hadn't had the heart to refuse the offer. Sunny must have misunderstood his earlier complaint to think his feet hurt. In fact, he was just so unused to this bipedal form, it made him clumsy.

Hakko, the eldest of the hatchlings in his broodnest, had always warned he spent too much time in scales and feathers, hardening himself to the softer side of his nature. How he wished now that he had listened to those incessant "suggestions." As he stumbled over another tree root, his big toe clumped into the unyielding wood, and Emile cursed.

Sunny's hand landing on his arm was both welcome and a scalding reminder of why he should really move away from the man. Only he didn't, and a spark of crystalline light flickered between them.

"Are you okay?" Sunny asked. He blinked but gave no sign he'd seen the shower of sparks. Given the way Sunny excited Emile's magic, it was disappointing to realise Sunny was no more aware of the magic than most humans.

"I am." Emile tried not to let his irritation penetrate the words. He wasn't irritated by Sunny, just by his traitorous body, his sore toe, and the idea that his manipulative broodnest companion might have been right about this.

"We're almost there," Sunny assured him, replacing his support at Emile's back.

That was both better and worse. Any skin-on-skin contact called his magic to the surface far too easily. If he wasn't careful, he might set them both on fire. The insulation of the blanket was a blessing. But the steadying hand low on his back, so comforting, made him long for things he probably shouldn't.

"I think I have some burgers thawed," Sunny said, then cast a look over Emile. "But maybe soup…." He drew his brows down as his gaze skated over Emile's torso.

"Is there a problem?" At least he was getting a handle on the cadence of Sunny's speech. He'd managed to smooth his accent out enough he didn't sound quite so alien.

"No, I…." Sunny's smile this time was muted. "How long have you been out here?"

Emile could tell him only a few days, but Sunny probably wouldn't believe him. Even for his kind, Emile had grown thin. For a human, he would appear obviously underfed. His stomach snarled at the thought, and Sunny pursed his lips.

"Soup," he decided. "You need to go slow and keep the food down." He guided Emile toward a narrow plank bridge arching over a lively creek. "This way."

Emil's shoe caught under the first board, and he grunted, pitching forward a few slapping steps until Sunny caught him.

"No rush," Sunny admonished.

A damp, heated breeze, like an echo of Hakko's disapproval, blew against Emile's back, and he glanced over his shoulder. The dog stopped in his tracks, a low rumble in his throat. Even Sunny furrowed his brow and glanced back the way they had come.

"Hungry," Emile blurted and moved quickly over the bridge, even while he scanned the trees and frowned.

Sunny hunched his shoulders as he hastily followed, tugging the dog to heel as he made it to the other side.

The dog lingered a moment, one front foot on the bridge, the other lifted, as though he thought about going back. The forest seemed to breathe out another heated waft of air, and the dog's grumble rose in pitch.

"Ferny." Sunny's stern command got the animal's attention, and he trotted over to them. "Good boy." Sunny led them both across the grass toward the house, ignoring the dog's obvious reluctance to leave whatever he sensed in the woods behind them.

Emile spared one last glance into the shadows under the leaves. There was nothing to see, but he didn't need his eyes to sense Hakko's presence. Had his broodnest companion actually followed him through the Fold? After all his zealous preaching about the dangers of opening their world up to the human plane on the other side, would he do such a thing? Surely not.

But Hakko was strong. His magic did many things. It wasn't impossible that he could follow Emile without ever physically leaving their homeland. It wouldn't be easy, even for Hakko. But it wasn't impossible.

"Emile?" Sunny's voice, all warmth and welcome, billowed over the shiver that had started under Emile's skin. It calmed him. He rolled his shoulders and turned to follow.

Behind him, the forest rustled, but he refused to look back.

CHAPTER 5

A SENSATION skittered over Sunny's skin as they crossed the little bridge. It left his palms sweaty, his instinct divided between reaching the cottage and stopping to peer into the shade under the trees. He opted for forward momentum. As soon as Ferny and Emile had crossed the threshold, Sunny closed the door with a satisfying click.

"There." He rubbed the damp off his palms onto the fabric of his shorts. A little of his unease was soothed away by the click of the door behind Emile, shutting all of them inside. Strange to feel so protective over someone he didn't know and who was technically trespassing on his private haven, but there it was. For the moment, the desire to keep the world away from Emile overruled Sunny's lately developed aversion to people in general.

He could only chalk it up to Fernforest's odd behavior, the unfamiliar forest, and Emile's obvious need. Emile was nothing like the soul-sucking media circus that had surrounded the accident and Sunny's departure from the family business. He was a weak, perhaps lost man who needed help that Sunny could give.

After motioning Emile to the tiny loveseat that served as his sofa, Sunny scraped curls off his face and wrapped a tie around as much of it as he could manage as Emile lowered himself onto it. "You sit. I'll find you something to wear, and you can have a shower." He paused next to the sofa. "Are you sure you don't want me to call anyone? A friend? Family? I can take you to town to the clinic."

Emile stared at him for a long moment. Then he sighed. "I left home and family behind." He offered a small, only slightly reassuring smile. "I am hungry, but I don't need any… clinic?" He said the last with a small hitch at the end, like he didn't quite recognise the word, but then snugged the blankets tighter. "Clothing would be good."

"Right. But if you change your mind—"

"I will not." Emile worked himself deeper into the sofa. It had to be more comfortable than the lumpy, mouldy cot. He pulled a few of the throw pillows closer with a sigh, creating a snug nest.

Fernforest immediately hopped up next to him, curling his furry body against Emile's thigh. The dog's ease with his affection soothed Sunny's remaining anxiety at inviting this stranger into his new home. He laid a hand on the animal's head. Stiff fur tickled his palm, and he smiled.

"Watch out for him, Ferny. I'll be right back."

Ridiculous. Where was the guy going to go? What would happen to him in the amount of time it took Sunny to go up to his bedroom for clothes?

He didn't dare look down as he hurried to his wardrobe. He found a pair of cut-off track pants—ideal, since any of his pants would be inches too short for Emile and the drawstring would keep the garment from sliding off his lean hips. From his dresser, he pulled a T-shirt and the package of briefs he'd recently bought but hadn't opened. On his way back to the main space, he fetched towels and necessities from the linen closet under the stairs.

Emile was staring at his dog, hands cupped under his jaw, head cocked to one side. His eyes, bright and intent, seemed out of focus. The dog panted happily at him, occasionally flipping his tongue up over his nose.

"Does he have anything interesting going on in there?" Sunny asked, tapping the top of the dog's skull.

Emile jerked his hands away. "Sorry. No. Nothing in there."

Sunny chuckled. "Really? Not even a story about that time he chased pigeons and ended up in Mom's pool because he wasn't watching where he was going?"

Emile flushed. "No. Sorry." He looked entirely serious. "Nothing like that at all."

"Okay, then." Sunny held out the clothes, at a loss for how to take the man's comments. "Bathroom is right through there." He pointed to the door below his loft. "Take your time. I have to thaw the soup, so…."

Emile rose and took the offered clothes and towels. "Thank you."

"Sure."

Dropping his gaze, Emile sidled past Sunny, dodging his shoulder aside so as not to make contact. What had happened, Sunny wondered, that left Emile alone and without even the clothes on his back? What made him nervous about touch? And how did Sunny frame that question when Emile had already shut down any mention of contacting anyone? He would have to ask. Eventually.

He was turning his back, headed for the kitchen end of the room, still contemplating how to bring up such a delicate subject, when Emile spoke.

"Your dog."

Sunny spun, maybe too fast, because Emile shuffled back a step, one hand up. Sunny sidled back too, leaving space between them. "Is he okay?" Sunny glanced at the mutt, who now sat on the couch, watching them, gaze shifting from one to the other.

Emile smiled wide. "Very much, yes. He's very bright."

"Yeah." Sunny couldn't help an indulgent smile at his little buddy. "He's brilliant, actually. Well. For a dog."

"For many a creature, he is quite smart, but that isn't what I meant." Emile scratched Fernforest's ears. "Is it, my friend?"

The dog licked his fingers, thumped his tail, then cocked his head at Sunny.

Why do I get the feeling there's some joke on me that I'm not getting?

And then he realised he was imagining some kind of conspiracy between his house guest and his *dog*. He shook his head. "I'm going to get your dinner started. Ferny, if you want to eat, you'll find your ball, buddy."

Fernforest yipped and jumped down, beginning the hunt for his food delivery ball, which Sunny had hidden, this time behind the woodpile next to the door. It would keep the dog occupied and out from underfoot while he got the soup on.

ONCE BEHIND the closed door of the bathroom, Emile let out a small sigh. He'd been holding his breath that Sunny didn't ask any more about what he had meant. He wasn't sure he could explain without using words like *magic* and *fey* and *bloodlines*. Fernforest wasn't any more an ordinary dog than Emile was a run-of-the-mill human.

Well. That wasn't entirely true. Ferny *was* a dog, whereas Emile was not even a little bit human. With a sigh, he dumped his armload onto the chair—no, that was wrong. He picked up the clothes again and lifted the cover. The name for this water-filled little stool escaped him at the moment, but he understood its use.

You'll never learn enough to pass in their world, Emik-kik. Stop this foolishness and take what you've been offered.

Hakko's voice rumbled in his head even when there was no possible way he could be hearing it on this side of the Fold. Even right down to the hated child's name Hakko used in place of the name given him on his hatching day. *Emikku.* It was a good name. Their Bearer, Bethakke, liked to translate it from its ancient tongue into modern speech and often called him their joy-chaser. Hakko, the chosen Sire of their broodnest, of course, delighted in reminding him the traditional meaning was something closer to *jester.*

Like a king's fool, he used to say. *And I will be your king—or close enough—one day, Emik-kik. Best you stay on my good side.*

Emile snorted. What did it matter what any of them thought now? He'd made his choice. Emikku had flown to the stars with Bethakke on the night they had shed their last scale and feather. He was Emile now, and Emile he planned to remain.

Even as he had that thought, a ripple of excruciating pain undulated along his spine. He jerked, the lid slipped from his fingers to close with a clatter, and he had to bite his tongue to keep quiet. Pushing his shoulders far back, he arched his spine and moaned softly. Magic dug into bone, pushing it outward to stretch his skin.

"Blast." Twisting, he arched until he could see the spines of his other form stretching the soft pink skin to its limit. *Not good.* From between his shoulder blades to midway down his back, his vertebrae had elongated to protrude in a wave of rounded humps. They were merely a shadow of the true spikes that coursed down his neck and back when he transformed to his hard scales, but no way would any human look at those humps and think them a normal variation on human anatomy.

The stretch of skin stung where it turned white at the tops of the protrusions. He didn't dare round his back even a little, in case he tore the delicate membrane. The last thing he needed was to try to figure out how to explain newly opened welts on his back as the blood trickled onto Sunny's pretty black-and-white tiles.

"Everything okay in there?" Sunny sounded close, and the door handle rattled.

"Fine!" Emile swung around to face the door, but it didn't open.

"Heard the toilet lid fall." Sunny chuckled, and the sound was endearing in its embarrassment. "Just making sure you didn't fall in or something."

Toilet. Of course. "No. I'm fine. Just clumsy."

"Well, good to know." There was a soft shushing against the door. "No rush, Emile. Just take all the time you need, okay? And let me know if you change your mind about a doctor or calling someone."

The calm in his words eased Emile's panic, and he breathed in. "Of course. Thank you." He listened to the padding of bare feet retreat towards the kitchen. The pain in his back eased, and when he managed another glance in the mirror, the spikes had diminished, though his spine was still too prominent.

He frowned. Normally shifting was a seamless, painless magical process. *When* he controlled the magic. He'd witnessed the agony of shifters who were at the mercy of their magical transformations, and tried hard not to panic. All he had to do was maintain his grip on the magic and he would be fine. The shift to scales wouldn't—*couldn't*—happen if he didn't will it.

Humans' disconcerting habit of washing in huge quantities of water aside, Emile was certain he'd have the magic under better control once he was feeling more himself and less like a dirt devil. He'd just have to endure the discomfort of the water, since he was pretty sure the smell of heated scales as he burned the dirt away would raise some serious questions for Sunny.

It took some fiddling and intuitive leaps to figure out the knobs and levers that released water from the overhead sprinkler, but he managed. He stayed under the spray as short a time as possible and rubbed his skin pink in the effort to get it all off again.

Dressing was quick, as the clothing was far less complicated than the fashions currently in favour at home. The odd packaging for the underthings made his skin crawl in its unnatural, slick, impenetrable texture, but the fabric itself wasn't so bad. He was definitely a fan, he decided. There was some magic-resisting element to some of the clothing, but the bulk of the content came from natural sources. He could live with the unusual feel of the synthetics sliding over his skin if it came with the stretchiness that allowed for virtually no fastenings to fiddle with.

Clothing had been a big deterrent to this form for him all his life. Few places in the enclaves he visited growing up allowed bipedal nudity.

Ironic that his flight into the human realm had landed him in a culture where clothing was a must.

He envied the water sprites and forest nymphs and dryads. As far as he could tell, even on this side of the Fold, they had a lot more freedom than his kind ever had. In fact, according to Fernforest—if he could trust the flitting thoughts of a dog—most fey had as much leeway as they liked, as long as they remained out of sight of humans.

Humans, he had been informed, were a scary lot. But not Sunny. Fernforest was wildly in favour of Sunny. It was the best recommendation Emile could ask for.

CHAPTER 6

SUNNY WASN'T going to wonder too hard why, fresh out of the shower, Emile still smelled like forest light and cool earth. He knew it wasn't his shower gel. That was unscented. No, he didn't have to know why. He would simply enjoy that it was so.

"Here you go." He set a bowl of soup on the table in front of Emile and pushed the plate of soda crackers closer before picking up the empty bowl from the place across from him. "Take your time. If you eat too fast, it might mess you up. Not eating for a long stretch makes your guts do weird things when you do eat again."

Emile nodded and eyed the bowl.

"Lentil mostly," Sunny offered.

"Meat?" Finally, Emile picked up the spoon, but instead of eating, he poked around in the bowl with it.

Sunny's heart sank. "Ham. Are you a vegetarian?"

The way Emile's lips curled back from his teeth, he looked positively feral. The snarl stirred Sunny's gut, tiny licks of interest igniting in his belly.

"Hardly," Emile growled. He scooped up a spoonful and swallowed.

"Careful! It's hot!" Sunny almost grabbed his wrist to stop him but managed to curb the impulse.

"Oh. Um. Yes." Emile blew across the top of the bowl, pursing his lips to a pretty O. "I guess it must be." He stirred the soup, but the next mouthful was just as large, and eaten with as little care. The guy must have a cast-iron mouth.

And really. Sunny had to stop obsessing over his mouth.

"It's delicious." The spoon disappeared past his lips once more, heaped with chunks of ham.

"Thanks." Sunny blushed, heat rising to his hairline. Hastily he turned back to the stove to serve his own meal.

So many impulses to control, not the least of which was one to protect. He didn't understand that at all. Attraction he got. But this urge to protect Emile confused him. He'd come here to be alone, and here, on his first day in his new sanctuary, he was feeding a strange—intriguing, yes, but strange—trespasser at his kitchen table. He should be eager to get rid of him. He *was* eager to get rid of him. He'd feed him and send him on his way. As soon as Emile was stronger, of course. And rested. Then Sunny would send him along.

No, I won't. Daisy would be proud of him.

A little pang darted up his sternum, and he stifled a gasp. He missed her. He should call her. Shaking off the sadness, he set his bowl on the table.

Emile's head cocked slightly on an angle, poised over his bowl. His spoon hand stopped midscoop. "Are you well?" He turned his head more, until Sunny could see the blue of his eyes and couldn't look away.

"Fine."

Emile gave a single, gentle nod.

More of Sunny's resolve crumbled.

When Emile returned to his meal, Sunny scooted into the chair across from him, then focused on his own food.

They ate mostly in silence, though Sunny couldn't help but watch the eager way Emile downed his soup. He had to be starving to eat like that.

"Is there more?" Emile tipped the bowl back, lips to the edge to get every last drop. His Adam's apple worked as he swallowed, and Sunny lost the plot for a moment. "Sunny?" Emile's bowl clunked onto the table.

"Uh." *Brilliant.*

"More soup?"

"Yeah. I mean, no. There were only two bowls. You should really let that settle for a bit anyway. If you eat too much—"

"It's fine." Emile smiled at him, and there went Sunny's focus again, right to his lips. "Do I have something in my teeth?" Emile grinned, obviously teasing.

"Oh my God." Heat flashed up to Sunny's hairline. "I—" *God. What if he isn't gay?*

"I've made you uncomfortable."

You're making me horny, if you want to know. But he wasn't going to say that. And now he'd gone too long saying nothing at all.

"I should go." Abruptly, Emile stood. His chair rocked on its back legs, and he grabbed for it, moving so fast Sunny could swear he might have blurred.

He blinked. "Where would you go?" Sunny stood. Faced with the immediate idea Emile might vanish as if he'd never been there, Sunny realised he didn't want him to go. "Please. I was being awkward. You don't have to go."

Emile's eyes widened. He flared his nostrils. "I hadn't thought that far." He blew his cheeks out. "Hence my stay in your little shack. I suppose I didn't think things all the way through."

"What things?" Sunny blurted, curiosity controlling his mouth for an instant.

"I—had to leave." Emile stretched his lips in what was not a smile, no matter what he might have thought to show Sunny. "My home, I mean. I had to leave everything behind."

"Literally," Sunny agreed. "You were naked. Did something… happen? I mean—"

Emile's eyes got wide for an instant; then he lifted both hands. "No! Nothing like—no." This time his smile was more genuine. "I am fine, Sunny. Hungry. And tired, but otherwise fine. I left at an… inopportune moment, nothing more."

Sunny was more relieved to hear that than he'd expected. "I'm glad." He motioned at the sofa and the pile of pillows. "Sit. Relax." Sunny shoved the nearest book, a tropey romance he considered a bit of a guilty pleasure, into Emile's hand. "Read for a bit. I'm just going to clean up. Then we can talk. Or… something."

This time only one of Emile's eyebrows rose.

"No! I mean. Talk. Play cards. God. I wish I had a TV." But he'd never been one for screens and watching. Reading, yes, but not watching.

Emile just stared at him.

"Okay. Read the damn book." He turned on his heel, rushing for the safety of dishwashing and tidying. If he kept talking, he was going to choke on his own foot. Proof positive: he sucked at social intercourse.

Fuck me. Or not. *Or…. Fuck!* He couldn't even *think* without tripping over his thoughts and kicking up innuendo. But at least he hadn't said it out loud. He could feel Emile watching him, but he kept his attention firmly on the dishes, hoping it would take him long enough he'd have time to regroup.

THE MORE Sunny tripped over his words, the more endearing he became. If Emile was going to escape this human unscathed, he was going to have to do so soon. He wasn't sure he could withstand Sunny's accidental charm. He wasn't sure he wanted to.

Since it was obvious Sunny was hiding the only way he could in the small cabin, Emile turned his attention to the book he'd been offered. The slick, colourful cover was a far cry from anything he was used to at home. Books there took themselves altogether too seriously, with their leather bindings and pages thin as a gossamer pixie-dragon wing. His people only wrote down their own personal history, the stories of their accomplishments, and the counting of their offspring.

This book didn't look like any of those things. *Romancing the Ugly Duckling*. Curious, he opened to the beginning of the book and began to read.

He had to be grateful to Hakko and his predecessors for one thing, at least. They had all been adamant the Corcaird House learn to speak, read, and write as many human tongues as possible. As a rule, their kind had a gift for language, so it hadn't been a hardship. Emile was especially adept, and the near-impossible rules of the English language had intrigued him. His studies served him well, drawing him deep into the third chapter. Then the hairs on his arms stood on end. A warmth skittered over his skin, and he looked up.

"Hey." Sunny smiled. He rubbed a hand over the back of his neck. "You look comfy. I'm just going to be going in and out. I want to get the rest of my boxes in before the sun goes down. If you need anything, just shout, okay?"

"Thank you. You've been very kind."

Sunny's smile brightened. "Not every day I find a handsome stranger camped out in my shack."

Emile caught his breath. That was a declaration if ever he'd heard one, and the hopeful expression underneath the shy smile Sunny offered made it impossible to ignore, no matter what his better judgement was screaming at him from behind the scenes.

"It's not every day I'm rescued by such a lovely host. So I guess we have that in common."

"I guess we do."

For a moment Sunny hovered, hand scrubbing rhythmically over his nape. "So. I guess I'll let you get back to your book. If you need anything...."

"Thank you."

Emile watched him leave, captivated by his plump behind and bouncy step. Fernforest followed his master, but he stopped on the threshold, and Sunny left the door open so the dog could sit half in and half out of the house, like he was guarding them both.

Emile didn't want to think from what. He had a harder time sensing things here, but the dog clearly had no such encumbrance. Something had him on alert.

Easing into the soft cushions, Emile was glad to find his spine seemed to have relaxed into the proper form. The ache was almost gone now, and once he had pulled enough pillows and blankets around himself to form a simple nest, his discomfort eased. He lost himself for a little while in the love story and was almost drifting off when Fernforest yipped sharply. A blast of air drove into the house through the open door, flinging it back against the end of the counter. It bounced halfway closed again, blocking the sunlight, leaving the cabin muted and dull. The pages of Emile's book flapped and turned. The fringe on the throw pillows whipped up.

Emile started so violently he almost fell off the couch. His foot hit the floor with a thud and a clatter as pain jolted up his leg. The twist and crunch of bone sent agonising spikes up his shin, and he curled his toes in reaction. The scrape of claws on the hardwood jerked him completely alert.

Claws. He glared at his feet. The right was perfectly human-looking where it rested on a lemony cushion. The left, however, stopped looking human just past his ankle, where iridescent auburn scales morphed out of his skin and over the top of his foot, arched into a bony-knuckled claw.

Even as the violent pain knifed into Emile's consciousness, it ebbed again. The claws remained. Magic coursed just under his skin, and he grappled with the slippery tendrils, fighting back the incursion of more scales up his shin and the sensation that the magic wasn't exactly his.

"Ferny?" Sunny's voice came from just outside the door, still half-closed in the aftermath of the breeze. "What's up, buddy?" Sunny pushed the door open with a foot, arms filled with yet another box. He set that on the counter and stopped to stroke Fernforest's head. The dog was staring out into the yard, tail straight out behind him, head lowered.

Emile snatched his foot off the floor and shoved it under the throw pillows at the end of the couch. The points of his talons tangled in the fabric, and he grimaced. That was going to be tricky to explain later.

"Everything okay?" Sunny asked as he poked his head inside.

"Fine," Emile croaked. His voice was hoarse, and he ran a hand over his throat. More scales cascaded down over his Adam's apple and onto his chest. In a panic, he dropped the book over the exposed area just as Sunny lifted his gaze from the dog's face to his.

Please don't let anything else be scaly.

Sunny's expression didn't change, though. "Were you sleeping?"

Emile blinked, realising it wasn't the cabin that was in shadow. It was his eyes, slitted to guard against the bright glow haloing Sunny. "Yes, I suppose I drifted off." He yawned, closing his eyes to better focus and get a handle on the recalcitrant magic. It eased grudgingly around his control, and he pushed it down. Scales melted away, leaving tender skin behind. His eyes watered, but as he blinked again, they focused on Sunny, taking in the light and shadows as they should.

Fernforest trotted across the floor, nose twitching as he weaved through the maze of bins and boxes Sunny had brought in. He stopped near Emile's hidden foot and dug his muzzle under the pillow. Wet warmth twined between his toes, and he almost jerked his foot away. Almost.

"Ferny!" Sunny reached for him, but Emile stopped him.

"It's okay. He's just being friendly." *Nosy, more like.* Fernforest tipped his head so he could lick Emile's toes and look at him at the same time.

"Well, I've brought everything in. Are you hungry?"

"Sure?"

"You don't know?"

"I could eat."

Sunny smiled. "Good. I'll make sandwiches. Tomato or beef?"

"Beef." As Fernforest licked between his toes, Emile gathered the magic's residue and swept his thoughts over his body, making sure he was all skin and no scales now.

The effort of forcing the magic to conform left him breathing hard and feeling wrung out. Like good sex without the orgasm.

"You look beat," Sunny observed from where he was assembling sandwich fixings. "You're definitely staying here tonight."

Emile was too weary to argue.

CHAPTER 7

SUNNY GRIPPED the rounded handrail and peered down. Shadows trickled across the floor in undulating patches as moonlight flowed between the poplar trees and into his living room. He was reminded of the dancing pebbles in the bottom of the stream and blinked.

Just shadows. He dragged his gaze away from the dance of moonshine on hardwood to find the paler, uneven lump on his sofa. His eyes adjusted to the dim silver light, and he studied his sleeping guest.

Long, slender feet poked from the edge of the blanket. Equally long-fingered hands rested on the rough weave of the afghan covering Emile's abdomen. A book peeked from under the afghan fringe, and another, this one open under one elegant hand, rested on his stomach. He'd evidently shucked his borrowed T-shirt, because his skin was pale in this light, even more than it had been in the bright sunshine. Strands of deep burgundy hair, washed nearly black by moonglow, trailed over the backs of his hands and tumbled across his bare chest. Small, enticing nipples peeked between the locks.

He looked ephemeral and too delicate to be real. Too beautiful to be lying on Sunny's couch. Stirring in his sleep, Emile crooked a knee, pushing one shapely calf out from under the covers. The hair on his head seemed to be the only hair on him.

Great. Perving on your house guest. Classy.

But he wasn't perving. Concern that Emile was resting comfortably wasn't perving. It was being a good host.

At two in the morning, it's perving. Go back to bed.

Sunny was just turning from the balcony rail when he felt the heated prick of attention lift the hairs on the back of his neck. He looked back at Emile.

Dark eyes gazed up at him, pools of near black in the dimness.

"Sorry." Sunny took a step back. "I was—"

"Checking on me?" Emile offered.

"Um. Yes. You're settled, though."

Amusement flickered over Emile's face. "I was."

Shit. Embarrassment tingled up his neck to his cheeks. He opened his mouth to apologise again but was cut short by Emile's low, sexy chuckle.

"I'm not offended, Sunny."

"I have better manners, I swear."

Emile actually smiled, and in this light, Sunny could swear his teeth had points. It should have been creepy, but his skin tingled, and the heat of embarrassment sank lower, along with an awkward amount of blood flowing straight to his groin. He was glad it was darker up here than down there, or Emile might have been less forgiving of Sunny's observations. Still, he took a step back from the railing and waved, revealing he was a complete dork as well as a creepy host. "I'll let you get back to sleep. Sorry again."

He could have sworn he heard Emile's quiet laughter as he scuttled back to his bed. He was also fairly certain the moonlight dancing on the far wall of his loft bedroom was laughing at him too.

MANNERS WERE a funny thing. Where Emile came from, admiring someone was never considered ill manners. Admiring them while they slept… that was a human thing. His kind didn't have the same reticence when it came to expressing admiration or attraction. One of his own kind would never have hesitated to admire openly and in daylight.

As moonlight flitted across the cabin's interior, he watched the rail above, but Sunny didn't reappear. He could hear him breathing, knew he hadn't gone back to sleep, but he didn't come back to look over the rail and watch Emile. Too bad. Emile would have invited him down if he had.

But then, if it was too soon for Sunny to admit his attraction, it was probably too soon for Emile to suggest they act on it. Besides, he didn't yet know if Hakko would be able to track him or find him, or if he'd try. No. He knew he would try, and if he succeeded, Emile might be better off moving on, father from the Fold itself.

A ripple of sensation floated just under Emile's skin. He tensed, but the magic didn't surface this time. It hovered, waiting, as if to see what he did with his own arousal. When he lay still and did nothing, the power slowly tapered off. Perhaps he should gain some strength and get a better grip on how his magic reacted to this new environment before he indulged in a situation that had the potential to strip away his control.

The magic rolled over, another faint ripple before Emile slipped back into slumber.

He woke to the gentle clatter of dishes and sunlight playing among the leaf shadows on the floorboards. Idly, he twitched his tail and watched the cavorting patterns of light and shade, glancing periodically at Sunny working in the kitchen. He had his back to Emile as he worked, and Emile scooted upright.

It wasn't until he braced himself with his tail to sit up straighter, then flicked the edge of the blanket with the tip to cover a chilled foot, that he even realised he *had* his tail. The magic hadn't dissipated after all. It had chosen perhaps the most obvious of random ways to manifest.

Emile yanked it under the blankets as Sunny turned.

"You awake?"

"Mmm." Emile hunkered down, pulling the cover up to his chin as he frantically took stock of the rest of his body for any signs of scale, feather, or claw. "Sort of."

"I made coffee. It'll be ready in about eight minutes. You want to use the bathroom?"

"I'm good."

Sunny tipped his head to one side. "Cold?"

"Just cozy."

"Good. Relax. If you don't need the throne, I'm going to take a quick shower. I'll be back in time to pour coffee, and we can figure out what comes next. Okay?"

"Perfect."

"You're sure you're not cold?"

"I'm perfect." Emile smiled. It was all he could do to keep his tail from twitching. He'd never realised how unconscious its movements were until he needed to keep it hidden.

"About last night." Sunny dragged a hand over the back of his neck and stared resolutely at the floor.

"Not to worry. I'm sure it is disconcerting having a stranger sleeping in your parlour."

One of Sunny's eyebrows went up. "Parlour? Who's the spider and who's the fly in this particular scenario?"

Now it was Emile who was confused. "I'm sorry?"

There was a stretched pause; then Sunny's face flashed bright red and he scrubbed his neck frantically. As if realising the nervous motion, he dropped his hand. "Nothing. Sorry. I'll"—he pointed to the bathroom door—"go. Shower." And he was gone, darting into the washing room and all but slamming the door behind him.

You'll never pass for one of them. Why even try?

Hakko was wrong. The voice in his head was wrong.

Closing his eyes, Emile concentrated. In a heartbeat the magic was back in his grasp and the tail gone. He repressed the first few shivers, but eventually he had to pull up another blanket to compensate for the heat the magic stole as it retreated into his core.

By the time Sunny returned, Emile had warmed enough to sit up and accept the steaming mug Sunny handed him. It smelled heavenly, and when he sipped, the flavour danced over his taste buds. There was nothing like this back home. It sang in his veins, replacing the vibrancy of magic and warming him down to his toes.

There was so *much* on this side of the Fold he never knew existed. He met Sunny's gaze and was greeted with a sun-tinged smile that heated his blood in such a radically different way, he couldn't even remember why it might be a good idea to move on as soon as possible.

CHAPTER 8

"SUNSHINE, COME *on*." Daisy was a champion wheedler. "One afternoon. It won't kill you to come visit. Everyone misses you. One lunch with a few staff won't kill you."

"Will there be people?"

There was silence over the phone, and Sunny tucked it between his shoulder and ear, awkwardly because it was really too thin for the manoeuvre. But he needed both hands to pick up the wheelbarrow handles. For the past week, he'd neglected his yard in favour of nursing Emile while he regained his strength, as well as unpacking the rest of his personal belongings Daisy's friend hadn't moved for him. His new house truly felt like home now, with all his photos and collected souvenirs on display.

Since his house guest was showing definite signs of improvement, even if he hadn't shown much interest in leaving his nest of cushions on Sunny's couch, Sunny had thought it prudent to begin work on the outside of the property.

Over the week, Emile had read his way through a good third of Sunny's book collection and oddly hadn't replaced the books on the shelf. They were tucked carefully into the crevices of the couch, between the cushions and lined up along the arms. Like he was hoarding them as he read. Sunny couldn't help but wonder if there was any correlation between how much Emile enjoyed each story and how deeply he tucked it away.

"You're kidding, right?" Daisy's deadpan was almost as good as her wheedle, and it brought Sunny back to his current dilemma.

"Do I sound like I'm kidding?"

"How could it be lunch with friends if there were no friends there to lunch with?"

"You know how I feel about people."

Daisy sighed loudly, and Sunny was going to reply when a tap on his shoulder gave him a start that sent the phone to the ground. He turned to find Emile next to him. The hairs on his arms rose, and he couldn't help but smile, even as he had to retrieve the phone.

"Let me," Emile offered. Sunny relinquished the barrow, juggled the phone, then pointed to the corner of the yard behind the tool shed. He followed as Emile slowly pushed the wheelbarrow across the yard. He set it down more than once as he crossed the grass but refused Sunny's offer to take it back. A sheen of sweat glistened on his forehead by the time he had upended the load of grass roots and weeds onto the pile in the corner.

"People aren't the problem, Sunny," Daisy was saying when Sunny tuned back in to the conversation. "People are mostly fine. It's only when they get around you that things get dicey."

"So see? You don't want me there. It'll make everyone uncomfortable."

"You don't even have to say anything. Just get here, nod, smile once in a while. Let people see you're okay."

"Oh, and you almost had me at the 'don't have to say anything' part too," Sunny teased.

"You know what?" Her bitchy was beginning to show, and Sunny sighed inwardly. He could even alienate her these days. "Maybe if you smiled once in a while, you wouldn't have so many issues with people."

"Sis, I don't think I can do that."

"Sit and eat with people?"

Pretend I'm okay. But he couldn't say that to her. Any time he talked about his discomfort around their employees, his dislike of the sad smiles they gave him, the virtual pats on the head and the sympathy, she got uncertain. She wondered why she didn't feel so devastated by their loss, or so debilitated.

"Never mind." Selfishly, he couldn't listen to her be anything other than the powerhouse sister and boss who ran their company. "Let me think about it, okay?"

"You have to come back to reality sooner or later, Sunny."

Sunny watched Emile settle on the pile of cedar logs by one of the sheds and turn his face up to the sun. He looked like he was soaking up energy through his skin. He seemed so content just resting in the bright midmorning rays. Like he belonged to this place as much as Sunny wanted to belong here.

If this was the alternative to the reality where he walked the halls and labs of their company, always expecting to see his mother elbow-deep in plants, or his father hunched over a computer, this was what he wanted. Maybe it was a fantasy. Maybe he didn't care that it wasn't "real life" according to most of society. It was his life. This was what he wanted.

"Look, sis, I gotta go."

"Sunny, I'm sorry. I didn't mean—"

"I know you didn't. I know you *don't*."

"It's been a year. I know it's hard, but if you got back to work, if you—"

"Sis. I love you. That worked for you, and I'm happy it did. You needed the distraction and the company needed your stability, but I can't be there."

She was silent for a few heartbeats; then, "I miss you."

He had to smile. Sometimes she still sounded like his little sister. And sometimes, like yesterday, he had a pang of missing her too. It had surprised him with the sharp pain of it, but also with the comforting *normalness* of it. Like he'd begun to at least feel something again other than the vast emptiness where his parents had once lived. "I miss you too."

"Do you?"

"Actually, yes."

"Will you come have lunch with me? Just me?"

"Let me—" Sunny broke off as Emile stood, the movement abrupt, his attention focused on the trees past the refuse pile, his expression grim and cheeks pale. "Um. I have to go."

"Your carrots are calling?"

"Rutabaga, actually."

"Sunny."

"I'll think about it. Promise."

"Wednesday after next? I have the afternoon free."

"I'll think about it."

"Wear pants!"

"Blasphemer!"

She laughed. "You'll come?"

"Love you, Daisychain."

"Jerk. Love you and your little dog too."

He chuckled as he listened to her say something away from the phone, probably to Bobby, her assistant. Then the line was dead. God.

He *did* love her. He missed her. He did *not* want to drive to the city—dressed in slacks, no less—and enter the building where he still expected to see his parents chatting and joking with their employees. How Daisy could go there, day after day, and not die from missing them, he had no idea.

"Are you all right?" Emile's palm against the bare skin of Sunny's shoulder made him jump. Heat passed between them, and Sunny felt an immediate vibration, like Emile's touch was enough to excite every particle of his being into motion.

Part of him wanted to brush the touch away. It was too alien, what it did to him. More of him wanted to curl into it, see how it would feel to have his whole body light up like that. Before he could do anything, though, Emile's hand fell away. "Sunny?"

"Oh." He tucked the phone into a pocket of his cargo shorts and snapped the flap closed. "I'm good, thanks."

"You looked so sad there for just a moment." Emile shivered, his body undulating in a delicate wave, as though Sunny's distress had caused him physical discomfort.

"It's nothing."

"What were you talking to yourself about?"

Sunny blinked at him. "Sorry?"

"You were talking. Like you were arguing with yourself."

"I was talking to my sister." He pulled out his phone again and held it up. "On my phone?"

Emile stared at the device, nodding, but his expression was one of confusion.

"You've never seen a cell phone before?"

"Like a telephone?" Emile touched the screen, and since it was still unlocked, it lit up. He jerked his hand back. "I thought they were more…." He waved his hands, making a vague shape in the air. "Bigger."

Sunny wanted to laugh, but the look on Emile's face, so open and sincerely boggled, was too real to risk it sounding like Sunny was mocking him. "Where did you come from?" he wondered aloud.

Emile's expression abruptly closed, and he took a step back.

"No, it's okay." Sunny smiled what he hoped was a reassuring smile. "I don't mind. I just don't think I've ever heard of anyone who didn't at least know what a cell phone was, even if they'd never seen one. It's… odd." He touched Emile's arm, not wanting to scare him off, not wanting him upset. "But it's okay."

It was sort of adorable, actually, and another nail in the coffin of Sunny's tragically short-lived hermit life.

"I suppose I have been sheltered somewhat. Things are different where I come from."

Maybe he was Amish or something. Although northern Ontario was a long way away from Amish country. "Do you miss it?" he asked impulsively. "Home, I mean. You said you left in a hurry."

Emile drew in a deep breath and let it out, long and slow. "I did. And yes, I do. But I can't go back, and I wish I could tell you more, but…." He gazed off into the trees over the bridge. "Most of it you would never believe," he whispered. "And the rest you wouldn't understand."

"Emile." Sunny touched his arm, and this time, Emile didn't flinch, and the shock of contact was mild. Emile pulled his gaze from the forest to look at him. "You're welcome to stay here as long as you want. And I won't ask questions if it makes you uncomfortable. But you can understand I worry. You were alone and hungry and naked. That's not okay. Whoever you're running away from—"

"Is a long way away. I'm here now." He smiled something of a sharp, toothy grin that had the hairs on the back of Sunny's neck standing on end. "I had a difficult patch, which you rescued me from. But I am not helpless. I promise you."

"Of course not."

Emile's expression softened. "I did need your help. But I'm much stronger now. So thank you."

"You're welcome." He glanced at the wheelbarrow. "I have another six or seven of those to load up and move before I can start building the raised beds."

"Do you have another shovel?"

"Oh no. You are stronger, but I saw how much that took out of you. I'm glad you're out in the sunshine at last, but you need to take it easy still." He glanced to the trees that had drawn Emile's attention earlier. The depth of shadow under the branches limited his view, but as far as he could tell, there was nothing there to see.

"Please. It is the least I can do for you. I feel like I've taken over your life, not to mention your sofa."

"If I didn't want you here, you would know, believe me." Sunny hadn't quite figured out why he wanted Emile around. Or why he hadn't told Daisy about his presence. *Because she'd freak out and tell me to do a background check before kicking him out on his ass.*

If Sunny didn't particularly *like* people lately, Daisy was the one who tended to be more practical about who she let into their life. Hippies their parents might have been, but they had still managed to make a very healthy nest egg out of their research and the technology they had created for greener food production. Neither of their kids had to work if they didn't want to. Daisy thrived on carrying on their legacy, though, and Sunny… well. He was still figuring out where he'd landed after their deaths.

Emile touched his arm again, sending another, stronger shower of sparkling energy cascading through him. "Such kindness to a stranger is worthy of some repayment."

Sunny took a step closer to Emile, gazing up at him, breath caught as the heat grew in the pit of his stomach. Emile's fingers had closed around his arm just above his elbow, and the touch was electric, almost hot. "You don't feel like a stranger," he breathed. And that was the heart of the matter, wasn't it? Emile felt like part of this world Sunny had purchased for himself. He'd thought to get away from people, to be by himself, but already, he couldn't think of this bit of land and life without Emile's presence.

Emile blinked down at him, his eyes darkening, his pupils blowing up. His fingers tightened, and Sunny gulped, breath short, blood rushing south.

"Ferny likes you, I mean." *And so do I, apparently.*

"Fernforest is an excellent judge of character." Emile bent his neck, face looming, close to kissing distance but just out of reach.

"He really is." Sunny licked his lips, the parchment dryness alerting him to the fact he'd literally been panting.

"Are you all right?" Emile brushed fingertips over Sunny's cheek. "You're flushed."

Sunny groaned and closed his eyes. Too close. Too hot. *Too—*

Lips pressed to his and thought fled as Emile placed a careful, steadying kiss on his mouth.

If the touch of Emile's hand had been electric, the kiss was an explosion of brilliance and heat that burned through Sunny and left him—oddly—calm and still in its wake. Like a missing piece had flared and blazed, but then snicked perfectly into place somewhere inside him.

He pulled back to find Emile leaning in, eyes closed, a breath easing out of him in a long, slow exhale. His features were serene, lips curled in a tranquil smile. He practically glowed for a split second, and the sight of his beauty awakened a pulse of need so strong, it made Sunny gasp.

He took a step back, startled by the intensity.

Emile blinked, straightened. His expression sharpened. A look of panic flicked through his eyes. He, too, stepped back. The motion made him waver. His knees folded, and Sunny reached out to catch him. As tall as he was, he still weighed practically nothing.

A fetid breeze blew over them as Emile's weight settled in Sunny's arms. It smelled sulphurous and weighed Sunny down. He shuffled one foot, then the other, but it was like he was glued to the ground, unable to move.

At the bottom of the yard, the trees swayed, branches clacking together, leaves flailing in a wild dance of air that coiled and crawled up the yard, curling around their legs in tendrils of hot breath and stinging sand and twigs. Tiny sharp stones drew spots of blood up on Sunny's calves and shins, and he yelped.

That sent Fernforest into a frenzy of yipping barks. He drew back his lips and grabbed at the air, teeth very nearly brushing Sunny's skin. Like he was trying to sink his fangs into the offending wind, he danced and snapped, as irritated by the fact he couldn't catch it as by the weirdly cloying wind itself.

"Ferny!" Sunny tried to step away from the dog's frantic nipping, but still his feet didn't want to move very far very fast. The bridge over the little creek groaned loud enough they all turned to look. Shadows under the trees shifted, out of time with the madly whipping branches. The little creek splashed. The sounds of rushing water reached them, and a heartbeat later a cooler, fluttering breeze chased up the yard, brushing the heat and smell of ozone away.

Fernforest barked, reared up on his hind legs, still yipping, then took off for the bridge and the water. He skidded to a stop, barking across the water a few times, like a little kid taunting something that couldn't get to him from the other side. The trees shook vehemently one last time, then stilled. Fernforest raced back up the grade and past them to bark from the doorway of the house.

"Shush, you stupid dog," Sunny told him, then turned his attention to Emile, bracing the weight of his long, lean frame better against his side. "Can you stand?"

Emile nodded. "I'm fine." He struggled upright and tried, though not very hard, to push Sunny's hands off him.

"Let me help."

With a small nod, Emile let Sunny lead him back inside. Fernforest remained in the doorway, staring out, gaze fixed on the bottom of the yard, where the trees seemed to throw deeper-than-normal shadows, and their branches rustled in a wind that didn't travel past the creek now, let alone as far as the house.

"Ferny," Sunny called. "Come inside."

The dog obeyed, and Sunny kicked the door closed. Immediately the feeling of oppression eased, and Emile sank into the centre of his little nest, drew his feet under him, and pulled an afghan up to his chin, all but his face hidden under the blanket. A few books tumbled to the floor, and he gazed at them, distressed.

"You need to rest more," Sunny declared, determined to ignore the weird weather, the gooseflesh still crawling down his spine, and the way Ferny paced in front of the closed door, hackles half-raised. Instead, he focused on what he could actually do. He gathered some of the books from the couch, about to return them to their places on the shelf, but stopped at the soft sound Emile made.

When he glanced up, Emile's expression was half-greedy, half-distressed.

"Okay." Sunny tucked them back into the space between a pillow and the arm of the couch while Emile watched him closely, body visibly relaxing once the books had been tucked away. "Try to rest."

Emile nodded, fingers caressing the spines of each book in turn, though he was no longer looking at them. Something about having them where he could touch them seemed to calm him, so Sunny let them be.

He fetched a new towel out of a drawer and wet it down so he could clean up the specks of drying blood on his shins caused by the sharp sand the wind had whipped up.

Emile sighed. "I can't stay here."

Throwing an uneasy glance out the window over the sink, Sunny frowned. "I think you have to stay here, actually." A few quick twists of the towel expelled the excess water, and he used it to wipe down his legs.

There was no real damage. All the spots of blood wiped away with no effort, and the pricks were too small, dusted over by the fuzz of leg hair, to bother trying to bandage. He straightened and went back to the sink.

"Lie down for a few minutes. I'll make us some lunch."

"You don't have to."

Sunny tossed the rinsed towel into the hamper and sat on the coffee table, where he could reach to touch Emile's cheek lightly. "You're clammy still. Pushing that wheelbarrow was a bit much for your first time out."

Emile looked at him through his lashes. His expression was unreadable, but he said nothing, just turned enough to kiss the tips of Sunny's fingers, then nod.

"Good deal." Sunny smiled as best he could, knowing they were both ignoring something inexplicable. "We'll eat, then we'll talk."

CHAPTER 9

EMILE REMAINED perfectly still, glad when Sunny didn't push, instead returning to the kitchen. At least that way, Emile could keep the scales on the back of his hand hidden, and the burning itch of them emerging wouldn't tip Sunny off if it showed on his face. With Sunny's back to him, Emile could concentrate on easing the scales back where they belonged—hidden under a veil of magic.

Halfway between where Emile sat and where Sunny worked, Fernforest settled into a squat, gaze fixed on the door. The dog knew, even if Sunny was remaining willfully ignorant.

Or was he?

Talk. And tell him what?

You know that weird breathing forest thing that just happened? That's my intended mate watching us from a magical realm. He's spying on me, trying to work out how to make me go back so he can enslave me to carry a new brood. Brood of what? Oh. Right. Dragons. Did I mention I was a dragon? A sort of gender-fluid dragon princeling. But I ran away from certain... expectations *because I don't want to spend the rest of my life doing what other people tell me to.*

He couldn't stay here.

He'd never planned to stay longer than the few days it took him to get his strength back. This new development made him even more certain it was time to go. Hakko was getting bolder. Or more desperate. But either way, remaining so close to the place where he'd crossed was dangerous. If Hakko figured out where the Fold bent over itself enough to allow passage from one world to the other, there was no telling what he might send through after Emile.

Not to mention he was beginning to think his proximity to that opening was allowing magic to seep through, mix with the native energy, and interfere with his ability to get his inner dragon under control. Every morning he woke with his magic searing gouges through his psyche, and he had to grapple it into submission. He was getting better at it. There were no more spontaneous shifts of extremities from human-shaped to *other*, at least, but often he remained cocooned in a blanket on the couch, hiding scales or feathers that would prove awkward to explain. The torn pillow had been bad enough, and when Sunny had reprimanded Fernforest for that, Emile had felt bad. Fernforest had given him a cold shoulder for most of two days.

He'd been forgiven eventually, but at some point he had to figure out what he was going to do next. Going back under the Fold wasn't an option. The lengths Hakko was apparently willing to go to to get him back made that obvious. Emile was beginning to suspect that the strange way his magic was behaving had more to do with Hakko than the human side of the Fold. If he went back, there would be no second chance to run.

So he had to go forward. But to where? If he didn't get hold of his wayward magic, he didn't dare go near more people. He didn't know for sure if it was just Sunny, or if any contact with humans would make his magic spike in wild and unpredictable ways. Or if that was Hakko's doing in some way. But if his few brief physical contacts with Sunny were anything to go by he had to be cautious. It was a convenient excuse not to leave this idyllic, safely human-free spot. Well, human-free except for Sunny. But he wasn't going to look at *that* impulse too closely.

He'd never known anyone like this man who glowed like sunshine and made his heart race. Somehow Sunny's tiny patch of cultivated, tamed ground in the midst of acres of nearly pristine old-growth woods and clear streams had a magic of its own. That magic had Sunny's touch all over it, and Emile was hopelessly ensnared.

And how is that any better than the gilded cage Hakko would build around me?

At home he'd faced relentless pressure to accept both sides of himself. He'd been assured his bipedal form was as strong as his dragon, though at home many of his people only wore skin when they were too tired, too sick, too old, or too much in their heads to carry the weight of their scales. They tried to convince him the Egg-bearer he was destined to be was as virile as the Sire that was to be Hakko's role. As an Egg-bearer, his softer, scale-and-feather form would be celebrated. And as much as he preferred his hard-scale form, that wasn't untrue.

Egg-bearers were protected, coddled, even. He would spend his life shrouded in luxury, given his every possible desire. Except freedom. His need for freedom, for the forests and streams and open spaces, would be forever taken from him and replaced with decadence in a pretty, opulent prison. They'd wanted him to embrace his inner scholar to make up for the fact he'd never be allowed beyond the outer walls of Hakko's beautiful home. They wanted him tame. Controlled. Content to be their Egg-bearer, then their Hatch-guardian, and to accept his place in the halls of their pretty castle until he was ready to return to the stars as their own guardian had.

He wasn't about to give up scale and feather or skin. The magic made both forms his right. Steeped in the magic on the other side of the Fold, his scales made him stronger than most, his skin more beautiful, and the transition between as effortless as a thought. No one had understood his choice to remain in hard scales and feathers as much as he did, and certainly no one understood why he eschewed his soft scales for the harder, heavier form he most preferred.

Not that it mattered. His choices were his own, and he'd left in an attempt to keep them that way. He hadn't anticipated the way his magic and the odd, strangely unpredictable magic on this side of the Fold would play havoc with the shift that had always been so effortless.

"You're awfully thoughtful." Sunny stood in front of the couch, holding out what had, over the week, become Emile's mug. He didn't know what "My other dog is Chickie" meant, but he liked the golden-eyed image of what was maybe the close-up of a wolf's face. There was the soul of something powerful and loyal in the drawing that reminded him partly of Fernforest, and partly of the wilder things he'd left behind the Fold.

With his back resting on one arm of the couch so he could watch Sunny pour and doctor their coffee, Emile had let his feet poke from under his pillow nest. As soon as Emile took his drink, Sunny sat, thigh covering Emile's toes. The contact, even through Sunny's shorts, eased some of Emile's tension.

Fortunately the hand that had sported a few iridescent orangeish scales on its back just a few minutes earlier now only had an irritating itch to remind him he still wasn't quite himself. The hot breath of the forest on their heels had distracted his concentration enough that some of the magic Sunny's touch excited had seeped through. Fernforest had taken Sunny's focus off Emile just long enough to allow Emile to hide the anomaly under the covers.

There was no visual sign of the scales or the ridge of tiny feathers that had trailed up the side of his forearm now. The feathers themselves had molted almost as soon as they had appeared, and Emile had managed to secret them into a pocket. He would take them to the bathroom and flush them, with Sunny none the wiser, as soon as he could.

The thought that he couldn't tuck them in next to his newly acquired books saddened him, but he felt the time to reveal his true form hadn't come yet. He would have to deal with the disappointingly small collection of things in favour of keeping Sunny's help. For now.

Accepting the offering of coffee, Emile cradled his sore hand against his stomach. He had no shame in admitting the beverage was one of his very favourite discoveries of what the world on this side of the Fold had to offer. A lot of everything else was confusing, but coffee was a definite plus. He sipped, feeling Sunny's eyes on his face.

"I can't understand how you have any skin left inside your mouth," Sunny mused as he blew across the top of his drink. "It's like you don't feel heat at all."

Emile could hardly admit that heat meant very little to him. Cold was more problematic, and water…. He shivered. "I guess I'm tough."

"Not gonna lie, my friend. It's a little bit freaky."

You don't know the half of it. Emile just smiled and took another sip.

For a few minutes, they sat in companionable quiet. This had become Emile's favourite part of their day—sitting quietly, sipping coffee, and silently agreeing not to mention all the things they weren't talking about. It should have been awkward but never had been until today. This time, after the phone call Sunny had received—or maybe it was the unsettling brush with magic Sunny would have no explanation for—the silence was troubled. Whatever he was thinking about, Sunny was clearly unhappy. His brightness had been dimmed, and his closeness, which usually excited the magic always running just under Emile's skin, had a different, more disturbing effect.

The power Emile drew on to change between forms pulsed, a hard, heavy beat thudding against his chest, not quite in sync with his own heartbeat.

Sunny swallowed, and Emile's attention caught on his throat. He noticed the pulse there and felt the magic shift, beat, fall into rhythm with Sunny's heart. It was odd. For a few moments of utter stillness, it was like two hearts beat in his chest, slightly out of sync, their rhythms uneven and at odds. And then they weren't. They still beat separately, distinct from one another, but the magic fell into a counterpoint to Emile's slightly slower beat, complementing it, no longer sizzling and roiling just beyond his control, but relaxed and calm. Still there, the power thrummed with potential, but for the first time since he'd slipped to this side of the Fold, Emile didn't fear it might spike out of his control.

CHAPTER 10

CALM WASHED over Sunny, not erasing the unease the morning had brought but making it feel less daunting. He closed his eyes and let out a bone-deep sigh. "I'm not sure where to start," he admitted finally.

"Start?" Emile's feet shifted under his thigh, and Sunny glanced at him. Late-morning sunlight caressed his face, lighting his eyes, causing a sparkle in their depths. Sunny was reminded of a pair of sapphire earrings his grandmother had once given his mother for Christmas. She'd given them back, asserting that she'd rather have something more practical and that there was no reason to spend so much money on adornment.

Sunny closed his eyes and beat back the wave of sadness. His grandmother had replaced the earrings with the Land Rover Sunny now drove. It was one of the last things she had done for their family and had seemed trivial at the time. Sunny wondered now if things might have been different had his parents been driving it instead of the tiny electric car his father preferred.

"What is it?" Emile leaned forward, touching fingertips to Sunny's face. The heat of each fingertip was a distinct, searing spot of excited heat, and Sunny turned into the touch without thought.

"Nothing you can fix," Sunny said after a moment, words thick with syrupy bottled emotion. A sigh seeped from him. He blinked and looked at Emile again. Sunlight looked so good on him, his pale skin pearlescent where the rays brushed it. The blue of his eyes softened with compassion.

"I would try," Emile whispered.

"Why do I know that's true?"

Emile sat forward, setting his mug on the table. "Because it is." He brushed his lips over Sunny's cheekbone. Instantly the fire from his fingertips burned deep into Sunny, and a peck on the cheek was nowhere near enough.

Sunny turned his head, lighting his gaze on Emile's parted lips. "I need to kiss you," he whispered.

Emile's lips curled up at the corners. "Need?"

"I think so, yes." He licked his lips and imagined pulling back, giving Emile room. The thought pained him, and he closed his eyes. "Please."

Emile kissed him, at first gentle, no more than a soft touch of his lips to Sunny's as his long fingers cupped the back of Sunny's neck and held him in place. Sunny opened to him, willing him to apply more pressure. With a soft sigh, Emile licked delicately, like he was waiting for something.

"More," Sunny breathed against his lips.

Emile's consent was a soft-whispered "yes." So Sunny planted his mouth over Emile's and drove him back against the arm of the couch. He licked along Emile's lower lip, eliciting a tiny gasp. The sound and taste of him made Sunny's blood rush. He ran fingertips over Emile's jaw, trailing them along hard bone under satiny skin, revelling in the heat that spread through him as he touched.

Emile sighed again, tipped his head enough to allow Sunny to slip fingers back into silky hair.

And Sunny was lost. Between the kiss and the sensory appeal of Emile's hair sliding through his fingers, the sparks of heat dancing between his fingertips and Emile's skin, he couldn't pull away if he wanted to.

He didn't want to.

EMILE FLUTTERED between Sunny's brightly lit world of sunshine and his own uncertain control over his magic. If he let Sunny control the kiss, he risked the magic slipping his grip. It roiled just beneath the surface, sparking and fretting, pushing at the bonds he kept on it with every touch of Sunny's fingers along his jaw, his throat, his nape.

Just as Emile thought he might lose that small sliver of control over the chaos, Sunny eased off, cupped his cheek, and gazed into him. "Huh." He puffed out the nonword, then grinned. "I should let you up."

The idea of it suddenly panicked Emile, and he shook his head, eyes wide. "Wait." He placed his hand over Sunny's on his face. "Stay there."

"Okay." Sunny kissed the very tip of his nose. "Take a breath."

"Yes." Emile let his eyes drift closed as he concentrated on the whirling maelstrom of magic and emotion battering in his chest. The heat was almost too much, and he couldn't believe Sunny didn't feel the constant flow of sparks and incandescent light flashing between them at every point their skin connected.

"Okay?" Sunny asked, worry seeping into his tone.

"Fine." Emile heard the tightness in his voice and concentrated until he could once again focus on that dual thump of heart and magic in his chest. Finally, he opened his eyes, managed a small smile. "Been a weird morning."

Sunny's face fell and he sat back. "It has."

Immediately Emile's magic flared, rising in a tidal wave of searing heat and pain through his chest and stabbing bright spikes into his head. He groaned and clutched at Sunny's arm to ground himself before the agony ate through his last thread of control.

"I've got you." Sunny stroked a hand over the back of Emile's neck and leaned close to press their foreheads together. "What is it?"

"Feel…." *Better. I feel better.* He leaned into Sunny and let out a heavy breath. "Tired," he admitted. Slowly the magic regained its rhythm, attuning itself to his heartbeat and to the pulse of Sunny's blood Emile could feel where his fingers brushed Sunny's wrist.

"Then I should let you rest." Sunny made to move, let him go, maybe was even posing to rise, but Emile stopped him with a tightened grip on that faint pulse that seemed to speak to his magic.

"Stay."

"Okay." Careful not to let go, Sunny manoeuvred himself so his feet were tucked up at the end of the short couch, with Emile's legs draped over his lap. He slid an arm under Emile's back, yanked free a few books that he tossed to the far end of the couch, then pulled at Emile until his cheek rested against Sunny's shoulder. The couch was too small for them both, but somehow Sunny made it work. Emile melted against him, relief pouring through him as his magic settled to a manageable, if constant, ebb and surge that kept time with their mingled heartbeats.

"Better?" Sunny asked after a few minutes.

"Yes."

Sunny pressed a kiss to Emile's hair. "Me too," he whispered. "Me too."

CHAPTER 11

EVENTUALLY EMILE asked, as he always did, what Sunny had planned for the rest of the day.

"Gardening, I hope. If the weather holds out. That wind this morning was weird."

Blithely, Emile allowed Sunny to pass what he'd recognised as a magical surge of energy off as weather. The truth was "weird" in ways Sunny wouldn't believe. "I like watching you garden," he said instead of challenging the assumption. He wasn't sure why he said it. Or why it was true. It looked like backbreaking work. A twitch of movement against his hair had Emile imagining Sunny's sweet smile.

"That why you came out today? To help? Or to watch?" There was amusement in his tone.

"Mmm." Emile snuggled closer, giving in to the fog of sleepiness. "Looks hard. But rewarding."

"It's satisfying to see the work progress. To see a change from what it looked like when you began a task to what it looks like at the end. I like creating something from nothing more than a bit of dirt and some horse shit. I like doing it with my own two hands."

"Yes. Progress. Success you can see. I like that." Growing green things—life from next to nothing—was a magic all its own. Not one Emile excelled at.

The idea of nurturing life in his own body was alien to him. He'd had suspicions about Hakko's determination to have Emile as his Bearer. The night their own Bearer had left them, Bethakke had warned Emile that the other Houses were drawing further from the Corcaird House. That they didn't trust Hakko. Bethakke had counselled Emile to be wary, ask questions, study their House's history, and above all, trust his other broodnest companions' opinions on Hakko.

When Ananth had suggested Emile leave Hakko's home immediately after Bethakke's star-watch ceremony, he had agreed. Crossing the Fold hadn't been on his agenda that night. He'd planned to be better prepared, at least to have clothing for after he'd taken his skin form.

Hakko hadn't afforded him that choice.

"I take it your last job was less results-oriented," Sunny asked, reclaiming his attention.

"My last occupation had no appreciable way to measure success." What success was there in reading dry, boring tomes of fey histories, House conquests, following the lengthy root systems of intertwined family trees just to keep himself occupied? And when he was called on to do anything more than sit and read? It was to stand at Hakko's side, the picture of obedient adherence to a social system he abhorred. To proudly hold up the tradition and pretend he was happy to be the branch from which would spring the next generation. Once he accepted the eggs from the other Houses, incubated, and bore them, he would be their only support. The donators of those eggs would disperse back to their lives, and he would be left to rear their young alone.

So maybe he wasn't exactly speaking truth. A healthy, happy new brood of dragons would speak to success, after a fashion. However, once raised, once they fled their broodnest, there would be nothing left for Emile but the boredom of books and leisure he didn't want. Nothing for *him*. Nothing to build a life on. He could well understand why the Egg-bearers of the Ten Houses were often the first of their generation to choose the oblivion of the stars. At least the Bearers of the lesser Enclaves could have more than one brood. As a Bearer for one of the Ten Houses, he would be allowed only one.

He tried not to believe that Hakko had more sinister plans for him. The Corcaird House was a small one—powerful and respected, yes, but small. Hakko couldn't do much to change that. Not without more power than he possessed himself. The fastest if not the best way for a small House to grow was also the one way their laws prohibited. One dragon had to be stronger than all the rest. The only way for that to happen was if that dragon was the product of a Sire and Bearer who shared a magical lineage. Creating and fertilising such an egg was forbidden.

And yet, Hakko was an extremely powerful dragon. That strength made Emile wonder about the whispered rumours that Bethakke's mate had secretly done just that to create not only Hakko, but maybe Emile as well. It didn't bear thinking about.

And yet. Hakko was a very powerful dragon....

"Yeah, that would kind of suck." Sunny's sympathetic voice once again drew him away from that unpleasant contemplation.

"It was, as you would say, not so awesome."

"What did you do?"

Emile considered that.

"I mean, I basically know nothing about you."

That was truer than Sunny could possibly know. But how to explain his former responsibilities had entailed seeing to the comfort of a man who never seemed satisfied with Emile's best efforts, and who would never accept Emile's flight?

"I guess there's the argument that if you were desperate enough to hide out naked in my shack, there's probably a reason you ran away from your old life and that you maybe don't want to talk about it. I can see that." Sunny let out a breath, stroked a hand over Emile's hair, but there was a new tenseness in him now that hadn't been there a moment ago. "I get it. I do."

"But?" Emile asked, frantically searching his memories of the scant human artefacts and written stories he'd been able to find while avoiding Hakko's notice. He needed to explain where he'd come from, why he was here, how he'd arrived on Sunny's doorstep, and not sound like he was hiding anything. Impossible, knowing as little as he did about modern human society.

"You've lived with me a while now. I have no reason to kick you out that I can see. But you understand why I'd be curious. Maybe even a little worried. Like if cops are going to come knocking on my door looking for a criminal, for instance. Or if someone even nastier were to come looking for you?"

"In your experience, criminals tend to hide out naked in old forest huts to escape the law? Is that a thing around here?" *Deflect. Good strategy. Because he's going to just forget all about the fact he has no reason to trust me if I continue to avoid answering the simplest of questions.*

Sunny snorted. "Hardly. Still—"

"Still," Emile conceded, thinking of nothing he could use to explain his situation, "after all you've done to help me, you'd like to know where I come from and why I'm here now."

"My helping you doesn't hinge on you telling me anything," Sunny assured him. "And it never will."

"So curiosity, then?"

"Concern. You've been wearing my shorts strapped on with some rope and wandering my house barefoot. You're more hippie than I am, and that's saying something. I have no issues sharing my clothes and my books and my food. But I worry. Maybe you aren't going to want to hang out here in the forest with me forever. Maybe someone is going to come looking for you eventually. I'd like to know if I should be protecting you from them if that happens, or…."

When it was clear he wasn't going to continue, Emile finished the thought for him. "If you should be protecting them from me? Or protecting yourself from me?"

Sunny grunted, hand still moving lazily through Emile's hair. "Ferny likes you. I've learned to trust his instincts about people. As far as I know, he's never been wrong." He sat up, forcing Emile to sit as well, since he was all but sprawled on top of Sunny.

When he met Sunny's gaze, the intensity of it should have been unnerving. It was just… steady. The unwavering patience soothed the bubbling magic Emile could feel pushing to get free as they moved away from one another.

"Will you settle for an admission that I left an untenable situation to which I have no intention of returning? And that there is no reason your law would be looking for me? That I can assure you."

Sunny inclined his head. "If that's all you want to tell me, then yes, I'll have to settle." He did smile, though, and a tightness in Emile's gut eased. His magic rose, enthusiastic and bright, and he had to grapple it back.

"Thank you." If his voice sounded strained, Sunny didn't seem to notice, and a few breaths later, the magic tamed once more. Maybe someday he could tell Sunny more. Or, if he managed to get a handle on the magic plaguing him, he might keep his secret forever. As if in response, the fiery energy fanned high, and it was all he could do to hold in a gasp and wish it would make up its mind if it liked Sunny or wanted to burn him.

"Awkward segue, though," Sunny said after a moment, and Emile tilted his head. "You know that phone conversation I had with my sister?"

The phone itself was an interesting bit of human technology. Emile hadn't encountered cell phones in his furtive studies. He'd quickly realised most of the information his people had about this side of the Fold was grossly outdated. While the concept of long-distance communication wasn't alien to him, he and his kind simply eschewed the technical aspects for magical ones.

"Well, as much as I dislike cities and people in general," Sunny said, "I did sort of promise her I would visit her. It's been… a while since we saw each other." A wave of hurt and loss washed over Emile, accompanied by the deep shadow in Sunny's eyes.

Emile reached over and brushed his fingers over the back of one of Sunny's hands. Some of the pain in his expression eased, and he offered Emile a weak blink of a smile.

"We were pretty close growing up. Are close, except…." His frown and another wave of pain told Emile clearly that whatever had happened, Sunny wasn't prepared to talk about it.

If he was willing to endure that kind of hurt to be by his sister's side, though, the relationship mattered to him. Emile barely remembered most of his broodnest companions other than Hakko, who had hatched right next to him and helped him from his shell, and Ananth, the last to hatch and much smaller than the rest. Ananth had stayed by their Bearer the longest, listening to Emile's dreams of leaving the broodnest and never returning. He had thought to find understanding with Ananth, given that they had the same affinity for their soft scales that Emile had for his hard ones.

When their Bearer finally succumbed to their desire to join the stars, Emile had felt Ananth's ache and sadness. It had pained him to feel that loss, but Ananth had never asked for his help, nor wanted his support in their grief. It had been the one time Emile ever remembered seeing Ananth's hard-scale form. As beautiful as they were in razor-edged gold and bronze, it hadn't lasted long. Ananth had shifted to their soft form and taken flight, that final warning to Emile their last communication before Ananth was gone.

So Sunny wanting to go to his sister's aid was as foreign to Emile as cell phones and plastic. He was so lost here. Helpless, really, caged even more surely than he had been at home, through his own sheer ignorance.

"What is it?"

"Nothing." He shook his head, face tightening into a frown. He watched the coffee in his mug tremble, concentric rings forming on the surface. The magic, forced down for so long, burned deep and hot. He could feel the scales rippling under the surface of his skin and fought to keep them there.

"Emile." Sunny took the mug from him. "What is—"

Emile's bones ached with the tension of wanting to change. The magic railed against his control, simmering hotter with every breath, flaring with every doubt that assailed him. The breech, when a lick of his magic curled up through his net of restraint to wrap itself around his restless dragon-heart, was a searing flash of pain over every inch of his skin.

Emile vaulted from the couch.

The tiny cabin, the closed door, Sunny's proximity all crowded in on him. He couldn't breathe. In seconds he'd flung open the door, headed for the bridge and the woods beyond, no thought in his head but that he had to free himself from his constraints, not even knowing exactly what those constraints were.

"Emile!" Sunny pounded after him, the hollow thump of his footsteps reminding Emile of the sound of a dragon walking over a brownie nest as Sunny ran down the yard after him. He called again, even as Emile ducked into the cool green shade under the trees. Water gurgled under the bridge, but the sound quickly died with distance.

Air brushed over his skin, soft and shaded, a crisp ruffle of a breeze. Grateful, he pulled it into his lungs, closing his eyes as he finally slowed and breathed in the woods. The smells of warm earth, emerald shade, blue-and-gold air washed through him. Fernforest barked somewhere behind, spurring Emile back into action. He took a narrow path at a quick jog, hoping the forest and its inherent magic would help him get a handle on his own.

As if in answer, the forest herded him, opening up as he moved, swaying back together in his wake. He soon found himself across a clearing and on the edge of the brook by the willow where Sunny had first followed him so long ago. He skidded to a stop.

Just on the other side of the fast-flowing stream, the pulsing undulation of the Fold curling over itself, enticed his magic to rise. Emile moaned, the pull of his magic to the familiarity of that leaking from the Fold calling to his dragon.

The water, though, was too wide to cross and moving too fast. He followed it until he was once more sheltered, this time by the intertwined arms and fingers of spruces and pines. The creek laughed up at him, bright even in the deep, mossy shade of these prickly trees.

A spruce nymph morphed out of its tree's shadows to bare spiked teeth in a leering smile. He flicked green-and-rust clawed fingers in

Emile's direction, catching his cheek with a lightning-fast caress that drew a drop of blood. His eyes widened, the faceted depths unfolding like a dried pinecone.

"Magic is drawn to magic," Emile told him, and the nymph bent its long neck to one side. "Sorry if I pulled you from slumber."

A shiver rustled the nymph's needles in a muted rattle, and he offered that toothy, salacious smile again. The invitation was clear. Magical beings were inherently compatible on many levels, and it wouldn't have been the first such dalliance Emile had. His dragon half rumbled, restless and hungry for the infusion of magic such a coupling would bring.

A sunshine-bright memory of Sunny splashed through Emile's mind.

"I can't," he whispered.

His dragon rumbled.

The nymph shrugged with a shiver of needles and tiny twigs.

The creek bubbled and roiled, merriment flooding over Emile and the nymph, who vanished back into the dimness, needlelike fingers at his lips. That only made the creek laugh harder, water splashing upward in tiny fountains.

"Laugh it up," Emile growled down at it—at *them*. Glittering sprites hovered over the surface of the water, giggling and flicking droplets of water at him. They were dazzling and mesmerising, playful but deadly if you didn't know they were there or didn't understand their game. They found everything funny. And if they didn't, they simply rolled over it to wipe the ground clean of whatever distressed them.

Amuse them, and they let you remain. Anger them, and there was no stopping their wrath. Not even dragon fire could withstand the ire of a pissed-off water sprite.

Emile usually gave them a wide berth. Now they demanded his attention. The sparkle they threw into the air sprinkled down over him to the tune of their tinkling laughter. His magic slipped its bonds so quickly and thoroughly he was jolted fully into scales and feathers, wings unfurling to smack against tree branches.

Ow! The sound of his reptilian grunt carried through the sudden stillness of a forest holding its breath. A flutter of needles sprinkled down over his hide, tickling where the scales were the most sensitive along the edges of his feather ruff, making him shiver where they tumbled along the hypersensitive membranes of his wings. The bright-fire burn of the transition faded almost instantly, and he settled into the dragon, pulling his wings tight against his back to protect the delicate skin.

With a soft huff, he dropped to all six feet and slipped, near silent, between the tree trunks along the bank of the ever-widening creek. As he turned, peering back in the direction of the house from the deepest, purpling shadows, he saw it—the golden glow almost too bright to look at.

Sunny. The thought sprang, a complete package of man, light, comfort, excitement, *want*, into his head. A heady moan crawled up his throat, rumbling out to roll along the forest floor, a wave of magical sound and heat. Leaves curled and tumbled in its wake. Grass shivered. A long-dormant deposit of devil's paintbrush seeds sprouted to life, pushing the orange-tufted flowers into the open in the wake of the magic pouring from him. The forest drew in another collective breath and held it.

At the edge of the trees, Sunny stopped. For a long moment he peered into the forest. Puzzlement showed on his face, as if he'd noticed the aspen leaves behind him frozen midtremble, and the utter silence under the striped shade of the pines. He cocked his head, and the soft thrum of his voice drifted into the shadows. "Emile? Are you there? Please. Let me help."

As if released from a spell, the forest rustled back to life.

Next to Sunny, Fernforest yipped, then trotted gamely into the brush, path unerringly leading to Emile's hiding spot.

Emile gave himself a mental shake. As if he trusted the dog to lead him, Sunny turned in Emile's direction and began walking.

His footsteps were slow. He glanced from side to side, as if he couldn't see Emile's brightly patterned scales flashing red, orange, and fuchsia under the deep green of the forest canopy where sunlight filtered through and bounced off him.

He'd heard that humans couldn't see what they didn't believe in. That nymphs and sprites and dryads walked free here because humans couldn't wrap their minds around their existence. That humans saw shadows and light patterns rather than living, breathing creatures of magic and lore. The thought that Sunny could look right through him, not believe he was real, hurt like nothing Emile had ever experienced.

A shudder sent razor-edged shards of magic coursing just under his skin, and it was all he could do to hold back the bellow of pain. As it was, the trees around him recoiled, their dryads feeling the burning splash of magic like acid. The forest shuddered with him.

Sunny stilled, frozen in the maelstrom of shaking leaves and branches. Needles rained down around him, caught in his hair, and stuck to sweat-damp skin. Then the wave of raw magic passed, absorbed by water sprites and tiny flower feys. The world stilled as quickly as it had flared up.

"Emile?" Sunny called. His tone was soft, pitched to coax a frightened, shy animal out of hiding.

It almost worked. Emile took a step, another—then remembered if Sunny *did* see him, discovering Emile slithering from the woods on six legs, with a muzzle and fangs, would terrify him. With a thought he was in his skin so fast, the burn fading to the localised scrape of twigs and stones on his palms and knees. He scrambled to his feet, leaning on a tree to catch his breath.

A spiky, rough branch-arm draped over his shoulders, sheltering and protective. He laid his forehead against the tree, silently thankful for the nymph's support.

The change always took his breath away, but unlike his experience trying to keep the magic—and the change—at bay, letting it happen left him energised. Clearly his magic liked the power flowing freely on this side of the Fold. At least, it did when he let it have some freedom.

Carefully, he lifted the nymph's arm from him and took a step. Something soft cushioned his footfall, and he looked down at the not-inconsiderable pile of pink feathers and iridescent scales littering the forest floor.

"That's going to be troublesome to explain," Emile muttered. He glanced back at Sunny, who had stopped at about the same spot near the edge of the stream where Emile had earlier. Rather than lifting his face to breathe in the breath of the forest as Emile had, though, Sunny was frowning at the forest floor.

"Emile?" He bent, picked something up, and Emile groaned. Sunny held the shorts Emile had been wearing when he'd run for the trees. Until that moment, he hadn't really noticed his nakedness. "What the hell?"

CHAPTER 12

EMILE MELTED back into the shadows. He couldn't walk out of the bush naked. Again. Certainly Sunny would already be concerned that he had fled in the middle of a conversation. There was no telling what he might think of this.

Behind Emile, the nymph shifted, a faint movement of shadows and tree limbs swaying slightly against the breeze. Emile glanced at him. Eyes in shades of bark and pinecone gazed back; then the nymph turned his attention to the creek. He raised an arm in the water's direction and tilted his head.

"No," Emile whispered. "I can't."

The water sprites laughed at him, splashing his feet, muddying the bank. He took a step back, damp soil squishing up between his toes. Sunlight splashed over his bare ass, and he scurried back into the shadows. Deciding to take a swim was as logical a reason to have doffed the shorts as anything, but it wouldn't explain why he'd run in the first place.

The nymph proffered another toothy grin as water lapped up and over the bank of the creek. A spiky hand on Emile's back made him jump. His feet went out from under him. He landed hard on his ass on ground that gave beneath him with a wet squelch. He sank into black, sticky mud, sliding down onto his back, then went feet-first into the creek with an almighty splash.

Water sprites surged around him, buoying him up, laughing at him, but keeping his head above water until he'd regained control of his body.

"Emile!" Sunny's shout cracked through the forest.

The nymph shivered into shadow and dappled sunlight like he'd never been there. The water flowed around Emile's waist where he sat, picking up the ends of his hair as it swirled and lapped at his skin. He trembled, unwilling to move. If it got deeper, if the stones beneath his ass and palms were slippery, if his head went under—

"Emile." Behind him, Sunny's footsteps slapped through the mud on the bank, and a warm, strong hand landed on his shoulder. "There you are. What happened?"

"Fell," Emile muttered, jaw tight, skin breaking out in gooseflesh under the layer of mud coating his back. His hair plastered against him in a solid mass of mud and twigs and leaves.

"You are a mess." Sunny stroked fingers over his head, catching in the tangles of mud-crusted hair. "Hang on."

Emile remained stock-still, not even daring to turn around to see what Sunny might be doing. The water remained just turbulent enough to hide his privates under the roiling surface. He heard the faint laughter of the sprites, though they were clearly disguising their voices and forms in the bubbling brook.

He hated water sprites. So much. When he scowled down at the water, they crawled up his chest, tickling over his most sensitive areas, then trickling innocently away as Sunny returned to crouch in the stream behind Emile.

"Let's get the mud out of your hair first. Can you lie back?"

"No!" The mere thought of putting his head anywhere near the mischievous sprites made him bark out the word, and he was sure the dragon voice came through, though Sunny's only reaction was to squeeze his shoulder.

"It's okay. It'll just take longer this way." He cupped some water and let it flow through his fingers over Emile's head. The cool silver slid along his hair and scalp and skin. Maybe because Sunny had touched it, the water was just water, clear and calming and cool, like magic that meshed with his and settled it.

Soon Emile closed his eyes, and before long he was leaning back against Sunny's chest, body, magic, and mind calm despite the water still flowing past, rippling around his waist and over his legs.

"Why did you take off?" Sunny asked finally. "What did I say?"

"Nothing. It wasn't you." And yet, it *was* Sunny. Or his house. Emile couldn't be sure. Right here, right now, he was calm, his magic quiescent. Even sitting waist-deep in the lap of the aggravating water sprites wasn't enough to stir his dragon. Because of the forest or his proximity to the Fold or Sunny's arms around him, he had no idea.

He wanted to stay this way, wanted to never, ever leave this place. This moment. And the thought of remaining closed like a trap around his mind. Caged, just as surely as if he allowed Hakko the golden chains of the Egg-bearer's lot.

"No." Emile sat up. He couldn't stay. Magic flared under his skin, and he fought it back.

"No what?" Sunny placed a hand in the centre of his back. Heat spread outwards from the touch. The magic burned bright and strong. The dragon reared up, roaring inside his head, demanding and covetous. Emile whirled.

SUNNY SCRAMBLED back. He'd been leaning on his shirt, which was draped over a boulder at the edge of the stream. When Emile turned to face him so suddenly, he was pinned. For a split second, the light in Emile's eyes blazed the fiercest blue, flames so intense the heat licked at Sunny.

Sunny held up a hand. "What?"

"I—" Emile stared at him, lips parted, gaze so heated it set fire to Sunny's tenuous control over his libido. It had been all he could do to ignore his body's response, knowing Emile was naked under the waves.

The mud had been everywhere, providing a convenient excuse to get close, but now only clear water remained, sliding lazily down Emile's chest from the splashes he'd made turning around. It teased, trailing over Emile's pale, freckled skin, daring Sunny to reach over and follow.

"Gah! I want to kiss you again." Emile's voice, so smooth and cultured any other time, had a growl now, an underlying heated snarl that Sunny's body responded to instantly.

"Then you should," he breathed, leaning in to take the kiss if Emile didn't offer it.

They met halfway. This was nothing like the exploratory introductions they'd had at the house. Emile pushed him back, crawling over him on hands and feet, not touching, yet still aggressive, pinning Sunny under him by force of will.

Sunny's spine pressed against the rock. He could retreat no farther. Either he gave in, or he pushed back. As Emile ran his tongue along Sunny's lips, Sunny's will to resist evaporated. He pressed a palm to the centre of Emile's chest. The skin there, slick and heated and smooth, felt glorious.

"I had no idea," Sunny breathed.

"About?" Emile latched his lips on to Sunny's throat, all heat and sucking pressure.

Sunny wasn't sure exactly what he'd been talking about, though he did know he'd never been kissed quite like this. "We should get out of the water. Oh. Wait—that—do that again." And he lifted his chin.

Emile trailed his hot mouth down over Sunny's throat. Sunny granted whatever access Emile wanted. A low rumble, on the verge of inhuman, vibrated over his skin where Emile's lips scalded his soul. He was going to melt.

"Come." Abruptly Emile backed away, flowing like silk and sin to his feet, where he stood over Sunny. "Now."

Sunny placed his hand in Emile's, palm to palm, and allowed Emile to haul him to his feet. In moments, much faster than Sunny imagined possible, they were back in the clearing. Emile parted the hanging fronds of the willow and guided Sunny underneath. Green and yellow and gold light filtered through to them, creating a dome of delicate shadows, fragile streams of light, floating dust: a cocoon of pure magic.

Sunny didn't protest as Emile drew him down to the bed of soft moss. He had a fleeting thought of ants and other crawlies, but it evaporated as Emile knelt over him.

"This should be weird," Sunny noted.

Emile was naked, Sunny clad only in a pair of boxer briefs he'd had on under his own shorts. They both dripped, though the remaining water had warmed with their body heat. Sunny imagined faint steam rising off Emile's back, but before he thought to examine that more closely, more immediate matters distracted him.

Like Emile's smile. For the first time, Sunny saw more than a beleaguered stranger. There was something princely and majestic about Emile. And sad. So very sad and alone. The impression made him gasp.

"What do you see?" Emile asked, like he wasn't the least bit shocked or surprised by any of this.

"You." Sunny touched his cheek, expecting skin cooled from their time in the water. The contact was all heat and sparks. If he squinted, he imagined he'd see *actual* sparks. And then Emile was kissing him again. He closed his eyes and the sparks were real, flooding his vision, making the world spin around him.

Emile's birdlike weight settled over him, a welcome grounding. Sunny let his hands roam, smoothing over flawless skin. Long, lean muscle rippled under his fingertips. Emile's ribs no longer showed. His ass was a firm, sleek mound beneath Sunny's palm and his cock even firmer, pressing into the hollow of Sunny's hip.

Emile undulated against him, soft grunts and huffs puffing air over Sunny's skin in hot blasts between kisses. Emile snaked fingers into the hair at Sunny's temples, though he couldn't get far because of Sunny's curls. The gentle pressure, slender fingers against Sunny's scalp between the coils of hair, soothed and centred him in the moment. The simple touch kept his attention focused.

The gentle rocking of their bodies soon increased to a grind that Sunny knew was going to end in a sticky, delightful mess. He moaned softly, hands clamped to Emile's ass as they rocked together.

Kisses trailed off. Emile buried his face in the crook of Sunny's neck, and Sunny wrapped an arm around his waist. Their soft grunts sank into the moss around them, absorbed into the forest. When he lifted his face, his gaze on Sunny ignited heat deep inside, beyond physical.

The blue of Emile's eyes sharpened, taking on gem-bright edges. Sunny couldn't look away. He brushed fingertips over Emile's cheekbones. "Beautiful," he whispered.

Emile licked parted lips plump from kissing. "Close," he breathed, the word like a prayer slipping over skin, sinking into muscle and bone, and deeper. Sunny's gut tightened. His body flushed hot, cold, hot again, and he was right there with Emile, on the edge of something so much more than orgasm.

The willow branches creaked, leaves jostling and whispering. In the distance, the water gurgled—too loud, Sunny thought, but then, the sun was too bright, the moss too soft, everything too *much*, amplified and intense. And then he was coming, long, pulsing shots of lightning and hurricane washing through his body. He clung to Emile, breath caught as his release flowed from him.

Emile's hands on his shoulders were just as tight, his body rigid as he reached his own peak. They melted down from the height together, Emile lying limp on top of him, kissing lazily along his neck, stopping to catch his breath, then kissing some more.

Sunny stroked a hand through his hair. The long strands flowed like water between his fingers, and for what felt like a very long time, he drifted, half his attention on the feel of Emile draped over him, the other half floating off in a haze of satisfaction.

CHAPTER 13

THIS HAD been a very bad idea. Emile had run from the house to avoid giving in to the magic, and here he was, subject to its whims anyway. Staying very still was probably the best way to avoid talking about what had just happened. Sunny would have questions, and Emile wasn't certain he'd have answers.

He could feel the magic popping, bubbles of warmth or contentment or fizzy excitement or sunshine-bright insistence over his skin. The stream babbled incessantly. Even the willow, old as the earth, with roots so deep its dryad should have been long asleep by now, stirred above them. How Sunny didn't notice any of it was beyond Emile.

"I love days like this," Sunny murmured. He had an arm up, fingers weaving gracefully through the invisible strands of energy like he was playing the sounds of nature just for Emile.

"Like what?"

"*Alive* like this. Like if you reached out you could touch the sunshine. Cup it and hold it and form it into dreams that you can make come true. You know?" He moved his head a bit, and Emile just *felt* Sunny will him to look up.

He did.

Green and gold light, coloured by the willow's leaves, hit the side of Sunny's face. As he'd noticed before, Sunny's eyes turned a molten amber when the light slanted sideways through them. If Emile weren't sure he was human through and through, he might believe Sunny actually did know about the magic, maybe even knew how to manipulate it.

There was no doubt their lovemaking had awakened something. And there was no doubt that something belonged wholly to Sunny. He *was* magic, raw and unfiltered, and together they had trained the energy to something softer, stronger, easier to control.

Touch as gentle as the softest brush of a feather, Sunny stroked Emile's cheek, sweeping away a few strands of hair Emile hadn't realised had been floating near his face. He gave his head a small shake, willing the errant strands back into place.

Sunny grinned at him. "I'm talking shit, right?"

"Not at all." A smile found its way onto Emile's face, despite his worry. For a moment he managed to let his fear go and really study Sunny. "No." He dipped low enough to peck the very tip of Sunny's nose. "I know exactly what you mean."

If he was brave, it was the perfect segue. Now was the time for him to reach out and do exactly what Sunny had suggested: cup the sunlight, form a dream. Make it real. The magic would respond to him after this, he knew it. His connection to it was stronger in that moment than it had been since he'd crossed the Fold. Maybe because his connection to Sunny was strong in that moment.

Merging with Sunny had somehow merged his magic with the flux of this place. At least for a time. He could reach out and use it to show Sunny his other form, if he dared.

A twig snapped. Fernforest started baying like a bear was after him, and something crashed through the underbrush, coming nearer and nearer.

Under him, Sunny's body tensed. His face tightened to a mask of fear. "Ferny!" He all but shoved Emile off him just as Fernforest bounded across the clearing and into the sanctuary of the willow's arms, then Sunny's.

He wiggled his ass, tail waving furiously as he burrowed deeper into Sunny's embrace. "What's wrong, boy?" Sunny tried to capture the dog's face in his hands, but more crashing sounded through the forest, and the dog wiggled free. Turning to Emile, he began barking again.

"Stop." Emile crouched and laid a hand on the top of Fernforest's head. "Stop," he said quietly, using his grip on the magic to push calm at the dog. The effort cost him. His own magic bucked, unused to this strange meld of foreign flux and innate energy. But it was enough. Fernforest settled onto his haunches and stared directly into Emile's eyes.

"Is that so," Emile breathed after a moment.

"What?" Sunny crouched next to him, staring at his dog like he could see what Emile had, just by looking.

Fernforest couldn't show Sunny what he had shown Emile, though. Not really. He whined softly and turned pleading eyes on his master, but Sunny didn't have the same insight.

"Okay," Sunny said, matter-of-fact. "Can I get my pants, though?"

Fernforest yipped, danced to the edge of the willow's cave, and waited.

"What did—" Emile almost said *what did he tell you* but stopped himself. He knew what the dog *thought* he'd seen. A giant squirrel, bigger than the dog. Impossible. Except maybe not, with the way the magic distorted things so close to the Fold. And, after all, he was a dog. A giant squirrel could be anything. How else would a dog explain something inexplicable?

"Come on." Sunny took Emile's hand. "Let's go see what all the fuss is about."

They returned to the creekside to fetch their clothes and had only just managed to slip back into them, Sunny having doffed his sticky underwear and stuffed them into his pocket, when the unmistakable sound of a person tromping through the underbrush met their ears.

They glanced at one another. Heat rose up Emile's neck, and then Sunny burst out laughing. "That was close," he whispered loudly and once more latched on to Emile's hand. "Hello?"

His call went unanswered for a moment, but the footsteps ceased. Emile would have held him back, hoped for whoever was there to go away. If it was someone from his side of the Fold, how would he explain that? If it was someone who knew Emile, how would he reassure Sunny that there was no danger? No reason to fear for the sanctity of his home?

"Can I help you?" Sunny called again, heading forward in the direction the steps had last sounded. "Is someone there?"

Trees rustled on the far side of the clearing. Pine boughs jerked in the light breeze that shouldn't have been enough to stir them. They were hiding something, Emile was positive. Or someone?

Emile's skin crawled. He could sense the ripples in the native flux. Dryads and nymphs tended to exude the raw energy in spurts when agitated. At home, the excess was absorbed by the salamanders that lived in symbiosis with them. Here, he wasn't sure what was going to happen as the waves of energy escalated, making his own magic surge up to meet it.

"That's big," Sunny muttered, coming to a stop. "Hello? Come on out. Are you looking for me?" He turned to Emile. "I expect the neighbours might be wondering who moved in. I haven't introduced myself to many of them yet." He shrugged. "I was hoping to keep it that way indefinitely, but you know how people can be."

Emile tilted his head. He had no idea how most people were, only how Sunny was.

"Curious," Sunny supplied. "Annoyingly so, most of the time. Hey." He raised his voice and turned his attention back to the far side of the clearing. "You're on private land, so if you want to talk to me, now would be a good time to step out. Otherwise, I'd be quite happy for you to just go away."

Emile blinked. Sunny sounded downright cross. He'd never sounded that way towards Emile, even when he'd first found him squatting in his old shed. A heavy curtain of flux swept into them. Sunny frowned. Emile had to take a physical step back.

Fernforest barked, stopped halfway between where Sunny and Emile stood and the oddly wobbling pine trees. His bark was neither welcoming nor threatening. A warning, perhaps?

"This is *my* land," Sunny repeated, the power of his ownership strengthening his voice. "Either come out where I can see you or leave."

All around them the forest seemed to quake. A whisper shivered through the leaves. It could have been a breeze, if one wasn't attuned to the sound of dryads gossiping.

Fernforest gave a last bark, as if to add his support to Sunny's words; then he turned around and trotted back to Sunny's side, tail wagging.

"Fernforest doesn't seem concerned," Emile said. Whatever was hiding from them, it wasn't the giant squirrel. *That* creature—whatever it had actually been—had sent Fernforest into a positive frenzy of excited disbelief.

"No, he doesn't, does he?" Sunny, on the other hand, was beginning to sound more than just annoyed. "We should get back."

They walked—Emile's hand still firmly clasped in Sunny's—directly through the centre of the clearing. The place was infused with old and stable magic of a kind that his dragon knew well enough to respect. If it didn't exactly calm the dragon, it at least had it sitting back, behaving, for which Emile was grateful.

"Trees," Emile said, thinking out loud that the magic felt so stable because it *was* stable. As stable as, say, an ancient willow anchored in fertile soil on the edge of an excitable brook.

"Trees?" Sunny glanced at him, then at their surroundings.

"They calm me," Emile said.

They calmed the dragon. The magic under their feet was the willow, he was sure of it. If its dryad wasn't asleep—and he was fairly certain now that it wasn't—then it would be extremely powerful, given the age of the tree itself. That would explain the liveliness of the water sprites and the appearance of a dryad in the flesh. So to speak. The pine nymph he'd seen was about as corporeal as they ever got, in his experience. And he hadn't expected to see anything like it on this side of the Fold.

"Me too," Sunny said and his expression lifted. Some of his good cheer returned, if not the lethargy. "Let's go find out who's poking around under ours, shall we?"

Ours. Emile glanced at him, but if Sunny had said it on purpose, he wasn't admitting it. He was once more focused on the trees as they stepped under the first branches, following the narrow path that would lead back to the house.

CHAPTER 14

WHATEVER HAD so wildly excited his dog, Sunny saw nothing as they strolled back to the house. The feeling of being watched, though, that wasn't his imagination. He didn't think it was a person. It didn't feel threatening, but it was definitely there. And whatever was watching them didn't bother Ferny.

At the bridge, he stopped to look back the way they had come. The forest made only the regular forest noises. Sunlight filtered down through the aspen and birch leaves, just as it should, leaving gold-streaked motes of dust in its wake. A light breeze made the aspen leaves dance delicately.

But someone had been on his property. Whoever it was had ignored his calls. Sure, it might have been someone innocently following a path, walking their dog or enjoying the summer day. It didn't matter. It was his land, and what if he wanted to, say, walk around on it naked? He shot a glance at Emile.

"You seem unhappy." Emile pulled his hand free of Sunny's. "Perhaps we should not have—"

"That is *not* what I'm upset about," Sunny insisted.

"Then what?"

"What if whoever was wandering on my land saw us?"

"This is a problem?"

"It's a problem because it's our business. It's my space, and no one else should be on it."

"You didn't seem to mind my being here," Emile pointed out, taking a step back. "Was I wrong about that?"

"No. Of course not. You're different." Though he still had no idea what about Emile was different. He didn't want to examine *that* too closely because Daisy would have something to say about him letting his better judgement be overruled by some undefined *feeling* he couldn't explain.

But his instincts were right this time. Daisy would love Emile. Wouldn't she?

"Sunny?" Emile squeezed his shoulder, and Sunny blinked at him.

The look of concern on Emile's face hinted that it might not have been the first time Emile had said his name. "Sorry." He swallowed a lump that had formed in his throat and turned away from the woods.

Emile was different. He wasn't after anything of Sunny's. Look around. Sunny didn't have anything Emile—or anyone else—could possibly want. A tiny house in the middle of nowhere. A crazy-sweet dog and a whole lot of trees. And Emile showed no signs of leaving any time soon, and that, weirdly, was perfectly fine with Sunny.

"Let's get back." He took Emile's hand. "Are you hungry? I never did make us anything to eat."

EMILE FOLLOWED Sunny up the yard to the house in silence. Whatever was on Sunny's mind, it was best to let him work through it. No rocking his precarious boat. Especially not since his dragon's lethargy was already wearing off. Even a good orgasm, it seemed, wasn't enough to withstand whatever it was this place did to his magic.

He had a few ideas about all the things they hadn't quite seen out there. He'd come through the Fold when there was still a bit of snow in the shadiest parts of the forest. Now it was full summer, and he had to wonder. He felt more magic in the air than he had when he'd first arrived. Was that because of the season's change?

Warmer weather brought more of the fey, more of the delicate creatures out at home, and that was often enough to make the world feel like a more magical place. Maybe it was the same here.

Or maybe his own presence or his disturbance of the Fold had awakened something latent in the world, like the willow dryad. Maybe the unrest of his repressed dragon stirred up other uneasy power in the forest around him.

He didn't want to think too hard about a third option—that Hakko was somehow responsible for the creatures they had sensed, that Fernforest had apparently witnessed, but that they hadn't quite seen. If Hakko could send something through the Fold to hunt Emile down, something capable of besting a dragon, Sunny and everything he loved would be in danger. Emile wanted to believe Hakko would never risk the exposure of so much to humans who wouldn't understand, but then, he hadn't expected Hakko's resistance to letting Emile leave their home the last time either.

If it hadn't been for Ananth stepping to his defence after the star-watch ceremony and their more rational argument for letting Emile mourn their Bearer in his own way, Hakko would still hold the keys to Emile's freedom. Ananth had pressed Hakko to let them both have the freedom to leave the broodnest for a time, to shake off the sadness. The argument had eventually swayed Hakko, as it must with the entire House and so many members of the smaller Enclaves they were responsible for listening to the disagreement.

Once free of the city, Ananth had instructed Emile to meet them on the bluff above the city before Autumntide, issued their cryptic warning, then flown off. He regretted fooling Ananth and slipping away to cross the Fold without warning them he was leaving, but he hadn't dared share his plan with anyone. And, he reasoned, he likely would never see them again anyway, so if they were angry, it was unfortunate, but he'd been willing to pay that price for his liberty.

Back inside the house, Sunny was quiet a long time, face troubled as he puttered at the kitchen counter.

"Do you need help?" Emile finally asked. He was accustomed to sitting in his nest of cushions and books watching while Sunny cooked, but there was no reason for that any longer. He wasn't ill. He had his strength back. It was more than time for him to pull some of his own weight. He was more than a house guest to be waited on, and after their time under the willow, they had a connection they hadn't had before.

"I'm fine." Sunny's tone was flat. He didn't turn to face Emile but continued working. There was a substantial pile of sliced cheese on the cutting board next to the dwindling block.

Emil expected to feel jealousy over Sunny's obvious and sudden preoccupation. Instead he wished he could do something to bring back the lazy rapport they'd shared under the willow. He wanted to see Sunny's smile make a reappearance. He wanted to feel his magic again.

CHAPTER 15

THIS ISN'T rational. So someone walked across my land. They didn't hurt anything. He wasn't even sure what he was feeling. It felt like anger. But he suspected it was something else. Something deeper. He glanced at Emile, who was watching him closely. "What?"

"I want to help."

It was hard to tell if Emile meant help with the food or help with whatever was clearly bothering Sunny.

At his feet, Fernforest whined, a sound that emanated from deep in his chest.

"Sorry, buddy." Kneeling, Sunny cupped the dog's face, made kissy noises at him, and ruffled his fur until Fernforest touched noses with him. "I shouldn't let it get to me, right? It's a forest. Things live there." He tried to smile, but no matter how rational an explanation he tried in his head, he just couldn't make himself believe whatever they had just missed seeing out there was all that benign. And if it was just another person, well. He'd already let Emile into his life and nothing terrible had happened, so why was this such a big deal?

Closing his eyes, Sunny leaned close and breathed in the scent of his dog's fur, pressed his cheek to Fernforest's neck. "You are so much better company than other people, I swear."

The subtle sounds of bare feet hitting the floor and padding across the room to him reminded Sunny he wasn't alone with his dog. Part of him wanted to kick Emile out before he got any more attached. Before Emile revealed some unforeseen agenda to prove Sunny was just a means to an end.

Part of him wanted those few, sweet moments under the willow tree back.

Emile brushed long fingers over the top of Sunny's hair as he passed, but he said nothing. He picked up the cutting board with the bread and cheese, carried it to the stove, and set it down. As Sunny knelt next to the dog, Emile frowned at the appliance. He ran his fingers in circles over his chin as he contemplated, then reached to turn a knob.

Blue flames sprang up through the iron grate on a front burner, and Emile yelped, jumping back, nearly knocking the cutting board to the floor. Only impossibly fast reflexes caught it before the food went flying.

"Well, that isn't right," Emile muttered. He tipped his head to one side, considering the flames, a delicate frown wrinkling his forehead. Without regard for the danger, he moved to turn the knob again.

"Hey!" Sunny sprang up, grabbing his elbow. "Careful!"

"I'm sorry!" Emile took a step away from him. "What did I do?"

"Just let me—" Sunny clamped down on his ire. "Let me turn that down before you set your hair on fire or something." He did that, then fetched margarine from the fridge. "You want to help, you can butter the bread." He passed the tub to Emile and pointed to the top kitchen drawer. "Knives in there."

Emile took the margarine, fetched a knife, then leaned a hip on the counter, arms crossed, the margarine tub in one hand still, the butter knife in the other. "I agree that your dog is very good company," Emile said, tone so neutral it made Sunny's chest hurt.

He hadn't said that to imply anything to Emile. He'd sort of forgotten the other man was there, so focused was he on his dog and the unsettled feeling in his own gut. "Emile—"

Emile held up a hand. "I'll ask this once. I know I landed in your lap and you felt you had no choice but to help me, and I feel bad about that. If you want me to leave, I will. First thing in the morning, I will move on. All you have to do is say."

"No. That isn't what I want. I didn't mean you when I said that. I just meant—" He sighed but made a conscious effort not to offload his paranoia on Emile. "Mom always told me I spent too much time alone," he said, focusing his attention on lining up the slices of cheese. "She worried I wouldn't make friends when I was a kid, then that I would never find a boyfriend when I got older." He shrugged. "I never really thought much about it. I didn't want or not want friends. I was perfectly happy by myself. Daisy and I always got along well. I liked hanging out with her. I never really thought about it beyond that."

"Sunny." The click of stainless steel on the countertop alerted Sunny to the fact he'd closed his eyes. He'd been looking so far inside himself and his memories, he hadn't even noticed.

The heat, when Emile touched his shoulder, was no less than it had been that afternoon, despite Sunny's tumultuous emotions.

Heaving in a breath, Sunny plunged on. "I was happy with my small life. My people. Daisy. Her assistant, Bobby, who practically lives in her back pocket. Mom and Da—" A physical pain gripped his throat, as it always did when he tried to talk about his parents. He tried to swallow around it, but that didn't ease it any.

"Sunny." This time Emile stepped right into his personal space and wrapped Sunny in his arms. "You don't have to say anything else."

Only somehow Emile's embrace—maybe not having to look him in the face, maybe the fact Emile couldn't see his—made talking easier.

"Bobby was great for Daisy when they died. She had him to help her do the work, sure. But they're more than that to each other. And he was her rock. She didn't need me to get through it like I needed her." He leaned a little more of his weight on Emile, who tightened his grip.

His arms were strong, stronger than Sunny expected given his recent convalescence, but it seemed he was feeling better by the moment. He held Sunny, his chin resting lightly on the top of Sunny's head, his body a firm support.

"I spent most of my time with Mom in the greenhouses, collecting data from the plants, managing the other staff there. We were a good team. When I had to go back and work, and she wasn't there… and then Daisy was always holed up in her office with Bobby. I know she was doing what she had to do to get through it and still keep the company running, but it hurt. I didn't have anyone like that. I couldn't go in and tend the plants Mom had worked with, always expecting to see her, talk to her, and instead having all those eyes on me, feeling sorry for me. It was too much."

He gulped and once more closed his eyes, taking some time to breathe in Emile's heated scent of spice and spruce and sun-warmed earth. The closeness calmed him, and he went on.

"A while after Mom and Dad died, when the company was still reorganising, I told Daisy I had to leave for a while. She wasn't happy about it, but she needed someone running the nurseries who was focused. I tried, but I was a mess. So I left. I packed everything up, and after a month of not hearing from me, she stopped by my apartment. I was sleeping on the floor in the middle of piles of boxes. I wanted to go but had no place to run to.

"It was Daisy who actually convinced me to look for something to buy that had space to garden. She hoped getting back to the plants someplace that didn't always remind me of Mom might help."

Emile rubbed his back and pulled him in tighter. "It is hard to lose the one who created you."

"Yeah." Sunny sniffed and steeled himself enough to pull free of Emile's embrace and go back to making the sandwiches. He set the pan on the burner and focused on it. "Anyway, when she realised I really was going, that I'd found this place, she hired a company to finish packing up all my shit, move it out here, and set up the house." He swiped a hand over his face. "You want to butter that?"

Emile glanced to the bread he pointed at. "Of course." He did as asked without speaking further, spreading an air of serenity that enticed Sunny into continuing despite the pain of remembering how lost he'd been.

"I was mad at first. Her letting people dig into all my stuff. But it was just stuff, you know? Books, dishes, linens. They didn't move the important things. The pictures or the gardening tools or anything really personal. And once I saw the place in person, even when it was still empty, I knew this was my home. This was where I belonged. Daisy didn't really get it. She doesn't like it being so far away, but she was made for that company, to run it. She's better at it than the folks were, and she loves it. She's in her element, and she has Bobby.

"Dad would have been so proud of her." He sniffled again, causing Emile to glance over at him. "And anyway," Sunny let out an enormous sigh. "Everything went tits-up after Mom and Dad died. I just wanted some peace, and now there are strangers in my woods, and I don't want creepers on my land. There's nothing here for them anyway." He snorted. "Unless someone wants my trees."

"You have some wonderful trees," Emile murmured as he handed over a slice of bread, buttered on one side.

Sunny placed it into the pan he'd set on the burner. As he spoke, he concentrated on laying out slices of cheese to cover the bread.

"I worked there because I loved working with my family. With Mom especially. Then she was gone, and it killed me to go there every day knowing she was never coming back. I was an asshole about it. It was poisoning my relationship with Daisy, because I wasn't pulling my weight. It got easier when I stopped going in every day. I still miss them, but at least out here, I have peace and quiet."

"Until I came along."

"But I love you being here," Sunny blurted, the words out of his mouth before he had time to think about holding them back. "I wake up in the morning and there you are, sleeping in your little nest. Ferny loves you." He cast a fond look at the dog, who had one leg straight up in the air and his head down, lapping happily at his own ball sac.

Fernforest stopped what he was doing to look up at them. His tongue lolled out the side of his mouth, and he grinned.

"Seriously?" Sunny asked.

Emile chuckled. "Trust me, you'd lick your own balls, too, if you could."

Sunny chuckled because the image of Emile twisting to reach his ball sac was funny. "You sound pretty sure about that."

Emile made a noncommittal grunt and turned all his attention to the bread and butter. The pink staining his cheeks was adorable.

ARE YOU insane, Emikku? Yes. Yes I am. Flame's sake. Licking your balls? He gave himself a mental shrug. It wasn't like he was the only dragon in existence who engaged in a bit of self-gratification just because they could. Dragons were hedonistic that way, which was one of the reasons he liked the form so much. He could indulge in his emotional side far more easily in scale and feather than skin.

Things just made more sense without the encumbrance of forethought, or worse, *after*thought, to muddy the pure emotion of a situation.

He heaved a sigh and tried not to bring attention to the flaming heat in his cheeks as he handed Sunny slices of buttered bread. He couldn't read in his scale form, could he? Or make fried cheese sandwiches, or care that his host was upset. Or comfort him. Because he wanted to comfort Sunny very badly.

"This will take a few minutes," Sunny announced as he situated the last slice over a layer of cheese and lowered the flame a notch. He turned to lean on the counter next to Emile. The heat he gave off went straight to Emile's groin.

Comfort him, Emikku. Not... that.

He shifted his feet. He wanted to do both.

"So." With an air of slightly soggy smugness, Sunny crossed his arms over his chest. "Tell me more about this ball-licking situation."

Emile stared at him, for a split second thinking he'd given something away, but then Sunny burst into a wide grin.

"Or...." He waggled his eyebrows, which encouraged a smile to creep over Emile's face. "We could exchange the licking bit."

That sounded like an excellent idea. Emile's cock liked it very much. So did his dragon, and that's what he listened to as he dropped to his knees and freed Sunny's equally interested cock from his loose cargo shorts. *Shut up and lick. This* is *comforting. In a way. The best of all ways.*

"Emi—oh." Sunny sighed softly, sliding his fingers through Emile's hair as Emile took him into his mouth. The salty tang was perfect on his tongue, the weight of Sunny's heavy cock a delight. He could be a hedonist in skin as well as he could in scale. He just hadn't had that many opportunities before now.

A glance upward, filtered by his lashes, revealed Sunny's face already flushed, lower lip caught under bright white teeth. He curled the side of his mouth up and cupped a hand at the back of Emile's neck.

The firm grip brought a groan direct from the pit of Emile's gut to rumble around Sunny's cock. It was comforting rather than confining, as it often felt when Hakko did the same thing. Sunny wasn't holding him still for the rough, immediate taking as Hakko often did, so much as holding him safe while he performed an act that gave them both pleasure.

The insistent bump of Sunny's cock at the back of his throat momentarily engaged his gag reflex, and Sunny paused, watching him intently. Their gazes locked, Sunny's golden intensity lighting tiny sparks along every one of Emile's synapses. Emile fought and conquered the instinct to back up.

"Oh, that's good," Sunny whispered, lips forming words Emile had to strain to hear. The effort set off a cascade of goosebumps over his scalp, and he groaned. His magic prickled along the disturbance, his ears twitched, but he held back the instinct to flick them forward.

"Jesus." Sunny curled his hips again and pushed deeper.

This time Emile swallowed around him, accepting the push of cock into throat. The satisfied grunt from Sunny made it worth the effort. He dropped his jaw and gripped Sunny's thigh for balance, welcoming the deeper penetration as Sunny began to rock his hips.

Sunny made the work of taking his cock deep pleasurable, whispering praise and encouragement with every stroke. His hands on Emile's neck, his fingers caressing his cheek, tracing lightly through a tear as Emile's eyes watered and spilled over from the effort, made his magic sparkle and sing in his head.

But it didn't try to escape. It hovered, ready to jump his bonds, but didn't push. It raced through him, lighting up his nerves, making his cock ache to be touched, but he was too busy holding on to Sunny, taking Sunny, to manage that much higher function.

Rather than fighting his magic for control, Emile let it course through him. Every prickle and surge made his blood race. Every scrap of skin Sunny touched heated, lit up from within by the flaring energy until Emile was certain he had to be glowing. Sunny's hands were like brands on his skin, his cock the entire focus of Emile's attention.

"I'm gonna—" Sunny bit his lip hard and huffed, shoving his hips forward, his cock deep. Emile swallowed and panted around him, breath cut short, but he didn't care. He had the bright, effervescent grace of the magic coursing through him. "So… close…."

Sunny whimpered. His body tightened, and the magic came to an abrupt, fiery halt, straining through Emile to get to Sunny. As Sunny's spend flowed from the pulsing end of his cock down Emile's throat, the magic reared up, flaring bright and unstoppable, gobbling up the essence Sunny spilled into him with greedy surges. Every inch of Emile's skin lit on fire, and he cried out with the shock, instant pain and equally instant and shocking relief as it washed away. His cock throbbed once, releasing a torrent of come into his shorts.

Startled at his cry, Sunny jerked back and the last spurts of his orgasm splashed over Emile's lips and cheek. He didn't care. The smell of it, of their sweat and the lingering, ephemeral scent of magical release, swirled through his head, and he moaned, swaying on his knees.

Sunny knelt just in time to catch him as he pitched forward. For a few heartbeats, he struggled to contain the heavy, sluggish residue of the magic's afterglow, to keep it from oozing out between his restraints and growing his horns or sprouting feathers. The warmth of Sunny's chest against his cheek, the smooth, sweet sound of his voice uttering pleased praise, and the strength of his arms encircling Emile went a long way to shoring up Emile's battered concentration. He soon had the magic back in its cubby, curled in a nest of satisfaction and drowsy contentment. Exactly where he would like to be in that moment, rather than slouched on the hard wood of the kitchen floor, Sunny's embrace notwithstanding.

"Come on." Sunny all but lifted him to his feet. "Let's get you someplace more comfortable."

Emile expected Sunny to deposit him on the couch, into his familiar nest of pillows and blankets, but they bypassed it without a pause. Instead Sunny guided him to the foot of the stairs leading up to the bedroom.

"Think you can manage this?" Sunny asked.

Of course he could. He was spent but not helpless. "I'm fine," he muttered.

"Maybe I worked you too hard." Sunny kissed his temple.

Another tendril of lazy magic curled around the ball inside and settled into the whole, its usual warm, green-gold glow encompassed by deeper, redder strands of molten, earthy power.

"It's… okay." And it was. Physically, yes, maybe he'd overextended. But the magic was taking less of a toll than he'd expected, and he felt an underlying strength returning that he had missed since crossing the Fold.

"Let's just get you lying down, and I'll come back and finish the sandwiches." He made a face as he sniffed. "Or probably make new ones. That smell…."

Emile hadn't noticed the scent of char, used as he was to the ever-present smell of baked heat just on the edge of his senses. It was a dragon thing, he supposed: that inner, constant sear of magical energy that left the sensation of deeply ingrained heat in the pit of his being.

Food would be welcome. Emile was starving. Not surprising given how much energy the magic had sapped as it spun through his body. He could still feel fingers of it poking at his control, threatening a partial transformation, but this time he thought probably he wasn't in any danger of that happening.

They made it to the top of the stairs, and Emile sank his grateful frame onto the soft mattress. Once more, Sunny kissed his temple and crouched to look into his face.

Emile didn't have anything to say, so he leaned close, taking Sunny's mouth in a kiss. He had no way to convey with words how thankful he was to have the magic—finally—as close to dormant as it had ever been since he'd come here.

So he thanked Sunny with the kiss. He poured his gratitude and happiness into the connection, surrendering when Sunny cupped his cheek and tipped his head slightly. Anything Sunny wanted from him, he could give, if it promised more of this kind of relief, of pleasure, of satiation.

This was a calm he'd never experienced. He was greedy for more. Giving up control of his body, his senses, to Sunny seemed to have done the trick. He'd gladly do it any time Sunny asked.

"Lie down," Sunny whispered, lips still touching his. "I'll get you a warm cloth. Some food. Water." He pulled back to look into Emile's eyes. "What do you need? Tell me what I can do for you now."

Emile shivered. "Kiss me again. Please."

Sunny did, long, lingering, releasing Emile only when *he* was satisfied. It took Emile a moment to catch his breath. He swallowed, nodded, and let Sunny push him over with a gentle shove.

"Be right back. Stay put."

Oh, Emile did not need that instruction. He was not going anyplace. In fact, he watched as Sunny retreated back downstairs, keeping his eyes glued to the other man until the straw-coloured locks had disappeared below floor level, then pricking his ears—with impunity this time, since Sunny couldn't see him—to listen to his movements below.

If this is a cage, at least it's one of my own making. And what a jailor I've found.

He was vague when Sunny returned, drank the water Sunny handed him, allowed Sunny to strip him bare and clean him up with delightful strokes of a warm cloth and strong, capable hands. He was half-hard again by the time Sunny was finished, which earned him a rich, indulgent chuckle.

"Food first," Sunny admonished when Emile whined at Sunny stepping away from the bed. He leaned close again, tucked a strand of Emile's hair back from his face, and handed him a book. "But don't worry. Now I've got you here, I don't expect I'll be letting you leave this bed for some time."

His magic roiled, a low simmer of heat and want in his belly, and accepted the sentence with a lazy smile. *I can be a happy prisoner here.*

CHAPTER 16

THE INTRUDER they had not managed to lay eyes on that first time returned over the course of the next few days. They still didn't see who— or what—it was, but Emile had no doubt that they weren't alone. Every time it made its presence known, Emile's magic surged. It wanted him to change, wanted him to grow his fangs and claws, sharp horns and a whipping tail that could protect his Sunny from any danger.

"He grows bolder," Emile muttered as he followed Sunny's gaze to the woods at the bottom of the yard. Fernforest glanced up at him as though hearing his mutterings. The dog's tail was out stiff behind him. He swivelled his ears back, not pinned, but clearly showing his displeasure at the intrusion.

"I just wish whoever it is would stop sneaking around and show themselves." Sunny's frown tugged at Emile, making him wish the same thing, if only to appease Sunny's mood and ease the unsettling effect it was having on Emile's already heightened magic.

If he hadn't already convinced himself this wasn't the garden-variety trespasser Sunny expected, Emile would have forced the issue and gone looking for them. He could no longer pretend he didn't feel his magic responding to the native flux, nor could he ignore that he wasn't the only magical being to notice that the world around them was waking up.

"Feels like a storm coming," Sunny muttered, even as he glanced up at the cloudless blue sky. He wandered over the grass to the end of the driveway and peered down to the road, but there was nothing to see.

All around them, the air charged and crackled. Emile's magic rippled under his skin, arching out to Sunny standing just beyond Emile's reach, as though it would draw Sunny closer, within its circle of protection.

The branches of the nearby rose brambles shivered, and Fernforest cocked his head towards the bushes. Soft, ruffled sighs rolled between the shivering leaves, and Emile was sure he caught a glimpse of the prickly dryad within, stirring.

"Sunny."

Sunny grunted, attention still fixed on the empty drive.

The rose bush rattled again, seeming to expand outwards under the caress of a nonexistent breeze. The movement caught Sunny's attention, and he stared at it.

"Is that a porcupine?" He squinted and took a step closer to the bush, leaning in to get a better look.

Emile's magic sparked.

The dryad convulsed and formed fully, its magic that same heated red-gold that intermingled with Emile's after he'd been with Sunny. Turning in its crouch to look at Emile, the dryad inhaled, pulling at Emile's magic, bolstering its new form with strands of his thready, twining energy winding around its own. If it stood and revealed itself, there was no telling how Sunny might react.

Emile made a soothing sound and extended his magic willingly towards the bush. The first time a dryad took a corporeal form was the only time it needed the magical input from a source other than its own tree. If sharing his magic would calm the spirit, Emile would gladly do so.

He felt his energy brush against Sunny's body in passing, and Sunny shivered, running one hand down his arm, smoothing the hairs as they lifted away from his skin. His focus moved from the bush to Emile just as the dryad shook itself and began to soak in Emile's magic. Rosebuds furled open. Tiny new leaves stretched to their full potential, and the soft new wood of the twig-tips burst with fat leaf buds before Emile could pull his magic back.

The dryad sighed, settled cross-legged in the centre of its bushy home, and closed its eyes. It should have vanished back into twig and bark, but it didn't. It was hard—nearly impossible—to make out amidst the riot of blooms and leaves, crisscrossed by shade and light, but it was there, corporeal and alive. Awake.

Emile took a step back, but fortunately Sunny's attention remained on him.

"We should go inside," Sunny said, voice husky, eyes bright and wide.

"We should?"

"Uh-huh." Sunny grabbed his hand. "Now."

"I thought we had yard work."

"Yard's not going anywhere." Sunny placed a hand in the centre of Emile's chest. Instantly his magic spun to a standstill, poised, emitting an excited thrum Emile could hardly ignore.

"I suppose it's not," he agreed, caught in Sunny's intense gaze.

If Sunny wanted him, Sunny could have him.

They made it as far as the couch, and this time it was Sunny's mouth on Emile's dick, and oh, did the magic love that sensation. Emile wasn't completely in control of it when he came, nor could he be sure some hadn't escaped, flowing out of him along with his release.

He only knew the room seemed brighter, the little cabin cozier, and Sunny unnervingly energetic after they were done. There was no mention of trespassers or any talk of weird weather for many hours. The garden work went fast, and Emile was pretty sure the plants leaned towards Sunny's touch as he worked around them, digging fingers deep into the soil as he spoke softly to them, pulled weeds, and pinched away pests and wilt.

The sun was nearly down by the time Sunny called it a day and stood back from the raised beds to survey his work.

"That went well, I think." Sunny rested fists on his hips, satisfaction flowing from him. "Faster than I expected too."

"That's good." Emile moved to take his hand in hopes of soothing some of the frenetic energy. He could feel the thrum of Sunny's pulse through the skin-to-skin touch. It melded with his own heartbeat, their energies twining and curling around each other. "This is good," Emile murmured.

Sunny's grin lit up the dusk.

Nearby, Fernforest hopped about, snapping and tumbling over his own feet, chasing fleeting splashes of light and colour.

"What is he doing?" Sunny tipped his head to one side. "Is that a firefly?"

Emile squinted. *Pixies?* He thought he saw the flash of iridescent wings, and then Fernforest got his mouth around something, and Emile gasped.

A pixie-dragon. They weren't any bigger than a robin, though they were more scales than feather, and had some limited shifting abilities, able to tweak their forms to resemble the tiny winged pixies they were named after. They retained their brilliant colours and most of their scales, though, as well as their batlike, membranous wings. Actual pixies had wings more like those of dragonflies, were much smaller, and tended to be far more level-headed and less troublesome than their namesakes.

"I don't know what he has." Sunny let Emile's hand go. "Ferny, drop that."

Even as Sunny was approaching the dog, the pixie-dragon shifted in Fernforest's mouth, no doubt hoping the smaller, more humanoid form would slip free more readily. One of the things pixie-dragons could do that real dragons could not was shed their thornlike spikes as they changed and use them as weapons in their skin forms. This one did just that, wielding two spikes, nearly as long as the creature itself, to poke at the inside of the dog's mouth.

Fernforest yelped and shook his head, mouth wide open, feet scampering backward, fortunately away from Sunny, until he hit the rose bush at the end of the drive.

The dryad hidden within the bush gave a mighty shake, walloping the poor animal in his backside with branches covered in thorns.

Fernforest whined and danced, then shot off in the direction of the forest.

"Ferny!" Sunny pelted after him, but Emile called him back.

"He won't go far," Emile said, hurrying down to the bridge where the dog had vanished along the trail. "Sunny, please." He didn't want his lover disappearing into the forest just as dusk was falling. If anything was bound to happen that couldn't be explained away, this was the hour for it.

"But he—" Sunny stared into the deepening gloom under the trees.

"He'll be fine." Emile pulled him back across the bridge to the yard, but Sunny refused to go any farther as he kept searching the darkening forest.

Emile used Sunny's distraction to find the pixie-dragon and scoop it up from where it sat, slightly dazed and dripping dog drool in the grass. "You'll go find him and bring him back."

The creature glared at him, flame-bright eyes flashing.

"He's harmless. He wasn't going to eat you."

You don't know that. He was going to swallow *me.*

"Emile?" Sunny called from the bridge. "I can't even hear him anymore. I should go find him."

"Please," Emile whispered. "Fernforest isn't an ordinary dog. If you take a moment to think at him as hard as you just thought at me, you will see. I'm sure his attempt to capture you wasn't completely unprovoked."

The pixie-dragon crossed scaled arms, showing off spiked forearms and lime green feather ruffs along his shoulders. His face took on a defiant pout, and he still clutched his tiny spears in clenched fists.

"As I thought." Emile quirked an indulgent smile. "Go find him. Be nice."

He's not that bright.

"He's a dog." Emile straightened, sensing Sunny's approach without having to look. His magic undulated, reaching for the comfort of Sunny's presence. As he turned, keeping the magical creature behind him, he felt the disturbance of the weave of magic that happened when someone shifted, the sharp dig of claws into his palm. He managed not to grimace as the pixie-dragon, now in a tiny dragon form, fluttered off into the night.

"What was it?" Sunny peered around him.

"A robin. He didn't hurt it. He was playing, I guess, but it flew off."

"What if he doesn't come back?" Sunny glanced once more at the now-black wall of leafy darkness.

"He will. Don't worry. Let's go inside. We can leave the door open for him." He wrapped an arm over Sunny's shoulders and turned him for the house. He hadn't had time to quiz the pixie-dragon about where it had come from or how it crossed the Fold, or why, but the feisty little creatures rarely travelled alone. Where one went, dozens more were sure to follow.

Emile was fairly certain there was nothing like a flying lizardlike creature on this side of the Fold. It would be best not to have to try to explain it if he could avoid it. If things kept on like this, he worried he wasn't going to have a choice. Sunny wasn't blind. He was going to start noticing things, and Emile didn't think he'd be able to play dumb for very long, once that happened.

SUPPER WAS easy—fried eggs and toast—cooked up and plated as soon as Fernforest reappeared. Sunny's relief at having the dog safely inside went a long way to calming the extra energy he'd had all day. When they turned in, there was no real conversation about both of them cuddling into Sunny's bed. Their lovemaking was long and tender. As Emile lay in Sunny's bed, arms around his lover and night whispering over his bare skin, he fell asleep to the sensation of his very personal magic seeping through the bones of the building to the land beneath, anchoring itself in bedrock, tree roots, and rich, dark soil.

He should be concerned about that. When dragon magic soaked into the land, it woke things. It reminded the weaker magics how to flow and nudged deep, sleeping currents back to life.

That should be worrisome.

Sunny shifted, mumbled something, twisting restlessly, and Emile heard a snatched whisper of pain and loss. He held Sunny tighter, stroked his back. After some time, Sunny settled. Emile's magic curled around them, lending warmth to the cool room, soothing Sunny's distress.

There was going to be no disentangling himself from this place. This man. Emile felt it in his marrow. His magic had chosen, and he could not find it in his heart to argue. An anchor was not a cage, after all.

CHAPTER 17

SUNNY WASN'T at all surprised when Daisy called a week later to remind him of his pseudopromise to have lunch with her.

"You did promise."

"More like I didn't say no."

"Close enough." He could hear the grin in her voice. "Why do you want to hang out there all alone, anyway?"

"I can come into town if you need me." He descended the porch steps, kicked off his flip-flops, and dug his toes into the grass. He *would* go if she needed him. Turning his face up to the sunshine beaming onto the lawn, he tried not to hope she wouldn't ask. He wasn't ready to tell her about Emile. He wasn't sure why.

"No." There was a long pause. "Sunny?"

"Yeah?"

"I worry about you."

Sunny glanced to where Emile nested on the swing on the front porch, a book in hand, a few more sticking out from under the cushions, and Ferny curled against his thigh. Long magenta hair cascaded over his shoulder and glinted in the sun. No doubt his original darker dye had faded in the sun until it was rosy pink at the tips, setting off his perfect pale skin. Though he couldn't see the soft pink freckles from here, he knew they were there, and imagined the delicate splash across the bridge of his nose, across his pectorals....

"Um. Yeah." He shook himself. "I—guess we have a lot to talk about."

"We do?" Her tone was an odd mix of interested, and trepidatious. "Do I get a preview?"

"Patience, Daisychain."

"Something is going on and you haven't told me. Why not?"

"It's new."

"Oh?"

"I wanted to tell you in person, I guess."

"When do I get to meet him?"

As usual, Daisy made a leap Sunny hadn't expected.

"More to the point," she said, not giving him a chance to reply, "when did you meet him?"

As if knowing he was being talked about, Emile glanced up. His sapphire eyes shone, an inner fire sparking when he met Sunny's gaze. He looked curious, but there was a hard edge to his features, defensive almost, and Sunny offered a smile.

Emile cocked his head but didn't smile back.

"I have to go, Daisychain. I'll call you later. Or you call me, if you need anything." He hung up even as her voice rose in a demanding spike, asking again about Emile. He wasn't ready to tell her—or anyone—about Emile. Daisy wouldn't understand him keeping a man who'd just wandered out of the forest with no history and no discernible plans for the future. He was perfectly happy to keep Emile to himself—to keep *them* to himself.

"Eess everything okay?" Emile asked. His accent, which had smoothed out so much Sunny had all but forgotten about it, thickened to a hot hiss.

"Fine." Sunny frowned. "It's just Daisy being curious."

Emile set his book down and flowed to his feet. There was something preternatural about the way he moved, something too sharp in his eyes as he approached. Sunny ought to feel nervous about that, but all he felt was turned on.

"Trouble?"

"No. Not at all. She's just curious. And worried. We haven't seen each other in a while. I guess I sort of… ran away." Sunny was suddenly tired and sad. His mother would have known what he should do. Go to Daisy? Bring Emile and introduce them? Keep to himself? Keep Emile to himself?

Emile's nostrils flared. His eyes darkened as he stepped off the porch onto the grass.

A distinct rumble vibrated up through the soles of Sunny's feet, and he gasped. "Did you feel that?"

A slight wisp of scent caught Sunny's attention, like the faint hint of coals and woodsmoke, there and gone so fast he knew it had to be his imagination. At the bottom of the yard, the sharp crack of a branch breaking shattered the tense quiet between them, and they both turned to the forest.

Branches rattled and swayed, but only for a moment before stilling again. There was no breeze. Something big had moved in the bushes, and Sunny's heart skipped. "Wait here," he ordered and hurried to the bridge and over its gentle hump.

Ferns and asters crowded the bridge's railing at the far side. Moss curled over the bank of the stream, and the water itself burbled and splashed, wetting the greying wood under his feet. The gentle aspens reached over the arch of the bridge as though stretching to protect his gateway into the woods. Sunny didn't remember the forest hovering like this. He'd have to pay more attention to keeping it trimmed back from the path and the yard.

Now, he batted an outslung pine branch aside to take a few steps down the well-trod path. He had walked it often over the past weeks, pleased with the dapple of sun and shade the aspens provided on hot afternoons. Today, despite the sun, the shadows were deep, shading towards pine greens and twilight purple under the trees. He squinted into the gloom from his more sunlit spot on the path head.

"Who's there?" He didn't expect an answer and wasn't disappointed. Silence greeted his call, and after a few minutes, he took a step back, then another, until one foot rested on the smooth planks of the bridge.

He almost jumped when Emile placed a hand on his shoulder. Standing behind Sunny, on a higher part of the bridge's arch, he towered over Sunny's shoulder, brilliant blue gaze seeming to pierce the darkness under the trees much better than Sunny had managed. His face was set in a frown, and his fingers gripped Sunny's shoulder with near-bruising force.

"Come away," Emile whispered, and there was more of his accent, a spiced, flowing undercurrent to the words at odds with the gentle man Sunny knew. Or thought he knew.

Sunny didn't argue. The shimmering shadows behind the leaves moved too much at odds with the barely there breeze. Below their feet, the stream splashed along, a tumble of agitated sound. When Sunny glanced into the water, the flashes of silver and rainbow iridescence he would normally have attributed to tiny fish scales blinked at him from below the waves in a decidedly unfishlike manner.

"What's going on?"

"Come away," Emile repeated, and this time his tone rumbled under Sunny's skin, and Sunny followed without thought.

CHAPTER 18

"SOMETHING IS out there." Sunny hugged himself. They sat on the porch swing, Sunny crushing Emile's carefully built nest, displacing the pile of favourite books he'd brought out with him, and Emile next to him, bones aching against the hard wooden seat. Carefully, he squirmed, trying to get more comfortable as he followed Sunny's gaze to the bottom of the yard.

Something was out there. He was right about that. The small patch of wilderness felt more and more wild, more and more like Emile's home, and less like the alien, dry, magicless place he had entered on first breaching the Fold.

It was unnerving.

"Maybe hunters," Sunny rambled.

That made Emile shiver because his experience of hunters was probably not the same as Sunny's. Where a few weeks ago, he had felt the urge to move on, to keep from caging himself here, now he was torn. If he moved on, the land might return to sleep, with Sunny none the wiser. Or, he would leave Sunny exposed to whatever had followed him through, with no means of protecting himself against magic he wouldn't understand.

"It's like the forest is trying to tell me something." Sunny stood and wandered to the porch railing. "Look at the nightshade." Vines of it had crawled up the railing of the bridge, tiny purple flowers blooming prettily in the afternoon sun. "That isn't the really poisonous kind, but still. I've never seen it grow so fast. There was none on the bridge two days ago." It had twined itself halfway across the wooden expanse like it was deliberately covering and engulfing the man-made structure, trying to meld it into the woods and make it a part of the landscape.

Sunny's dreamy, distracted tone worried Emile. Humans had been known to fall into thrall to the constant, unyielding persistence of nature's force when it woke and decided to reclaim its own. Sunny's vacant demeanour stirred Emile's magic to a foaming froth, not violently agitated, but bubbling through the holes in its confines with gentle persistence. He could feel his scales shimmering just under his skin, and worried if he stepped into the direct sunlight, their sharp reflection would make him glow.

The forest *was* calling to them. There was no doubt about that. The fact that Sunny felt it was unsettling. "Maybe we should leave," Emile blurted. *We? That is unexpected, Emikku. Just where do you intend on taking him?* He wasn't sure he could outrun his dragon's need to answer the strong pull of the forest. *Answer it? Or battle it?*

If only he knew exactly what was prowling out there.

Sunny turned to look at him. His golden eyes, shaded under the house's overhang, seemed like extensions of the shadows under the trees. His hair, falling in corkscrew curls past his shoulders, reminded Emile of his home, wild and inexorable. With his bare feet, dirt-smudged shirt and shorts, and that hair, Sunny appeared as uncultivated a part of the landscape as any ephemeral dryad. Even the suggestion he should leave this place suddenly felt ludicrous.

"To see Daisy?" Sunny asked, voice firming, eyes sharpening. His expression lost the vague distance, and a smile curved the outer corners of his mouth. "You think?" He took a step away from the edge of the porch, towards Emile, and this time there was no need for direct contact. Magic arched between them, a feral surge that made Emile gasp and Sunny laugh out loud.

A sharp breeze and a burst of sunlight burning through thin clouds accompanied the spurt of energy. Sunny grabbed Emile's hand. "Yes," he agreed. "I like that idea. Now?" He nodded. "We should go now. I'll find shoes." He headed for the door, dragging Emile after him. "And keys. I'll need car keys. Come on. I want to see Daisychain. She needs to…."

Emile followed, the change in mood making his head spin. Whatever Sunny thought his sister needed, he didn't elaborate. His thoughts, though they had trailed off in words, were clearly racing. He skittered around the house, collecting things that made no sense to Emile.

Metal jingled to the sound of a triumphant "Aha!" from Sunny; then a square of folded leather disappeared into the pocket of his baggy shorts. He grabbed a metal vessel he called his "to-go" mug from a cupboard, and filled it with black, untreated coffee, as Emile had come to prefer. Another he filled with coffee dressed the way he liked, and he thrust them both at Emile.

The smooth metal surface was cool to the touch, a hard line up against which his magic stopped abruptly. Emile wondered at that, but there was no time to question. Sunny kicked a pair of leather sandals at him and a stretchy bit of cloth tied into a loop.

"You'll want to tie up your hair," he said. "I'm taking the top off the Rover. Could get windy."

It took Emile a few minutes to plait his hair and wrap the loop around the end of the queue. By the time he had, Sunny had rolled the sides of his vehicle up, leaving the back exposed. Fernforest sat behind the seats, tongue lolling, a happy grin on his face.

Sunny grunted when Emile came to stand beside him. "Cheekbones," he whispered, then shook himself. "Get in." He opened the door and hopped into the car. When he didn't move over to make room for Emile, Emile put a hand on the side, ready to climb in the back, next to Fernforest.

"What are you doing?" There was amused confusion in Sunny's voice. "Get in beside me." He motioned to the seat next to him, then leaned over to open the other door.

Flushing with his ignorance, Emile hurried around behind the vehicle to the other side so he could clamber in next to Sunny. He pulled the door closed after him, set his mug in a spot next to Sunny's, and sat, hands in his lap, waiting.

"Seat belt?" Sunny asked and reached over his shoulder to pull a strap out of an opening. He clicked the metal end into a slot next to his hip, and Emile emulated him.

Sunny narrowed his eyes. "Have you ever been in a car before?"

Emile's flush deepened. "It's been… some time… since I travelled under any power other than my own." Dragons, after all, had no need for any method of travel other than their own two wings or the muscled undulations of their bodies, for those who didn't have wings. Very few ways to travel outpaced them.

Emile had learned, since crossing the Fold, the disadvantages of only two feet for transport.

"Some time," Sunny repeated, cocking his head. "More questions than answers with you." But he didn't seem inclined to ask any of those questions. Instead he slipped one of the metal shards he'd taken from the house into a slot in the car and turned. The vehicle rumbled to life, and Emile grabbed hold of the seat, barely managing not to spring claws to dig into the soft leather as the vehicle began to move backwards.

CHAPTER 19

AUTOS WERE faster than Emile had anticipated. Much faster. He clutched the armrest of the door with the strength of ten dragons as Sunny spun them around another bend in the loose-gravelled road. Stones spattered up under the vehicle, the small pops and clacks of rocks hitting metal making Emile's ears twitch.

He gave his head a shake and focused on the uneasy roil of magic in his gut. The hard metal that surrounded him and the synthetic oiliness of what he now understood to be plastic jarred with his attempts to find a grounding force to steady his magical being.

"Doing okay?" Sunny asked.

Emile swallowed and nodded the lie.

"You look a little pale," Sunny said. "Should we go back?"

"No!" Emile flashed a wobbly smile. "It's fine. Just not used to this." He would have to *get* used to it. This was his home now, and Sunny wasn't going to suffer his ignorance forever.

"Sorry." Sunny shifted, moved the long metal stick between them around, and the vehicle slowed. "Better?"

It was, but at the same time, it wasn't. Nothing but setting bare feet on raw earth would satisfy Emile's need to connect the magic to its source. That wouldn't happen until he was out of this contraption. At least the slower pace eased the liquid defiance in his stomach.

"It's going to be a long drive at this speed," Sunny said, setting a palm on Emile's thigh. He tightened his fingers, and the prick of each fingertip against Emile's skin where his borrowed shorts left his leg bare sent a tendril of heat winding through him.

His stomach's disquiet eased. Even the magic wound itself around inside Emile, nesting down into a tight knot in his core, gathering some of the faint strands of energy from Sunny into the tangle.

"Now that is a much better colour." Sunny patted his cheek and winked. "That paleness wasn't doing you any favours. Really." Sunny's voice dipped to a sand-scratched huskiness. "Much prettier—er—better."

He jerked his hand away, but Emile caught it before it got far and set it back on his leg. "Please," he muttered when Sunny shot him a curious glance. "It—" He drew in a breath and let it out, long and centring. "Settles me."

"Okay, then." Sunny smoothed his palm over Emile's leg. "If I go too fast, just say so, okay?"

Emile *almost* shifted to nudge Sunny's hand higher on his thigh when the lurch of the vehicle picking up speed caught his attention. The *auto*—Sunny had been talking about the *auto* going too fast. He gulped and nodded.

"Need this just for one sec," Sunny said, lifting his hand. "Have to shift gears." He moved the stick again, did something with the pedals under his feet, then settled his hand back on Emile. "Okay?"

Any more okay, and Emile's cock would be answering for him. He bit his lip and nodded.

"Okay." Sunny squeezed his leg. "We got this."

The vehicle slowly but surely picked up speed again, but Sunny only let go of Emile long enough to occasionally shift gears. Each time he replaced it, another snaking coil of his warmth nestled into the knot of Emile's magic, intertwining and tangling until Emile couldn't quite tell which was which.

It should have felt alien and unsettling, but Sunny's sweet attention soon became an integral extension of Emile's own awareness, part of him, inextricable.

It was entirely too soothing for the path to disaster he knew it was.

SUNNY'S ENTHUSIASM for the trip into the city ratcheted up tenfold with the prospect of Emile's company. Schoolboy nerves rioted in his gut at the thought of nearly an hour in the close quarters of the Land Rover with him, but they had barely left the secure clearing of the yard when Emile's nervous tension began ricocheting around the cab.

Sunny made every attempt to ease Emile's worries. He figured it was natural for his new friend to be scared of the car's speed if he had lived as sheltered a life as Sunny suspected. He acted like he had no idea what to make of most modern conveniences.

The thought of a grown man not being used to cars or the overwhelming amounts of technology Sunny took for granted gave him pause. Was he ready to take on that kind of learning curve?

One look at Emile's fascinated expression as he gazed at the trees flashing past made him sigh. He'd been so happy with his little hut in the woods, far from all the people. He should leave Emile in the city once they'd made it that far.

Emile shifted, curling his toes under and chewing on his lower lip. Part fascinated kid, part mystery, part irresistible, magnetic man. All of everything Sunny tried to stay away from.

Shit. You're in deep already, Sunshine Rainbow. Don't kid yourself. You're keeping this one.

The thought was a giddy one, and he gulped down a sudden overflow of anxiety.

"You're nervous." Emile instantly fixed on him, intent, demanding a reply with his steady gaze. His brilliant eyes reflected shards of sunlight that sparkled through the cab, brightening the already glaring day with slivers of blue and aqua and diamond brightness.

"No. I'm fine." Sunny gripped the wheel a bit tighter, blinking Emile's glitter out of his eyes. He twisted his palms against the neon pink, faux-fur steering wheel cover his mother had given him with the car a lifetime ago.

"Do your people think you're a good liar?" Emile asked. His tone was so mild Sunny almost didn't catch the slight tinge of accusation in it.

"What? No, I—"

Dude, seriously. You couldn't lie your way out of a half-made bed. Something Daisy told him often. Though Sunny still didn't think it actually made any sense, it did make him smile.

"No," he conceded. "Daisychain just laughs at me when I don't tell her the truth. I can never fool her about anything."

"So what's wrong?"

"Your accent," Sunny blurted, cocking his head and completely sidestepping the question with one of his own. The there-and-gone-again nature of Emile's accent was a red flag Sunny had tried to ignore, but it popped into his head, as good a way to change the subject as any.

"My what?"

"Accent. You had an accent when I first met you. In the shack. What happened to your accent?"

"You… caught me half-asleep," Emile said, face flushing pink—again—sweeping in under Sunny's guard to turn his heart over. "It comes out more when I'm tired, I guess?"

"Who's lying now?" Sunny shot him half an ironic glance, though he didn't take the other half of his gaze off the road. They were almost to the edge of his property. Traffic would pick up along the highway he'd soon be turning onto. He glanced in the rear-view. Nothing to see but dust pluming out behind them.

Before Emile could reply, something dark and fast charged out onto the road.

Sunny slammed a foot on the brake and swung the wheel hard to the right. "Hang on!" A shadow of ink and smoke roiled in the wake of whatever had crossed their path, but it blew off and over the hood and windshield and was gone. The Land Rover came to rest nose-first in the shallow ditch. Sunny's knuckles ached with his hard grip on the wheel, and he felt the sharp pressure of the seat belt against his chest. Pink fuzz poked out between his fingers, and he stared at it, heart clogging his airways as it frantically tried to pound its way up and out.

"You okay?" he asked when he got his breath back. He turned to Emile.

The empty passenger seat gaped at him. Emile's door hung open. His seat belt clinked lightly against the frame as it swayed, caught from retracting into its slot by the plastic clip Daisy used to keep it short enough for her.

Fernforest whimpered against the side of the truck, where he was wedged between the metal and a wooden box of snow cleats and other emergency items.

"Ferny!" Scrambling with his own belt, Sunny fumbled out of the car and ran around to free the dog. No sooner had he shifted the box than Fernforest barged past him and across the road to where the trees swayed and fluttered, the only evidence that something had entered the forest ahead of him.

"Ferny!" Sunny raced after him, then remembered he hadn't been alone. "Emile." He scuttled back, but there was no sign of Emile inside the vehicle or out. "Emile?" He spun, his flip-flops making a squishing scrape on the hardpack. "The hell?"

The afternoon glared down, warming his back under the dark T-shit he wore. As he stood there, grasshoppers took up their high-pitched song once more.

Across the road, deeper in the bush, a loud cracking sounded, and Sunny jumped. A crow complained as it flapped up into the blue. Black feathers glinted with an unnaturally vibrant shimmer, gliding sunlight off his back like water.

Farther away, Fernforest barked, the alarm edged with frantic anger.

Sunny ran for the sound, crashing through the underbrush, losing both useless shoes after the first few steps. His feet hit every sharp rock and twisted tree root in his path, but he didn't slow down. "Fernforest. Where the hell are you?"

Keep him out of trouble for me, huh, Sunshine? In his memory, his mother's smile was as bright and open as the cloudless sky. *You know how he is. You have to keep your eye on this one.*

"Fernforest!"

A tree branch took a wicked swing at his face. Sunny had to close his eyes, batting at it to protect himself. A sharp twig dragged across his palm, and he swore. "Stupid dog." He ploughed ahead, scrubbing the back of his hand across damp eyes. Trees careened past him, branches reaching for his clothes and dragging sharp spines over the skin of his forearms. Trunks knocked into his shoulders like they'd leaned into his path on purpose. Dodging around the huge bole of an ancient white pine, he called after the dog again.

The tree threw up a knobby, razor-barked root to catch his foot, and he pitched forward. And landed smack in Emile's arms.

"Ungh." Sunny grunted. "The hell?" He tried to push past, but Emile grabbed him and hung on.

"Stop." Emile gripped both his arms. "Sunny, stop. You are panicking."

"I'm looking for my dog." Sunny struggled to get free, but Emile pulled him close.

"You are going to get hurt. Take a breath."

The strength of the arms folded around his back took Sunny by surprise. Against his first inclination, he relaxed, leaning into Emile's chest. The ironclad hold grounded him. Some of the panic soaked into Emile's calm, and Sunny breathed in the forest-and-sunshine smell of Emile. "Where's Ferny?"

The slap-slap of Fernforest's tail against his leg answered his question. Sunny glared down at him. "You're an idiot," he told the animal, sniffling up the residue of his panic and blinking back an unexpected sting. "Since when do you take off into a forest you don't know?"

"Be kind." Emile stroked a single finger over Sunny's chin, drawing Sunny's attention back to him. For an instant all Sunny could see were the brilliant gems of his eyes and the lush promise of his lips as they curled into a smile. "Everyone is okay now. Breathe."

Sunny hadn't realised he was holding his breath. He let it out in a huff and jerked his chin free of the tantalising touch. "Right." The loss of the skin-to-skin contact ripped a strip of raw nerves into him, and he gasped.

Fernforest yipped, distracting him from that sting to look down. The dog sniffed his toes. Blood oozed between them, and Sunny winced. "That sucks."

"Come on." Emile turned him forcibly from the deeper woods back towards the road.

"Never mind the dog. What are you doing running off into the woods?" Sunny asked, limping along at his side as they slowly made their way back.

"I went after Fernforest, of course."

Of course. He liked the dog. He would do that. There was something wrong with the explanation, but the fog of panic and the overwhelming crush of relief at finding the dog unharmed made it difficult to pinpoint the discrepancy. Then Emile brushed fingers down his arm, chasing goosebumps and a strong shiver, and Sunny let it go.

"The forest has damaged you." He touched a scrape on Sunny's palm and another on his shoulder, making Sunny wince.

All at once, all the little indignities the trees had inflicted on him began to burn with sweat and dirt. Sunny glanced down at his feet, and the throb of them was by far the worst of it. "You got better at running in flip-flops than me, I guess."

But Emile's feet were also bare. Only he wasn't bleeding or limping. His feet were filthy—not actually all that unusual for him—but unscathed.

"Come." Emile took his hand. "Let's go back and see what damage you've done to yourself." They headed back down what now appeared to be a mostly grassy path leading towards the road. Too bad Sunny hadn't found this nicely carpeted thoroughfare on his way into the forest.

"What even was that?" he asked finally as they were nearing the thinning edge of the trees and he needed something to distract from his aching feet. "Did you see it? It was huge. And the—I don't know, dust? Or smoke?"

Emile shook his head. "It must have been a bear."

"No bear moves that fast."

"They are faster than you might think."

"Not Speedy Gonzales fast."

"Speedy Gone-what?"

"Never mind." They had made it to the side of the road, and Sunny eyed the hot, stony gravel. The edge, soft and torturous with sharply cut grey scrabble, only led to the more packed brown hardtop, which itself was littered with tiny abrasive stones.

"Let me."

Before Sunny could utter a breath of protest, Emile had scooped him up as if he weighed nothing and carried him across the road like a child. He stopped next to the Land Rover, and Sunny climbed awkwardly from his arms to the truck's slightly inclined bed.

Emile knelt in the dust, gripped one of Sunny's ankles, and lifted his foot. "Let me look."

His fingers, hot pinpricks on Sunny's already burning feet, sent a bristling sensation spiking up along his nerve endings. Sunny tried to pull his foot free, but Emile's grip was iron.

"Stop," Sunny whispered. Tendrils of fire trickled up his leg as Emile poked and prodded.

"Be still so I can get the grit out." Emile sounded so different. So hard.

Sunny's dick muddled with that a moment, stiffening when Emile glanced up through his lashes to offer a brief, stern smile.

"Please," Emile amended. "Let me help."

"It's fine." Sunny drew his knees slightly together and tugged again at his caught leg. God. If Emile noticed....

"You're bleeding."

"A few cuts. No biggie."

"You need your feet to drive, yes?"

"Of course."

"So let me."

Sunny subsided and relaxed the tension in his leg. "There's a case of water bottles and some clean rags in the box in the back of the truck," he offered after a moment.

"Good." Emile finally released him and stood. "You will stay put. I'll get what we need."

He stared after Emile, his cock twitching at the tone, and he stayed put until Emile came back.

"Very good," Emile murmured as he knelt once more. "Now let's see what we have."

It didn't take more than fifteen minutes for Emile to clean and plaster up his feet. Then, while he poured more water into a bowl Sunny kept there for Fernforest, Sunny rooted through the box of odds and ends and found a set of mismatched flip-flops—one orange and one lime green with pink hibiscus all over it—and then they were on the road again. "We're going back?" Emile glanced behind them at the stretch of road leading around the bend they hadn't taken.

Sunny's reply was a shrug. "Maybe tomorrow" was all he said. The need to visit his sister had vanished, the desire to keep Emile close and under the cover of the forest's protection imperative.

Chapter 20

Emile's magic simmered. He held it with an iron will just below the surface. Having a handle on it now meant it couldn't sneak up on him, but it was funny how fear and adrenaline worked sometimes. Or maybe it was the anger. He had been hard-pressed not to show the anger at Sunny's injuries.

He wasn't sure he had completely succeeded, given Sunny's meek acquiescence, which had been out of character enough for Emile to notice. And now they had turned for home.

While he was glad they were headed back to their—to Sunny's—little clearing, he was also disappointed. He would have liked to see more of this world, to discover how his magic reacted in environments more human and less nature. The prospect both interested and worried him. He would have to figure it out sooner rather than later. Much as he would love to stay on Sunny's little farm forever, that wasn't practical.

Something in the woods was making that abundantly clear.

It hadn't been a bear or a cougar or a moose dashing across the road in front of their auto. It had been a creature that had no business on this side of the Fold.

Of course, he couldn't very well tell Sunny they had just witnessed the mad dash of a runaway salamander. The creatures were wildly reckless distant cousins to his own kind. They could loosely be equated to mountain apes in relation to humans, only salamanders were nowhere near as socially sophisticated as apes, or as mildly mannered. And ones that large were not the wild variety that populated his home forests. No. That salamander came from the old groves where they had once been purposefully created and reared for size and strength, both physical and magical. The groves were no longer used by dragons for their original purpose, but the trees and dryads that inhabited them remained, and the salamanders created there were not the timidly wild creatures of the deep forests.

While they never set out to hurt anything or damage property, they still managed to wreak havoc wherever they went. Emile had tried to catch up to this one, even allowing his magic to pull his feet to scale and claw to increase his speed, but the thing was damn fast. There was no way he could catch it in his skin, on only two feet. He needed full scale and claw and maybe even wing for that.

It worried him to find such a creature here. Most wild beings would shy away from that much unpredictable power, and salamanders especially would prefer to stay away from the strong magic energy of the Fold. It was one huge wall of fluctuating power wild salamanders—even a big one descended from those long ago released from domestication—would stay well away from.

Oddly, once in this world, the creature had seemed to bump up against the edge of the wood and careen back in a number of times like it was somehow confined to the old-growth stand. That was something, at least, though again, Emile wasn't sure exactly *what* it was, beyond odd.

He could only hope that soon enough the creature would run itself out and curl into a pocket of smog and dust to rest. That would take a few days. Emile might find time to sneak off and hunt it down. If he could catch it resting, he could bridle it. If he could bridle it, he could control it, young as it was, and it wouldn't cause any more damage or alarm.

He dreaded what might become of a salamander on its own here, where there was no chance for it to find another of its kind and slim chance for it to find a grove of dryads to feed it the flux it required to survive. It would be terrified and all the more dangerous.

"You're quiet," Sunny said.

Emile had been watching out the window, but he turned to Sunny now. "I was thinking."

"About?"

"Wondering about your city." Not a complete lie, anyway. That had been the thrust of his thoughts before the trip had been cut short. He wasn't sure there was a good way to explain salamanders and dryads to a human, so he didn't try. "I grew up isolated from a lot of people."

"You've never been in a city?"

Emile shook his head. The concept of cities the way Sunny knew cities—the way he understood human cities from his scant research—wasn't the same as communal living on the other side of the Fold.

"Lucky. By the time we came along, Mom and Dad had an apartment in the city. They stayed there all week. We only got to go out to the farm on weekends. They had to be near the office, and they wanted us close. Even though we were homeschooled, there was no hanging with the gramps even while Mom and Dad were at work. We went into the office with them and learned while they worked."

"Gramps?"

"Grandparents. It was their farm. Mom's folks. Dad's are all on the East Coast. He came here to work in one of the mines. Lasted a week, he said, when he met Mom and took a job on the farm. They got married a month later, had me, then eighteen months later, Daisychain, and never looked back."

"It sounds nice."

"It was. Dad was a genius. Between working on the farm and taking a few electrical engineering classes, he figured there was a way to turn any greenhouse into an automated plant nursery. Eventually between Mom's green thumb and Dad's computers, they built an entire company on the concept that the right automation, along with companion planting and multiculture planting and weather monitoring, could save water and turn any suburban yard into a high-yield, self-sustaining, environmentally positive space. They were pretty great."

He blinked, and the auto slowed. "Shit. I can't see."

Swiftly Sunny swiped at his eyes and drew in a soggy breath.

"I'm sorry." Emile patted Sunny's hand where it gripped the wheel in a white-knuckled fist.

"No." Sunny shot a hand out to grip Emile's before it got very far. "You couldn't know. It's okay." Sunny hung on, and for a little while, they remained quiet.

CHAPTER 21

THE RIDE back to the cabin was a quiet one. Emile watched out the side of the truck and Sunny sank into the silence, grateful not to have to explain anything else. He was exhausted not from running through the forest, but from the heart-stopping fright of thinking he'd lost his dog, from the confusing tilt of the world when Emile swept him up like he was a child who weighed nothing, treated his cuts, comforted his breakdown yet again, and showed himself in a different, more illuminating light.

Sunny wanted to think he was at a place of acceptance about his parents. It had been a year, after all. But a year was a blink of time compared to the whole rest of his life.

"You are still upset." Emile squeezed Sunny's fingers. They were holding hands across the wide centre console, and the touch grounded him, kept him centred and out of the haze of sadness. He squeezed back.

"Thinking about my dead parents upsets me," he admitted, belatedly thinking that probably sounded snippier than he'd meant it to.

"I can't say I understand," Emile admitted.

"Your parents are still alive?"

Emile said nothing for a long time. "Those who created me… didn't raise me. So even though the one who raised me… died… yes." He was quiet again for a moment, and Sunny risked a glance. He was staring out the windshield, a thoughtful look on his face. "I miss that bond. It was a loss."

"But it wasn't your whole world."

"It was the one connection where I was allowed to be who—and what—I truly am. No one else understood, and so I left. I don't miss the others, and I don't miss that bond less here than I missed it at home." He shrugged. "But it is gone. I am not. I honour it by continuing to fight to be myself." He frowned. "If that makes any sense."

Sunny nodded. "I grow my plants to honour Mom. I left the company to Daisy to honour Dad. She was more like him—more *liked* by him—than I ever was. It works out."

"Then we move forward with this new life. Yes?"

"We?"

Emile grinned, and Sunny would have sworn, before he had to look back to the road, that he'd glimpsed pointed teeth, and a wicked, brilliant gleam in Emile's sapphire eyes.

"We," Emile whispered, leaning close enough to blow the word in a hot breath against Sunny's neck, raising a flush over his skin. "Whatever comes."

He had to concentrate to keep the Rover in a straight line, but the promise was already made, and his cock had heard. He didn't want to ask what Emile meant by "whatever comes." One thing at a time.

FORTUNATELY THEY pulled into the yard only a moment later. Neither of them seemed to need to talk about what came next. Apparently running headlong through the forest got Emile going, and Sunny wasn't about to complain. The chance to lose himself in all the ways Emile was touching him came as a welcome relief. His parents wouldn't be any less dead and gone afterwards, but at least, as he lay sated in Emile's arms, blankets tossed over their legs, the scents of sex and sunshine permeating the warm air of the loft, he didn't feel quite so disconnected from the world.

Having Emile around was changing him. In his bones, he knew he wasn't the same man who had run to the woods to be alone, away from everyone and everything that reminded him of his loss. He had a connection now.

Next to him Emile moaned softly, snuffling in half sleep. He was so warm, and their sweat and come was drying between them. Sunny was content, but the sleepy lethargy that seemed to have overcome Emile didn't clutch at his own limbs. He watched Emile doze for a few minutes before deciding he needed to move.

Not wanting to go far, he merely went down to the bathroom to sponge most of the afternoon's activities away, and to make two cups of coffee. He dressed both with a generous dose of Irish cream and padded back up the steps. It would be nice to kiss Emile awake, share the coffee, and laze in bed for the afternoon. Being temporarily unemployed did have its perks.

For a heartbeat, as he topped the steps and viewed the bed from a few steps down, a slight motion made him think Emile had already woken. Then he thought Fernforest must have wheedled his way under the covers to snuggle in the crook of Emile's knees.

Then he saw the snake slithering, body first, out from under the covers and off the side of the bed.

Sunny screamed, charging up the last few steps, spraying coffee over his fingers as he dashed to kick at the coiling mass of scales.

Emile cried out as if in pain, spinning up into a crouch on the bed to glare at Sunny, whipping his tail around, knocking books, a glass of water, and a lamp off the bedside table with a crash. A framed picture of Sunny's parents bounced off the bed to the rug next to it, the muffled thump drowned out by the coffee cups hitting the floor in a splashing, shattering mess. Hot coffee splattered over Sunny's feet, and he cursed, dancing back.

"The fuck!" Sunny shouted.

"What?" Emile danced in his crouch, spinning this way and that as Sunny pointed. "What is it?"

"The fuck is that?" Sunny said at the same time, and Emile stilled.

He became so still, in fact, Sunny thought he had stopped breathing.

"Sunny?" Emile slowly reached out a hand, arms bent, fingers outstretched but not close enough to touch. Which was good, because the back of his hand glowed with iridescent splotches that, after a heartbeat, resolved themselves into neatly laid-out scales. Pink scales. *Pretty* pink scales. Feathers bloomed up the backs of his arms and around his ankles.

"Scales!" Sunny rasped, pointing. He finally tore his gaze away from what he'd thought was a snake—but obviously couldn't be because it was *fuchsia*—from Emile's hand, to Emile's ashen, terrified face.

Emile drew his hand back, covering the pink shimmering with his other, equally scaled hand. He settled on his haunches, partly supported by a thick, scaled tail, also in shades of pink and purple. "I—" He blinked. His eyes were huge, brilliantly blue, and haunted. A splash of what Sunny thought were more feathers poked from under Emile's long hair and drifted in fluffy pink lines farther up the backs of his forearms. "Give me a moment."

Frankly Sunny was too stunned to do anything but stand there in the pool of cooling coffee, breathe, and try not to gibber.

After a moment, the feathers rustled and floated to the bed. The pink iridescence to Emile's skin remained, though it didn't appear so scalelike anymore. The tail curled around him, hiding his feet, the end twitching like a nervous reflex. His eyes remained huge and frightened.

"I can explain," Emile whispered. "If you let me."

CHAPTER 22

"I-IF...." SUNNY gulped and tried again. "If I le—" He had to clear his throat. "If I let you?"

"You could throw me out," Emile pointed out as he curled his feet under himself and began to rake in the discarded feathers to pat into a rough circle around him. He used his hands and his tail, and Sunny couldn't stop staring at the very exacting way that appendage moved, as nimble as Emile's fingers. Once the feathers were gathered, Emile pulled the covers around his legs. He dragged pillows close, even hauled one into his lap with his tail, creating a nest for himself as Sunny watched.

"Can I?" Sunny asked, voice low, still shaking, but what the hell. He had a right to shake. If Emile could have scales and a tail—a *tail*—Sunny could shake for a little while. "Th-throw you out, I mean. If I wanted to?" He wasn't sure a—*something*—with a *tail* had to agree to be thrown out of anywhere if he didn't want to be.

"It ees your housse. You don't have to let me sstay."

"The accent again," Sunny said, because *that* was the elephant in the room.

"I am ssorry." Emile closed his eyes, swallowed a few times, and squared his shoulders. "Some of the changes you can't see on the outside," he explained in a more normal cadence. "My voice box does—weird things midshift."

"Right." *Midshift.* Because shifting was *real. The fuck!*

Silence. Exactly how did one go about asking their boyfriend just what kind of—of—

"Huh." Sunny blew out a breath. He met Emile's gaze.

"Huh?" Emile lifted an eyebrow, which was, Sunny noticed, a brilliant lemon yellow, like the tips of his hair and some of the feathers still gracing his ankles.

"The oddest thing here"—Sunny shuddered and pointed to the side of his head—"isn't even that I don't know how to ask you what... well. You know." He waved a hand. "The oddest thing is that I just thought of you as my boyfriend, and I'm not sure that's entirely, well...." *Normal.*

I should be freaking out. Running for the car, grabbing my dog, and getting the hell out.

He watched the last five or six inches of Emile's tail twitch and fiddle with the fringe on an afghan, mimicking the way he fiddled the edge of the pillowcase he held in his lap with his long, perfect fingers.

So then, I guess, just ask.

"What are you?"

"I'm a dragon."

They spoke at the same instant, both staring at the other, breath held at the end, waiting.

SUNNY CONTEMPLATED.

There was something in his woods. Something impossibly fast that spewed smoke and ash in its wake and easily outran his dog.

The nightshade was growing so fast he could all but watch it crawl along the railing of his little bridge.

His rose bush had bloomed overnight and slightly out of season.

His trees seemed to move on their own and watch him from their side of the creek.

And the creek. He remembered the fanciful images he'd "imagined" in the water that first day. A dragon and a dog, gambolling.

He'd found a naked, lost man in his old shack, and suddenly everything about that discovery took on a whole new shape. A shape that sported a pink tail.

Sunny glanced at Fernforest, who had jumped up to flop against Emile's side, heedless of the coil of scales he'd laid his chin on. "You." He approached the bed and Ferny's tail thumped a few light taps against the sheets. "You. Knew," he accused the dog.

Ferny yipped and grinned at him.

Emile stopped his fiddling long enough to pet Fernforest around his ears. He got a few licks on the bottom of one foot for his trouble, and then turned his attention back to Sunny.

"You're a traitor, Fernforest," Sunny growled. He lifted a foot, grimaced, and frowned at the spilled coffee.

Fernforest jumped off the bed and started licking it up. The caffeine and the whiskey probably weren't good for him, but Sunny had bigger issues at the moment that eclipsed a probably magical dog who could talk to his boy—

He mentally shook himself, but the label remained in place. *A magical dog who can talk to my* shifter *boyfriend.* "So many things wrong with that thought," he muttered.

Emile remained quiet, watching him.

"Okay," he said at last, relocated one pace to the side so Fernforest wasn't licking his toes. "A dragon. I don't… get it."

Sunny gnawed on his lower lip until the sting alerted him to the habit. He brushed the back of his hand over his mouth. Emile had been patiently waiting for him to ask something, only he had no idea where to begin.

Okay. Emile is a dragon shifter. Explains some things. He glanced at the appendage flicking at the edge of the rug on Emile's side of the bed, but looked away quickly. "How big are you?"

"What?" Emile blinked at him and his tail twitched more emphatically.

His tail *is twitching. Like a goddamn* cat. *A scaly cat. What the ever-loving* fuck?

"I'm…." Emile touched the top of his head. "This big. I don't understand. You know how big I am." He moved his hand, and it hovered for a heartbeat above his groin, but he must have thought better of the joke. Probably best. Sunny wasn't at the joking stage quite yet.

"No, I mean as a dragon? How big a dragon are you? Like, ten feet? Twelve? Bigger, even? Can you even shift in the house?"

Emile narrowed his eyes. "Is that a trick question? I'm as big as I am." He looked thoughtful for a moment, then tipped his head. "Though when I have scales and more legs, I suppose… then I am bigger than this." He indicated his body. "I never really thought about it."

Sunny's eyes got wide. "More legs?"

"Six. Yes. And a tail." He flicked said tail, and Sunny shivered as the tip caressed his bare calf. That was… oh. The tail moved up, curving over his knee and sliding along his thigh. "You really know nothing about us, do you?" Emile asked.

"That's distracting," Sunny pointed out, jerking his leg like he might if Ferny were licking him. "And hello. No. Dragons aren't—um, *weren't*—real when I went down to get coffee ten minutes ago. Sort of flying blind here. Stop that!"

Emile's tail had wiggled under the cuff of his boxers.

Emile just grinned at him. Sunny *would* find the only living dragon shifter with a dirty sense of humour. And a prehensile tail. *"For fuck sakes!"*

"Okay, okay. Sorry." Emile put his tail away and sat back. "Ask me anything."

"Can you breathe fire?" That might be cool. And was super relevant, but what the fuck.

Emile chuckled. "That's a myth."

"Oh." Disappointing, but not the end of the world. He still had the fireplace. "So dragons can't breathe fire?"

"Well." Emile hesitated. "Some can, I suppose. Sort of, although it wouldn't be breathing, exactly. I expect it's very difficult and probably as dangerous for the dragon as whoever he's breathing fire at. Mixing magic with physiology to that degree is always somewhat… problematic."

Now Sunny chuckled. "Whoever he's breathing it at? What? Girl dragons don't breathe fire?"

Emile stared at him, horrified. "Why would an Egg-bearer do anything that endangered their potential offspring? That makes no sense whatsoever."

"Oh. I—" Touchy subject, then. *Why, I wonder?* "Egg-bearer? Do they have names? Or just the designation?" He couldn't imagine Daisy allowing any guy, or, well, any *anyone* to dictate what she could or couldn't do with her body.

Emile pushed up straighter and crossed his arms over his chest. "Why would they not have names?" He cocked his head. "They're dragons, not property."

"You just called them Egg-bearers. Like that's all they are."

"*Egg-bearers* is as close as I can think of in English to describe how they think of themselves." He smirked. "Would you prefer 'vessels of all life, keepers of the Enclave, curators of our history and nurtures of the future'?"

Sunny thought about that. "Well. Yes, actually."

"Kind of a mouthful, don't you think?"

"But slightly more dignified than Egg-bearers."

"Being chosen to carry the eggs for your House or Enclave is among the greatest of honours for my kind. So to us, being called an Egg-bearer isn't such a tragedy. It means you will be pampered and cared for—worshipped, even—by the Sires whose offspring you will be blessed to raise, and by the House or Enclave they will eventually join. It is truly something many of us aspire to. A 'designation' any one of my kind would be proud of." Emile swallowed hard. "Most of the time."

"And there's the story." Sunny settled onto the bed. "Explain."

WELL. FOUR small words too far, Emile. How deeply his society was imprinted after all his attempts to buck the conventions. He shot a look at Sunny, who watched him expectantly.

"You came here for a reason," Sunny said quietly, taking his hand like he sensed the deep waters. "People don't leave their entire lives, all they know, their whole family and anyone who might love them, behind for no reason. What was yours?"

"You said 'girls don't breathe fire,'" Emile began.

"And you corrected me."

"You know there are some species, even in your world, where a gender switch for the good of the species is a fairly normal occurrence."

"Some amphibians, I think. And?"

"Even in your own species—"

"Gender isn't a fixed variable. I get it."

"Far from fixed, Sunny. For my people, gender, well, it *isn't*."

"Um." Sunny glanced pointedly down at Emile's crotch. "Do we need a graphic demonstration, Mr Dragon?"

Despite the clump of cold goo congealed inside, Emile chuckled. "Not if you want to get to the end of the lesson any time soon. And just because dragons have the ability to change our outward appearance with a thought, that doesn't always have any effect on how we think of ourselves."

"Fair enough. And true for humans, I suppose. Except for the part about changing our appearance with a thought. I expect there are a lot of people who would really like to be able to do that." Sunny leaned in and pecked his cheek, but Emile moved back. As gratifying as it was to feel the acceptance slowly untensing Sunny's muscles, some things were easier to talk about without distraction.

"Please."

Sunny nodded. "Sort of a rip-the-Band-Aid-off thing, huh?"

Emile furrowed his brow, trying to work that out.

"You know, now that I know you're *really* not from around here, that whole puzzled look thing makes so much more sense. All I meant was that now you're in it, you want to get the explanations over with. One fell swoop and all."

"Oh."

Sunny tapped one of the bandages on his foot. "Rip it off fast, get the hard, ouchy bit over with quick."

Emile nodded. "Yes. That exactly."

"Then have at 'er." Sunny spread his hands wide and leaned back against the headboard, shoulder to shoulder with Emile. He picked up Emile's hand again. "Amphibians."

"Gender."

"Your people don't have it."

"Not the way you think of it, no. There are various things it is easier to do, physiologically, in one scale form than in another. For instance, fire. Growing scales thick and hard enough to withstand that kind of magic, the heat needed to create fire would make it difficult to float. They'd be heavy. You'd sink."

"And so a dragon with thick, heavy scales wouldn't be a fan of the water." Sunny eyed him, head on tilt.

"Exactly." He shivered, and Sunny appreciated that afternoon in the creek on a new level.

"Anyway," Emile continued, "scales like that are also basically incompatible with a growing body flexible enough to accommodate an egg pouch and growing eggs, or with having enough follicles to provide feathers enough for a comfortable and safely warm nest in which to incubate them, once they have developed."

"And once you pick, you can't go back?"

"It depends. Sires have hard shells—nearly impenetrable, in fact. Egg-bearers are soft." He poked Sunny's ribs. "Almost as soft as you, with feathers and down all along their backs. Most others are somewhere in the middle and can fluctuate at will." He pulled in a breath. "A very few of us, who aren't Egg-bearers or Sires, don't care to fluctuate."

"As in?"

Emile tried to smile, but his heart wasn't in it. "I much prefer my hard scales and male skin form."

"And this is a problem?"

This time the smile Emile produced was a grimace and, he suspected, filled with sharper teeth than usual. "It is when the future Sire of the House I belong to has other plans for me."

"Oh." Sunny's eyes got wide. "That's—he can't force you to—"

"He—Hakko—is the dragon from my broodnest chosen to sire the next generation of dragons for my House."

"Like, the father?"

"Not in the sense you use that word. Dragons require what you might consider three parents: one who offers the egg, one who donates the genetic material that will fertilize the egg, and one who lends their magic to the union. The Offeror, the Donor, and the Sire. All three are necessary to make the hatchling viable.

"The Egg-bearer sometimes offers one of their eggs as well, but that isn't a requirement for being a Bearer. In fact, many Bearers choose that path because they have no eggs of their own but have the capacity to carry a clutch for those who prefer not to. They are the one who carries the eggs, helps them hatch, and cares for the offspring. They are the nurturing part of the creation of new life.

"Unlike Enclaves, where multiple broodnests are allowed in one generation and genetic siblings are not frowned upon, our laws dictate that every egg in a House's broodnest must come from a different Offeror and each egg fertilized by a different Donor. This dispels the magical bloodline, keeping any one dragon from growing too strong, and keeps even small Houses like ours genetically viable.

"Since Hakko is the oldest and strongest of us, he will be the one who lends his magic to the eggs once they have been given life."

"But he won't be allowed to be the Donor for any of them."

Emile stifled a sigh. That was the idea. Hakko, though, had other plans. Ones Emile wanted no part of.

"He wants not only my capacity to Bear the eggs for our House, but my eggs as well. I don't trust him. Because we shared the safety of our Bearer's egg pouch and broodnest, we are linked, through our magic, and"—he tapped his head—"in here. Sort of. He can't *make* me do anything. But he can... suggest I forget why I didn't want it. It's... ugly." He shivered. "Distance from him makes it easier to ignore his suggestions. I had hoped crossing the Fold would sever that connection."

"The Fold?"

"The barrier that keeps our magic on our side, and yours on your side."

"We don't have magic."

Emile frowned and studied Sunny. It seemed like he truly believed that. But then humans had always been an anomaly. "In any case, it has made it easier to clear my head of his ideas and see how dangerous those ideas were.

"Hakko is head of one of the Ten Houses. He will have a single Bearer, and they will be life-mated. The Bearer of a House's eggs carries a single clutch in their lifetime, and for many generations now, the eggs the House Bearer carries and the hatchlings they raise are never from the Enclaves under their protection, but from the Enclaves of the other Houses. It is the best way to share magical power, disperse genetic proficiencies, and keep the political peace."

"Because you are responsible for the offspring of someone else," Sunny said.

Email nodded. "It is in everyone's best interest to care for the hatchlings well, knowing your own offspring are in the hands of others." He frowned. "Hakko, and our Sire before him, make the other nine Houses nervous. It's been difficult to convince them House Corcaird is a fit House for their progeny."

"Do you ever go back? To the Enclave where your egg came from?"

"Many do, yes, once they are old enough and strong enough to leave the nest. There is a period of wandering, trying out our scale forms, experimenting, testing limits, seeing what skin fits us best, deciding what we want to do, where we want to call home. Many of us are drawn to the Enclave where our eggs came from, but there is a tight bond with our broodmates, as well, so when it comes time to settle, most choose an Enclave close to their broodnest."

"You are a long way from where your egg originated, I think," Sunny mused.

Emile sighed and looked sad. "Indeed."

"Why? If you belong to one of the ruling Houses, why would you leave?"

Emile covered Sunny's hand with his. "I'm getting there."

"Sorry."

"If you understand how the process works, perhaps you will understand why I—why it couldn't work for me."

"Okay." Sunny bit his lip, winced, and motioned for Emile to continue.

"The Egg-bearer carries the eggs for all the Enclave—or House in my case—once the eggs have been chosen and fertilised. In an Enclave, every egg will come from a different dragon and probably be fertilised and magically enhanced by different dragons as well. In a House, while the eggs come from the other Houses, and are fertilized by other dragons, only the Sire can enhance them. At least, that's how it is supposed to work. That will ensure some, at least, have the strength—the magic—to become the leaders of the next generation. They are incubated, nested, and hatched together, but seldom are there actual genetic siblings in a clutch. The age range of a single clutch might span as much as five years or as little as six months. And once the hatchlings have all reached their first shift, around the age of ten or twelve, the Bearer is free to leave the nest, bear another clutch, for those not bearing eggs for one of the Houses, or remain and continue to care for the younglings."

"So... a Bearer might be carrying some of those eggs for five years?"

"Hence my horror when you suggested that a soft-scale might take on the magic of fire-breathing. The danger to their eggs is—" Again, he shuddered.

"Makes sense."

"Five years is rare. It happens most often when a House chooses a Bearer. The other Houses choose those from their Enclaves who will offer eggs or become Donors of the next generation. In return, the House that takes those eggs offers one of its own."

"Which creates a natural alliance between them."

"Exactly. An exchange. But the trials for the privilege of being the enclave to donate the egg are gruelling and can take years to complete. From the time the first egg is chosen and incubated, a House is limited by the length of time an egg can be carried in a kind of magical stasis to choose the rest. Larger Houses have more Enclaves to choose from, and so they rarely run into an issue.

"Smaller Houses, like mine, are more likely to have many failures in the trials, and take longer to amass a viable clutch, since they cannot accept eggs unless they have eggs to give in return. A series of economic failures, natural disasters, and generally bad leadership decimated our House. It has taken a lot of work, and some very strict rule, to claw our way back into power. We are small still but have become a powerful House once more.

"Bethakke carried Hakko's egg for four years and three months. They were tightly bonded by the time he hatched. Bethakke loved him dearly, and Hakko was devoted to them. As a member of the Ten Houses, Bethakke was allowed only one clutch, small as it was, and they chose their successor before we hatched. Hakko never agreed with the choice. It was the one thing over which they fought, ever."

"Who did they choose?"

"A born soft-shell called Ananth."

"And who did Hakko want?"

Emile closed his eyes for a moment, but when he gazed at Sunny, the answer was right there, in the brilliant blaze of his eyes.

"Why you? Are you his true brother? Genetically?"

Emile shook his head. "Hakko came from one of Bethakke's own eggs. I did not, but there is a distant genetic link between us that should preclude me being the Bearer of our clutch, if only to ensure that an egg of mine could never be genetically or magically enhanced by him. Had Bethakke known about it, they may never have agreed to accept my egg in the first place, and when they discovered it, the choice for Ananth as the next Bearer became obvious. To everyone except Hakko."

"Why not just choose a different Sire?"

"Hakko was the natural choice. He has the power to lead our House despite the troubles we've had in the past. The next-best choice, Rokkan, hadn't the heart to contest it. It is not an easy thing to go against generations of tradition and fight a formidable hard-scale to do it. Kozinikk, who was the Sire chosen to partner Bethakke and the one to lead our House before Hakko, was not one to be gainsaid."

"And I take neither is Hakko."

"Not easily, no. He chose me as his Bearer because any egg of mine would be as close to his own genetic offspring as he can get, and since it wasn't coming from another Enclave, it would go undetected by the other Houses until it hatched. Then it would be too late."

"Too late?"

"Hakko was the product of the exact thing the mingling of House blood was supposed to avoid. Bethakke and Kozinikk were genetically very close. While their eggs came from different Houses, they still had mutual ancestors, and that gave them many traits in common, including a particular ability to harness enormous amounts of magic. Doubling any kind of magical ability like that makes it exponentially stronger in the offspring. That can be a good thing in some cases, but it can also be dangerous, depending what the magic can do.

"That kind of match doesn't happen very often, but it's not impossible. We keep meticulous records, so we can avoid it, but the Sire that chose them for their roles obscured those records. No one realised what he had done until Bethakke and Kozinikk mated and produced a dragon with more power than any in generations.

"When Kozinikk fertilised Bethakke's own egg, they effectively doubled the strength of their power in the offspring they produced—Hakko. It isn't at all unusual for a Sire and Bearer to fertilise one or two eggs of the Bearer's. There shouldn't be any danger in that, as Sire and Bearer should not be genetically related. Producing siblings is not prohibited, provided those siblings do not then reproduce in the same House or Enclave. But when Kozinikk's Sire did what he did, he took that choice from them. There was no way for Kozinikk and Bethakke to know how closely related they were until the hatching process started, and by then, it was too late." He looked up to meet Sunny's gaze.

"That's what happened? With Hakko?"

Emile nodded.

"And you."

"In a way, though my egg came from another House, it turns out the genetics are close enough to satisfy Hakko, and too close for my comfort."

"So. You're a what? Mega dragon?"

Emile laughed. "Hardly, no. It seems Hakko benefitted most from the situation. He is very powerful. And very power-hungry. I—" Emile swallowed hard. "There is only so much power one dragon can hold in their body before it starts to warp the mind. I suppose that's a necessary failsafe."

"Are you saying Hakko is crazy?"

"Our House was once the most powerful House in existence. They did great things with their power. They did terrible things with their power. Those things brought about a cataclysm for dragons—the Dispersal—that flung them to the far corners of our world. It has taken hundreds of generations for us to regain any kind of stability. The Breeding Rules exist for a very good reason, and they have worked for countless generations. There is peace. Balance. What brought Bethakke and Kozinikk together should never have happened. Their Sire was banished when his manipulations were discovered. What Hakko is trying to do now is unconscionable and I cannot let him do it."

"Bethakke tried to fix things when she chose—the soft-scale you mentioned?"

"Ananth. Yes. She couldn't do anything about Hakko's destiny. He was the strongest of our clutch. He will be Sire. But by choosing the softest, the gentlest, and the wisest among us for his mate, Bethakke hoped to mitigate his... shortcoming. Soften his edges, I suppose. And it helps that Ananth is in no way even remotely related to us in blood or magic."

"But he wanted you."

"He wants a hatchling who can begin a new dynasty. One as great as the Houses of old. But those Houses nearly destroyed us. They *did* destroy so much of our world, and so many other races suffered. If I took the role of Egg-bearer, I would be soft. Defenseless against him. Part of me wanted very badly to be that nurturer, to care for our young. I could have made that choice for any other Sire." He shook his head. His eyes glittered, and he scraped at a fraying edge of a pillow sham with a nail that was so sharp it was almost a claw. "I couldn't be that for him. I couldn't take the chance I would bow to his persuasion and give him the egg he wanted. So I kept my hard scales, what you would call a masculine body, and refused his demands. When he started using his power to sway me towards his wishes, to take the choice away, I panicked. I had no defense against what he was doing here." He tapped the side of his skull.

"So you ran."

"To a world where my choice is no choice at all. Where I can just be exactly what I am."

"Um." Sunny peered at him, head tilted to one side. "Dude." He leaned over Emile's hips and behind him to run light fingers down the scaled surface of his tail. "You're a fucking *dragon*."

"Well. Yes. But here I am dragon no matter what form I choose to take. There, I am Hakko's or I am... nothing."

"He'd cast you out?"

"Oh, he would keep me. I would choose his gilded cage and say thank you, or he would shackle me with much worse." The sadness in his sapphire gaze broke Sunny. "Is it still a cage if you don't realise you're caught? He has such magic, Sunny. I've seen him use it to 'persuade' others to his will, and they don't even realise they've been snared. They follow him happily, completely unaware they once opposed him. At least here I can be dragon without *being a dragon*. I can be who I am."

Sunny nodded. "I wish—"

"No. My one hope in coming here was to keep his power in check the only way I could. I met you. That is something I could never have hoped for. If you will have me knowing I am a dragon, then I cannot ask for more than that."

CHAPTER 23

AND *THAT*—BEING a dragon—was something Emile was going to have to learn to hide in this world. Sunny seemed bemused more than anything, and maybe that was because outwardly, most of the time Emile looked as human as Sunny himself. Sunny wasn't confronted with the otherness of Emile's nature as much as Emile was bombarded with example after example of how different this world was from what he knew.

The vacuum cleaner Sunny hauled out to suck up the glass shards of their coffee mugs, while fascinating, was just one more instance showcasing Emile's ignorance of human technology. If Sunny eventually made him leave, he had little hope of blending into human society, and he knew it. He needed Sunny. More to the point, he *wanted* Sunny. But since that afternoon of revelation, he wasn't sure the feeling was as mutual as it had been.

Over the next few days, Sunny's shock wore down to half-asked questions he often ended up saying he didn't need answers to, start-and-stop conversations about what to eat or plans for the day, and Sunny muttering to himself as he worked his increasingly verdant and fruitful garden plots. If not for Fernforest, Emile might have not talked at all for hours on end. It began to feel uncomfortably like his home, where he was a concept—a bit of tradition and societal necessity—more than a person.

Did Sunny see him as the *idea* of a dragon? A myth out of a fantasy story instead of a living, breathing, feeling being?

The only positive thing to come from his accidental outing of his other nature was that now that he had stopped trying to suppress any signs of his scale form, his magic had stopped rebelling. If the occasional blush of scales formed when Sunny's gaze lingered, Emile didn't have to hide it, and that made it all the easier to keep the magic in check.

Not having to fight his own nature left his body free to recuperate much faster. He'd not realised how much the need to clamp his will around the errant strands and surges of magical energy had been depleting him. Nesting became more about a desire for a comforting reminder of home than needing the security of a safe roost.

He was contemplating the porch swing with its pile of pillows and blankets, the small stash of books, and the drift of pink feathers beneath it when a prickle of magic lifted the hairs at his nape and along his arms. Like a cool breeze wafting up from the foot of the yard, a wave of magical energy buffeted his senses, and he frowned.

"Emile?" Sunny's voice quavered slightly. A tool clanked, and Emile turned to see Sunny with a shovel held in two hands and cocked over his shoulder. "Emile? You know this guy?"

Emile followed Sunny's gaze to the footbridge. The wood creaked under the weight of a creature that most definitely did not belong on this side of the Fold.

"So there you are," Emile whispered to it. "I wondered where you ran off to."

Dark fog and ash puffed up around the creature's feet as it shuffled a few steps closer. Its tail, a brilliant shade of turquoise that faded to deep pine forest green by the time it reached its rump, swished back and forth. Like a cat's, that tail gave away the mood of the creature with every twitch. It was nervous. Curious. Uncertain.

An uncertain salamander was not a thing to be trifled with.

Emile held out a hand, arm straight and strong, palm out, fingers splayed and pointing skyward. If the salamander had any training at all, it would know the gesture—and the accompanying push of magic flux—was a command to stay. If it was feral, the gesture was one of strength and command it would understand through instinct, and one it would—possibly—respect. Plus, the flux would appeal to it like a treat would to a dog.

Hopefully.

Emile walked slowly but steadily down the stairs and across the lawn. "Stay where you are, please, Sunny. And lower your shovel. It's not a threat." *I hope.* The animal's cautious but still posture was encouraging, but no guarantee.

Sunny grunted, shifted his feet, but only rested the shaft of the shovel on his shoulder. The blade remained up, his grip tight, ready to swing. Perhaps not a terrible idea, under the circumstances.

"It?" Sunny asked. "You don't know who—I mean—it's an it?"

"This is a salamander."

"So not a dragon?"

Emile chuckled. "No more a dragon than an ape is a man."

"He doesn't look like any salamander I've ever seen."

"Larger, perhaps," Emile agreed, remembering something about the differences in what his people called salamanders and what humans referred to as such.

Sunny snorted. "Just a bit, yeah. Also, he's got scales."

"How else would they defend themselves? They don't have tooth or claw. An impenetrable hide seems only practical. They are also rather intelligent, and social, if reared properly. Vicious and dangerous if handled with cruelty. A feral salamander is unpredictable but will usually leave you alone if you don't provoke it."

"How does one provoke a salamander?"

"Oh. Threatening or quick motions. Acting aggressive." He glanced at Sunny. "Like any wild thing. Would you poke a bear?"

"Of course not."

"Think of him as a… scaly… bear."

"A blue-and-green bear."

"Partially, yes. Also, he's magical."

"And has spikes on his tail."

Emile peered around the animal, squinting to see through the ash and smoke. There were indeed spikes on the creature's tail, easily three or four inches long, and wickedly pointed. Interesting adaptation, in general, only seen in populations that needed to protect themselves. So not one bred to domestic uses, or the spikes—if he ever grew them at all—would have been filed down for the safety of his handlers. Still, he remained preternaturally still as Emile approached him, head tilted, watching him. So neither was he feral.

"Where did you come from, little one?" he wondered aloud.

"Um. Maybe the same place you did?" Sunny offered.

"Well. Yes. But that's a big place. He didn't just wander across the Fold all by himself."

"Why not?"

"Salamanders are by far the most sensitive to magical disruptions of any creature we know. The Fold would make them… uncomfortable. One wouldn't cross it unless forced to."

"What's with all the smoke?"

"It's a byproduct. They absorb what we call magic flux. Something of a raw energy with magical properties, but not in a form than can be used to fuel, say, a dragon's shift."

"How do they absorb it? I mean, our salamanders breathe through their skin, but yours has those impenetrable scales you mentioned."

"Right now they are impenetrable, yes. He's got them locked because he's nervous." Emile grinned, showing sharp teeth. "You should see them if he feels threatened."

"Um." Sunny shifted his feet. "No, thank you."

"They are utterly beautiful."

"Deadly, too, I'd imagine."

"Quite. At rest, their form is much more skin than scale, although their shape changes very little."

"Does everything in your world have more than one form?"

Emile considered that. "I suppose… very nearly, yes. The more intelligently one can manipulate magic, the more varied the forms one can take. Generally speaking."

"You must think things very dull here, then."

"On the contrary." He stopped about ten feet from the salamander, who shuffled, curled its tail around its feet, and sat on its haunches. "I would think that if one were confined to a single form, one might have to rely on a different kind of genius to get things done. There, now." He lowered his arm and cocked his head at the creature. "You really aren't feeling well, are you?"

The salamander watched him, the tip of its tail flicking up at irregular intervals.

"How can you tell?"

"The smoke. Salamanders are magical constructs."

"O-kay." Sunny frowned, clearly not understanding.

"Made from flux and the element of whatever creature brought it into being. So a water sprite's salamander would be born of water and would release steam or ice along with the refined magic. One created by a brownie would be born of stone and would leave a trail of soil in its wake." Emile lowered his arm, took a few steps, and made a curling motion with his hand. "This one seems to be a wood salamander, created by a dryad."

"So, smoke and ash."

"Yes. But." He frowned. "I think it's sick. Or weak. Because the smoke should not be so black. The ash is crumbly and dry, more like coals than powdery grey ash. There's something wrong with it."

"Maybe the lack of magic?" Sunny suggested. "If it needs to ingest magic to exist, then there's an issue. No magic here."

"Oh, Sunny." Emile smiled. "How wrong you are. No. I don't think it is a lack of magic so much as the wrong kind of magic. Like someone fed it something that isn't agreeing with it." He curled his fingers again, and the salamander made a strange mewling sound, then lowered its long neck and crouched on all fours, head low to the ground.

"Well now you're just being stubborn." He made the curling gesture one more time, and with a sigh, the salamander lay down.

"It understands you?"

"After a fashion. I worked with them as a youngster. They seemed to like me. Other handlers treat them like animals in the manner a human might train a dog, training with treats and simple commands. I just talked to them. Told them what I wanted, coaxed them a bit, and eventually they listened. They really are smart. And they respond very well if you know how to use the magic flux to show them what you want. Something like how Fernforest tells me things, but not so primitive. He is a dog, after all, so his command of the flux and his understanding of the world are rather simple."

"What?" Sunny blinked and shook his head. "Wait. Okay, we're going to come back to the whole talking to the dog thing, because. Well. Because who knew that was a thing. Right now, though, there's a giant gecko in my yard, it's smoking, and I think also singeing my bridge." Sunny scrubbed a hand over the back of his neck as he eased the shovel to the ground. "I don't even know what I just said. It shouldn't make any sense at all."

Emile chuckled. "That is quite the beauty of magic, isn't it?"

As Sunny observed, Emile moved slowly closer to the crouching salamander. It watched him curiously, its tail swishing every now and then, its head on a slight tilt. It was interesting that while Sunny had no experience with anything like this and very little experience with animals, he could tell just by looking that the salamander wasn't well.

Its scales didn't glow, for one thing. He'd noticed that Emile's scales shimmered in sunlight, a rosy mother-of-pearl look that oddly suited his translucent skin. *Yeah, focus. There's a giant lizard on your doorstep, Sunny.* This lizard's scales were dull, the colours muted, and some around his nose and mouth were dry and flaking. Its sides heaved every now and then, and like Emile's when Sunny had first found him, this animal's bones seemed more prominent than was strictly healthy.

"What do we do with it?" he asked after a few minutes.

Emile glanced over his shoulder. "We?"

"Well." Sunny shrugged and stuffed a hand into his pocket. "It's here now. You said it won't cross the Fold or whatever on its own. So it can't get home, right?"

"Not by himself."

"Him. Okay." Sunny took a few steps, trying not to appear as tentative as he felt. Animals responded to confidence, didn't they? So confident, but not aggressive. How hard could it be? "And he's a tree salamander." Because that was obvious. Sunny shook himself. He'd seen the tail and feathers and scales. He knew Emile was a dragon. But the longer Emile walked around his house looking perfectly human, the more Sunny could ignore what he knew. This, though. It really did look like a giant gecko. And it was right there on his lawn. He was seized by the need to touch it. That would make it real.

"Sunny?" Emile held out a hand toward him much as he had toward the salamander. A bubble of resistance hit Sunny's chest, and he slowed his advance. "Please stay back, Sunny."

Sunny brushed at his chest. "Are you doing something to me?" He batted thin air, frowning. "Stop it."

"I need you to stay back."

"And I need to touch him."

"He might lash out."

"He won't." Sunny took another step. "If you're magicking me, you need to stop." He slapped Emile's hand out of the air. "I don't have magic, you can't use it on me. It's not fair."

"What?" Emile blinked at him. "Of course you have magic."

"You know"—Sunny lifted a hand and let it fall—"every time you open your mouth, you say another thing I don't understand. It's not helping."

"Television," Emile muttered. "Cell phones. Vacuum cleaners, for goodness sake."

"I'll let you use my vacuum if you let me pet your salamander."

"He's not *my* salamander." Emile's brows drew together, but he did drop his arm. "I'm sorry about the magic. It was instinct."

"It's fine. So was the vacuum cleaner."

"Instinctual vacuum-cleanering?" Emile asked, a hint of amusement creeping into his tone.

Sunny shrugged. "Something like that." He stopped one step in front of Emile. He had all of the animal's attention now. "And at this point, this guy is more yours than anyone else's."

"We don't own them, Sunny. Any more than you own Fernforest. You feed him, shelter him, love him, and he keeps your heart and your secrets. It's what dogs do."

"And what is it salamanders do?" Sunny might have challenged Emile's statement about Ferny not being his dog, but when he thought about it as Emile explained it, he couldn't argue.

"On a purely practical level, salamanders process magic flux into usable magical energy. The flux fuels them, and the energy we use to shift between forms and all the other magic we do is a byproduct."

"Like trees process carbon dioxide and pump out oxygen?"

"Very much like that. Magic flux can be toxic in large concentrations. As a source of energy to fuel our abilities, it's all but useless. Salamanders keep things balanced. They can also pull carts, protect sheep, and carry heavy loads. They are naturally very warm—good for nurseries, to keep it and the hatchlings warm." He moved closer to the salamander next to Sunny, lowering his voice as he did. "They can be quite beautiful. Many Houses once maintained them as decoration, chained or caged, floundering under the weight of jewels that kept them slow and pinned down. It gave the Houses a ready source of magic to fuel their lives."

"Sounds like slavery," Sunny muttered. His insides twisted at the thought of this lovely, lithe creature tied down in any way. He could feel the salamander's heat now, as he came to within arm's reach. It radiated off him in short, pulsing waves, and with it came a tingling sensation that rippled under Sunny's skin and reminded him of what he felt when Emile touched him.

"I imagine they would say the same, given the chance," Emile said darkly. "You're getting quite close, Sunny." His fingers clenched and unclenched as he watched like he wanted to reach out and pull Sunny back, but he didn't.

"I can't touch him if I don't get close, can I, Blue… no." He wasn't blue exactly. More greenish, but with undertones that reminded Sunny of the night sky right after the sun had disappeared and darkness and stars took over. "Nightshine," he said softly, holding out a hand not with his palm out, but with it up, offering his attention cupped in his hand.

The salamander stretched out his neck, nose twitching, body language perking up as if responding to the idea of a name.

"We don't name them, Sunny."

"Maybe you should."

"I'm sure they have names somewhere in their being. How are we to know what they are?"

"You said you can talk to my dog, and he's not a magical being. What's his name if it isn't Fernforest?"

Emile grunted. "Interestingly, Fernforest is his name. Or as near an approximation as human language is going to get."

Sunny took the last step right into the tooth range of the enormous animal and touched the tips of his fingers to his chin. Sparks flew—literal sparks, showering off his fingertips and bouncing off the salamander's scales. They lit up the thumbnail-sized plates of twilight purple, which were surprisingly soft around his lips, in the places they hadn't dried and flaked.

A glimmer sparked deep in the creature's dark, pine-hued eyes, and Sunny grinned. "Glimmerleaf," he said, and a wet, warm tongue swirled out to taste his fingers. "Glimmerleaf Nightshine."

The salamander moved forward, rubbing his head against Sunny's chest. Then he lay down, curling body, neck, and tail around Sunny's feet. Well, more accurately, around his feet, shins, and knees, nearly up to his hips.

"He seems to like you." Emile's voice, with an undertone of surprise, ignited a warm glow in Sunny's chest. It was something to surprise a dragon, after all. As Sunny shifted and eased a slight bit of his weight against the warm scales surrounding him, Emile observed Glimmerleaf, pleased surprise on his face.

"I seem to have that effect on magical creatures." Sunny met Emile's gaze, and his doubts fell away. Sure, he had been shocked to find out Emile's secret. But in the end, he was still Emile, still the guy

Sunny had come to know and want. The guy he was… *falling for. Admit it, Sunny. You're falling for the guy.*

For the *dragon*. Which he could still hardly believe. But why shouldn't he? After all, he had a smoking lizard curled around him, wrapping him to midthigh, radiating heat that was barely tolerable and, he was pretty sure, purring.

He had nightshade crawling along his bridge faster than any normal plant had a right to do. And he hadn't missed the way his garden was thriving out of all proportion to what the weather should be supporting at this time of year. He wanted to believe it was the application of all the research his parents had done over the years, along with a healthy dose of horse manure, but in his gut, he knew there was more to it.

He glanced at Emile, who met his gaze with something like admiration. Admiration from a dragon. Now wasn't that something?

CHAPTER 24

"How LONG do you think this is going to take?" Sunny whispered nearly half an hour later. He was staring at his dog, who stared back from about six feet away, a slightly accusing expression on his face. "Don't be like that, Ferny." Sunny wiggled his fingers in Fernforest's direction, but the dog only settled down to his elbows and lowered his chin to his paws. He didn't come any closer. "I still love you, you know."

Fernforest huffed.

"He's fine." Emile brought his attention from dog to salamander. "As for him, well. They can sleep for days."

"*Days*?" Sunny mouthed. He widened his eyes, which only made Emile laugh. The happy sound went a long way to easing the tension that had been growing between them.

"In this case, I expect he won't stay down long. He's restless." Emile pointed to the twitching tip of the salamander's tail. "Also, see how his front legs are clenching?"

"Like he's trying to grab something."

"And his scales haven't unlocked. He's dreaming. Normally that happens as they are waking. Be still. We don't want him startled as he surfaces."

"Do they bite?"

"A flare of magic would be more dangerous. He could expel a blast of energy or suck in a large quantity of flux. Either could kill you if it's big enough."

That got Sunny's heart beating, but he forced himself to remain still. The change in his heart rate was apparently enough, however, because Glimmerleaf lifted his head and blinked rapidly, swinging around to eyeball Sunny. He snorted a nearly white puff of smoke into Sunny's face. Through it, Sunny caught a glimpse of Emile, a long, sinewy body glowing in pinks, oranges, and purples, with long, slender coal-and-twilight wings superimposed over his bipedal form, like he was seeing a reflection of a dragon shimmering in a lake. Then the smoke dissipated, and it was just Emile again, as human-looking as ever, purple-burgundy hair pulled over one shoulder and cascading to his waist, Fernforest now standing, leaning on his legs. The afterimage of his dragon sizzled in Sunny's imagination, igniting all kinds of excited interest. He squirmed, surprised by his own reaction.

Glimmerleaf's long, slippery tongue came out to touch Sunny's cheek, then play with one of his curls. After a bit more exploring, which distracted Sunny from that unexpected epiphany, he rubbed his muzzle against Sunny's cheek and let out a soft sigh.

"You have to move, baby," Sunny murmured to him, motioning in an outward spiral with his hands. "I can't stand here all afternoon." He had things to do, not the least of which was explore the arousal that glimpse had set off.

Even as he thought that, though, his belly rumbled. One hunger at a time, he supposed. "You see? I have to eat." He ran fingers in a tickling path down Glimmerleaf's jaw and neck. "Think you can uncoil for me?" He made the circular motion again, like he was stirring the air.

After a heartbeat Glimmerleaf shifted, loosened his coil, and Sunny was able to step free.

Fernforest moved behind Emile's legs, flopped to the grass, and let out a heavy sigh. He lay with his back to Sunny and Glimmerleaf.

Glimmerleaf peered at the dog, head on tilt, a stream of silvery-grey smoke rising from his nostrils. "That's better, isn't it?" Sunny asked, pointing to the dissipating cloud.

"It is." In all the time Sunny had been standing in the centre of Glimmerleaf's coil, Emile had not approached any closer.

"What do we do with him?"

"They aren't pets, Sunny."

"Shush." Sunny rubbed Glimmerleaf's jaw. "Don't pay any attention to him. You're welcome here." He shot Emile a look. Just as Emile was welcome, so was this creature, also in need.

"You're right, of course."

Why was Emile even entertaining the thought that Sunny would turn Glimmerleaf away? Hadn't Sunny kept him?

Emile moved closer to them, and Glimmerleaf watched him, eyes bright. "You are calmer than I would have expected about all of this," he remarked to Sunny as he lifted a hand to touch the salamander's neck.

Glimmerleaf allowed a brief caress, then wandered off, nose to the ground, tail swishing behind him in slow arcs.

Sunny considered as he watched the salamander crawl slowly around the yard, tail sweeping in his wake as he investigated every corner. Fernforest rose and followed him at a distance of a few feet, sniffing at everything as the salamander moved on.

"I knew this place was special," Sunny said, keeping his voice quiet. "I felt it as soon as I stepped foot on it. It felt like… home, I guess, but more than that. It felt like I'd found a missing piece of something. Ever since my parents died, I've felt… lost. I worked so closely with Mom, and she had a way with growing things. Plants, animals—everything responded to her, and I learned a lot from her. I didn't have her innate way, but she taught me so much. After I lost her, I didn't want anything to do with plants or gardening. I thought it hurt too much, that I would never live up to her legacy, but then I found this place, and I knew the lack was what hurt.

"This place saved me. When I found you in that shack, I knew I had to help you. If the land was here to help me regrow my heart, I owed it to whatever brought me here to do what I could to repay that. I think he's the same." He held out a hand, and the salamander brushed the length of his body along his palm. "He's lost, and he needs help. He found us, so it's up to us." He knew in his bones this was right. And the more he thought about all of it, the less it shocked him that magic was drawn to this place, or even that magic existed at all. He knelt as Fernforest sidled up to him, tail wagging tentatively. He took the dog's face in both his hands and scratched behind his ears. "Do you understand?" He was looking at the dog but tuned when Emile answered.

"I'm beginning to."

They watched a few minutes more, and Sunny was pleased to see that the smoke trailing off his new scaly friend was much lighter than it had been before his nap. As it rose into the late-afternoon air, the shimmering view behind it caught Sunny's attention. The forest was so much more vibrant viewed through that veil, like there was more than simply leaves and branches moving just beyond his sight. As Glimmerleaf paused at the rose bush next to the drive, a distinctly not-rose bush shape moved in its depths.

"What is that?" Sunny pointed and moved a few steps closer.

The bush—all of it—froze, impossibly still in the light breeze.

"Softly," Emile whispered. "That's a dryad. They tend towards shyness, especially singles."

"Singles?"

"This rose bush is isolated here. Single bush, single dryad. He—at least I think it's a he—would have to cross a lot of open space to find another of its kind. They tend not to like doing that."

"Does every tree and bush have its own dryad?" Sunny asked, peering at the forest again. Without the screen of smoke before it, he saw only trees and bushes moving in the ways the wind dictated.

"Not exactly. It depends on the species. Willow trees, pine trees, they would each have their own dryads. A poplar grove, like yours, it depends. The trees themselves shoot up from suckers in the roots of their neighbours, so really, a grove theoretically might be all one plant."

"So one dryad."

"In a grove this size, a very strong dryad, but yes. Although it's also possible there is more than one grove intermixed here. We wouldn't know unless the dryads chose to show themselves and tell us. The willow, on the other hand, is a single dryad for each tree. And given your tree's age, it's also a strong one, because that willow has long outlived its natural nonmagic lifespan."

"So, like, a birch tree that lives to be about eighty would never have a strong dryad? Do they die when the tree dies?"

"I don't know that 'die' is exactly the right word. My understanding is that the healthier the tree, the healthier the dryad, and that if the tree begins to fail, the dryad lends its strength to its tree. They thrive or fail together. But… dryads don't die, per se. If your willow tree were to be cut down or destroyed in a fire, the dryad would… sleep? Its magical energy would be released back into the flux, but the awareness, while no longer corporeal, would still be there. If the tree sprouted again, the dryad would wake, regrow with the life of the new shoot. Or if you planted another tree, the consciousness of the ancient dryad would be there for the new dryad to draw on. It would, I guess, become a part of the new dryad. It's complicated, and I don't understand it all. I'm not a plant. I'm a dragon. I do know that the salamanders feed off the flux the trees produce, and the dryads draw on the refined energy the salamanders create."

"How does that work? We don't have salamanders."

"Perhaps your other wildlife serves the purpose our salamanders do? The squirrels maybe? I don't know."

"Or maybe that's why we don't have dryads here."

"But you do." Emile pointed to the rose bush, then more expansively at the forest. "I've seen them."

Sunny studied the rose bush. It was watching him now, and he didn't need the screen of Glimmerleaf's smoke to see the dryad within. "I promise if there had been a dryad in this bush a week ago? I would have known. If there are dryads here, it's probably because he's here." He pointed to Glimmerleaf. "Maybe there's a connection."

"Maybe. Like I said, I don't understand it all. Dryads are not the most outgoing of magical folk, plus we don't really speak the same language, so we don't know a lot about them. I think they have to be very old and very powerful to communicate through speech."

"Even still." Sunny watched the bush as Glimmerleaf nosed at it, and after a moment the dryad, a slim, prickly, humanoid shape of twigs and thorns, leaves and flowers, rose to a height that came almost to Sunny's shoulder. It was a tiny, brittle-looking thing, with eyes the colour of pink garnet glittering in the late sunshine. It—he?—was beautiful in the way of all magically delicate but menacing-looking things, as he was covered in an impenetrable layer of thorns and spikes and carried an air of aloof permission. Like he was allowing Sunny this up-close glimpse but looking was all that would be permitted.

Unlike with Glimmerleaf, Fernforest didn't seem the least bit fazed by his appearance. Like he'd known about the dryad's existence all along. Sunny was going to have to have a talk with him about keeping secrets.

"Hello." Sunny smiled, and the dryad made a slight curtsying gesture and lifted a hand to wave, petallike, in the breeze. His smile was kind, and then he swayed and vanished back into his bush.

Glimmerleaf watched it all with an air of interest.

"That was... wow. So much I didn't know," Sunny breathed. "We have to protect it." He looked at Emile. "All of it. Including Glimmer."

Emile held out a hand. "Come here?"

Sunny's heart lightened and a smile crept over his face. His gut, in turmoil for the past days, settled as his fingertips brushed Emile's. A shaft of golden sunshine broke through the trees and hit Emile's face, lighting his eyes to a glittering sapphire shine.

It was clear there was more to him, to everything, than the skin and bones Sunny could see—or even the scale and feather he could not, at the moment.

The difference was that Emile could pass as human. Glimmerleaf would pass as no creature humans had ever seen. "What are we going to do with him?"

Even as he asked the question, the salamander stopped moving, lifted his head, body perked like he heard something beyond Sunny's senses.

"Leeesin," Emile snarled.

Now he knew what Emile was, the draconic hiss to his words was obvious, and Sunny straightened. "What?"

But then he did hear what Glimmerleaf and Emile had heard: crackling twigs in the forest.

In an instant Glimmerleaf was gone, disappearing into the underbrush so fast Sunny blinked and could have been persuaded he'd never been there. Fernforest set up a cacophony of barking and dashed after the salamander, voice disappearing into the trees.

"Whatever it is, Glimmer and Ferny don't like it."

"*I* don't like it," Emile said, and to Sunny's alarm, a row of spiked, bony protrusions shimmered in the air along the tops of Emile's shoulders.

"Don't!" Sunny gripped Emile's wrist. "Emile, don't."

Emile straightened, and the shimmering of the air around him stilled. "Very well." He placed a hand on Sunny's shoulder and pulled until Sunny's back was touching his chest. "But I make no more promises if this is a threat."

"That's very sweet," Sunny murmured under his breath. "Shall we go see?"

CHAPTER 25

EMILE WAS much less enthusiastic than Sunny to go trekking into the woods to see what was out there. He already had ideas of what it might be and wasn't sure he wanted to introduce Sunny to the less wondrous side of his world. He couldn't say for sure if Hakko would dare cross the Fold himself, but that didn't mean he wouldn't send minions of one sort or another to track Emile down for him.

"Sunny?"

"Come on. I can hear Glimmer, but I can't see him. I don't want him to get too far ahead of us."

"He'll outrun us both if he wants to."

"Then he doesn't want to, because so far, he hasn't gotten too far ahead."

Emile pursed his lips but caught up with Sunny so he had a clearer view of what was ahead. Occasional glimpses of the salamander's tail spikes flashed between the trees, so Sunny was right. Glimmerleaf was keeping a pace they could match. But he was also approaching the sounds of disturbance ahead without slowing.

"Do you think it's another salamander?"

"I have no idea what it is, but generally salamanders aren't that noisy."

"A dryad, maybe?"

Emile cast Sunny a look. "Do you think a dryad would be that destructive in their own home?"

"Good point." To Emile's relief, Sunny slowed. He took a huge breath through his nose and grimaced. "It's not a bear."

Emile followed his example and sniffed. "You're right."

"It's smelly, but not bear smelly."

As they contemplated the stench, Fernforest barked excitedly and swirled past them, nearly knocking Sunny over as he dashed past between his legs.

"Hey! The hell did he come from?" Sunny threw his arms into the air. "I guess he's not afraid of whatever it is."

"Sometimes, Sunny, your dog doesn't show the prudence of, well." He sighed. "Any other dog, I suppose."

Ahead, Fernforest tried to dodge around a tree and misjudged, bouncing off the wide bole and landing in a scramble of limbs in the leaves.

"Seriously?" Sunny hurried forward, but Fernforest was up by the time he got there. "You're acting a little doofus-y, Ferny. Not gonna lie."

Emile knelt and took the dog gently by the head. "Is it the giant squirrel again?" he asked.

Sunny scoffed. "Giant squirrel?" But the question was barely out of his mouth when a tree branch overhead rustled wildly, dipping to tangle fine twigs in Sunny's curls. He looked up to see what might, to a dog, seem like it could be a giant squirrel.

It had as much area covered in brilliant red feathers as it did fur, along with a scaled, flexible tail and vestigial wings that glittered in the sun and that it held close against its back. It clung to a poplar branch that swayed precariously under its weight as it watched them.

"What the—" Sunny stared into curious brown eyes.

"Of course." Emile moved delicately, putting himself between Sunny and the creature. "A tatzel."

The creature smiled at them, revealing more than one row of spiky teeth.

"Not as cute as a giant squirrel," Sunny said.

"You have squirrels that get that big?"

"Uh, no. We have… well. Pretty much nothing that looks like that, actually."

"But you do have animals that eat only meat."

"Like dragons?" Sunny winked at him, which was both endearing and annoying. He'd never met anyone who defused their unease with the kind of levity Sunny used.

"Maybe animals not as intelligent as a dragon, though?" Emile asked.

"Okay, yes, sure. Lots of animals who hunt other animals to eat."

"Any that fixate on a specific prey until they catch it and tear it to shreds so they can eat it in strips?"

"*Really* not as cute as a giant squirrel."

"Well. The good news is that the salamander is too big for this one. This looks like a juvenile. Fernforest is too small for it to bother with. And it wouldn't take on a dragon in any form."

"Perfect." Sunny made his eyes very wide. "That makes me lunch."

"Which I am obviously not going to allow."

"How do you stop it? Feed it something else?"

"No. That won't work. Now that it's seen you, it won't stop until it catches you or dies trying."

"We have to kill it?" Sunny stared at the creature. "That isn't fair. Why is it even here? What does it normally hunt?"

"Others of its kind. Very newly formed salamanders. Bear cubs and the like."

"Of course. Because deer are too easy."

"Exactly."

Sunny made those wide eyes again. "I was *kidding*."

"There is one possibility I can think of that might save both you and the tatzel."

"I'll take it."

"If I shift—"

"You can scare it away?"

"No. When I shift, it will consider you under my protection. That will only present a greater challenge. It will want to hunt you to see if it can get you away from me."

"That's a lot of thought going into this for a wild animal."

"Magic creatures are not as bound by instinct as a mere wild animal, Sunny. Being magic makes them something more than that."

"Of course it does. So what happens if you shift?"

"We make for the Fold. Once we are close enough, we push it back through."

"Won't it just come back?"

"Very unlikely. As for salamanders, crossing the Fold is not a pleasant experience. It wouldn't have even done so if not forced."

"You're saying something forced it across to this side?"

"More than likely. And once back on its own side of the Fold, it will get as far from the barrier as it can, as fast as it can."

"But it won't want to cross."

"No."

"So you'll have to make it."

"Yes."

"Will it hurt you?"

"I sincerely hope not."

Sunny frowned. "I don't like that plan."

"Sunny." Emile cupped his face, detangling twigs from his hair as the tatzel looked on, tail swinging low enough to brush over Sunny's bare arm. Sunny started and a red welt rose on his skin where the tail had touched.

"That hurt!"

"Its scales exude a kind of venom, most potent just after it—she, in this case—has given birth."

"Not fair." Sunny shuffled away from the tree so the tatzel couldn't reach him.

"It's not as potent on other magical creatures, and many of the nonmagical creatures it hunts have a far thicker skin."

"Maybe it will think I'm too easy to be prey?"

"If you were an animal with no reasoning abilities, that might work. But you're not. And she won't wait very much longer for you to make up your mind to run. You have to trust me. This is the only plan if you don't want me to bring it down."

"If she was forced here against her will, then just killing her isn't fair either. Especially if she has babies somewhere."

"Babies that will die unless we send her home."

"This sucks."

"Are you ready?"

"I suppose I have to be."

"Make as direct a line as you can to the willow. The Fold is just past it. Tatzels live most of their lives in the trees, so if you can, stay on the path and out from under low-hanging branches as much as possible. I won't be able to reach her from the ground, and she's probably faster than me, so I can only protect you if I stay close. Watch out for her tail. That will be her primary weapon because she can use it from a distance. It will hurt, and if you absorb enough of her venom, she will bring you down. Once you stop moving, either you die, or she does. I don't have to tell you how that will end, babies or no."

"You probably think I'm crazy because I feel bad for her."

"No. Quite the opposite, in fact."

Above them, the tatzel made a chittering noise that set Fernforest off barking and jumping at it. The tatzel swung her tail at the dog, but Ferny was too small for her to reach. She chattered at him more noisily and bared her teeth.

"We should go," Emile whispered.

Sunny nodded.

Emile closed his eyes, shook himself, and, a heartbeat later, landed on all six feet. He roared at the tatzel and shook himself again, the rattle of his scales drowning out the tatzel's chatter.

"Now that is going to make the neighbours wonder," Sunny muttered.

Then the tatzel moved, and Sunny sprang away from the tree and down the path, running like his life depended on it, much to Emile's relief.

FOR ONE breath, between blinks Sunny had seen Emile, both as man and as dragon, in many forms at once, with spiky shoulders, with a tail, with claws and a magnificent feather ruff, and then he was all dragon, all scales, and taking up much more space than Emile the man did. In this form, he would never have fit in the tiny hunter's shack.

Sunny only wished he had the time to admire him. He was as impressive as anything Sunny had yet encountered, and the sound of him crashing through the brush on his heels did as much to keep him moving as the threat from the cat-lizard-squirrel-thing in the trees above.

Emile had been right about one thing, though. The tatzel was fast. It outpaced them quickly, then situated itself in the trees Sunny would have to run under in order to get to the willow clearing. There was no going around. Straying off the path under the trees only led him through even more trees that were more tightly packed and harder to navigate.

"Emile?"

"Do not slow." Emile's voice, as a dragon, was filled with gravel and steam.

"But—"

The ground shook under his feet, Emile's breath flowed hot over his shoulder, and he nodded even as he ran.

"Okay. Not slowing."

The lash of the tatzel's tail down his back as he entered the trees nearly knocked him off his feet. The fire that sizzled over the back of one arm and along his nape drew a cry from him. The rustle and snap of leaves and branches above as he ran sounded like the forest was tumbling down around him. Emile's hiss as he stretched his neck out to ward off another blow from the tatzel's tail buzzed in his ear like a giant snake rattle.

As he reached the wider path, the tatzel screamed at him, frustration evident in the sound, but it kept pace in the trees as he ran for the willow. It got one last whip of the tail in as he cleared the trees, wrapping around his arm and pulling him backward off his feet even as the spongy moss gave beneath him.

He tumbled and rolled, saw the flash of claws and scales above him; then the tail was gone, the tatzel was screeching again, and Emile also bellowed, a hot, stone-ground sound filled with pain.

Sunny rolled to his feet just in time to see them both disappear under the leaves of the willow. He dashed after them.

The tree itself shook, lancelike leaves showering down around them. The air sizzled and popped. The tatzel glared at Sunny, lunged, but Emile swung his neck, knocking her out of the tree. She landed, rolled, cringed back towards Emile, and glared.

"Go home," Emile said, voice now a rough, flat sound that shook Sunny to his bones. He nudged her towards the fringe of leaves on the far side of the willow's umbrella where the light had intensified. She hissed at Emile, tail lashing but not touching Emile's dragon form. After a moment he pushed hard, sending her tumbling head over tail out from under the tree to the far side. There was a splash, a brilliant flare of light and a sound like firecracker flares just before they exploded. Then silence. When Sunny parted the hanging branches of the tree to look, the tatzel—and the bright light—were gone.

The brook at the base of the tree jabbered at him, splashing over his feet. The faint scent of ozone drifted in the air, and the small hairs at his nape and along his arms stood on end. Squinting, he searched for any sign of where the tatzel had gone. Nothing.

He turned to Emile. "The Fold?"

Emile grunted and lowered his head in a nod.

"Is she okay?"

"I hope."

Sunny sighed, chest tight from running, from fear, from anger that anyone would use an innocent creature so viciously. He sank to his knees, thinking to dip his hands into the water to splash over his face.

Water gurgled and jumped, landing on his arms. He blinked, and where the water had been running uphill up his arm, he saw the faint, shining silhouette of a creature that fluctuated between human-looking and sparkling light. He couldn't quite get a good look at it.

"You're lucky." Emile's voice in his ear was back to very human-sounding, and Sunny glanced over his shoulder. The dragon was gone. Mostly. Emile's hair was now brilliant yellow at the tips, and there were lines of iridescent pink scales flowing up over his shoulders and the sides of his neck. Yellow feathers protruded from his skin along the backs of his forearms and up the sides of his calves. More scales, darker pink, covered the backs of his hands and the tops of his feet.

Otherwise, his pale skin and delicate freckles were very much in evidence everywhere else. An angry red line marched from his chin along his neck, marring the scales there, to disappear over his shoulder to his back.

"She got you too." Sunny touched the mark that darkened and curled some of his scales.

Emile winced and pulled away.

"Lucky?" Sunny asked, turning back to the water.

"They hardly ever show their true forms to anyone, magical or not."

Sunny watched in fascination as the water sprites danced up his arm. Everywhere their tiny splashing bodies touched the tatzel's tail lashes, the red diminished and the fiery pain cooled. He moved his hand to guide the sprites to Emile's injury, but Emile drew back.

"I'm fine."

"It helps," Sunny assured him. "Let them help."

The sprites shimmered on his arm and hand, waiting.

"Dragons and water sprites don't really get along."

"And maybe big bad dragons need to get over themselves just a wee bit," Sunny suggested. "They aren't going to hurt you. I should think it would take a lot more of them than this to do you any harm."

Emile rolled his eyes. "You'd be very surprised, then." But he held out his hand, wincing again as he moved, but allowed the sprites to traipse up his arm to the injured areas.

After a few moments of watching them splash over Emile's skin, Sunny saw the red and the swelling go down. The sprites launched themselves into the air, glittering in an arch that left multiple tiny rainbows in the air as they sparkled and floated back into the creek and were gone.

"There." Sunny touched the damaged scales again. "That wasn't so bad."

"They were helpful." Emile flexed his fingers, then his arm. "This time."

"They didn't fix your scales."

"No." Emile ran fingers gingerly over the damage. "I'll have to shed those." He got to his feet and held a hand out to Sunny. "Later, though. For now, we should get back. I would prefer to have you inside before dusk."

"Do you think there are more tatzels?"

"I don't know what to think right now, but I'd rather not linger so close to the Fold."

"Dare I ask what happened to your clothes?"

"They'll be back where I shifted."

"They just, what? Fall off?"

"For a short time, during the shift, I am… vision? Light, magic, energy. Not corporeal. The clothes have nothing to adhere to, and yes, they just fall."

Sunny narrowed his eyes. "That time. When you ran off into the forest. By any chance, did you…?"

Emile's cheeks brightened. "I was still adjusting to this world. The magic is different here. I had some difficulty controlling it, and I didn't want you to see me…." He shrugged.

"That's why I found your shorts next to the creek, then. You shifted right out of them."

"I have more control now."

Sunny smoothed a finger over the feathers on the back of Emile's forearms. "But not complete control?"

"Stopping the shift at this point let me keep the damaged scales for now. A complete shift back to skin will force me to shed them. That will… be unpleasant."

"Oh."

"It's part of the healing process. It stings, is all. The skin will be marred, but it will heal once the ruined scales are gone." He smiled. "Don't fret. Shedding the scales speeds the healing process along. I fear you will be in much more pain once the water sprites' magic wears off. If I could help you to shed your damaged skin, believe me, I would."

"I'll live," Sunny muttered, even as he ran tentative fingers over the numbed mark the tatzel had left.

"This time," Emile muttered, and Sunny heard the dark and the hot anger behind the quiet words.

CHAPTER 26

SUNNY DID find that the burns flared up again, but he also found the water sprites amenable to easing the worst of the burning sensations.

Emile refused their help, and his description of his skin as "marred" when he shed the damaged scales was the worst understatement Sunny could think of. It looked like someone had taken a cheese grater to his shoulder.

"That's horrible!"

"It will heal." But he said that with clenched teeth and sweat sheening his face.

"You sit down," Sunny ordered, gently pushing him onto the loveseat. Fernforest jumped up next to Emile and snuggled against his leg, tongue working over his uninjured arm.

Once Sunny had rinsed away the blood and loose skin, he could better see that the damage was due more to the loss of the scales than the tatzel's fiery venom. It reminded Sunny of the skin of a plucked chicken, only with crescent-shaped wounds where the scales had been pulled from their beds. "This looks bad. Will you have a bare spot there now?"

"The scales will grow back."

Emile leaned on his good side and closed his eyes, fingers playing over Ferny's head, and let Sunny wrap up the shoulder in gauze and some kind of cream that smelled too sharp and alien. He wrinkled his nose.

"It will help keep infection out," Sunny said. "You'll heal faster."

Emile just grunted. The shifting and chasing and the effort of removing the ruined scales had taken their toll.

"Come on." Sunny glanced to the dark outside the window. "Let's go up. We can both use a good night's sleep."

"Are you not going to ask why the tatzel was here?" Emile let Sunny drag him to his feet.

"If you're right and it didn't come here on its own, then I suppose we have to assume Hakko sent it. Why? If he knows they won't hunt dragons, why send it here? Just to try and reveal you by sending a dangerous magical creature to our side of the Fold, in hopes some random human sees it? Or gets eaten by it?"

Emile made a neutral sound. He didn't want to think that maybe Hakko knew about Sunny and had sent the tatzel precisely to hunt his lover. But Sunny's theory made more sense, especially if they added Glimmerleaf's presence to the equation.

Salamanders fed on flux. They weren't any greater danger to humans than a moose or a mother bear if she perceived danger to her cubs. A salamander wouldn't hurt anyone unless provoked.

If Hakko hoped to persuade Emile to return across the Fold by threatening to reveal all of the magical realm to the humans, he was far more dangerous than Emile had ever thought. He didn't think Sunny's reaction to discovering magic and magical creatures was at all typical. Stories that told of dragons interacting with humans never ended well for anyone.

If that was the ploy Hakko was using, it might work. There were creatures more dangerous than tatzels he could send across. There were also creatures much more vulnerable to human interference than salamanders or dryads. The realms were separate for a reason, and what Hakko was doing threatened both sides.

"I don't know that he did send it," Emile said as he settled into the bed.

"You don't know that he didn't either."

"No." He rolled to face Sunny as he snuggled under the covers, twining his legs with Emile's. "And if he did, I don't understand what he hoped to accomplish. All he did was risk revealing the Fold and everything on the other side."

"You said he could get into your head."

"Not nearly as well when I'm here." He touched Sunny's face. "And he's even further from me when you are close."

"So then he knows about me."

Emile thought about that. Hakko's presence in his head had lessened a great deal when he'd crossed the Fold. It was even fainter now, and especially so when Sunny was close by. There was every reason to think that Hakko understood why the connection had dimmed so much. "I suppose, yes, he likely does," Emile conceded.

"So then the tatzel was aimed at me, most likely."

"But why Glimmerleaf?"

"Maybe he thought that would be enough to scare you back home rather than risk revealing everything magical." Sunny smiled and kissed him. "It didn't work, so he upped the stakes. You think he'll try again?"

"I'm sure he will. But Glimmerleaf and the tatzel aren't the only creatures I've seen that shouldn't be here. I've seen pixies and pixie-dragons. They are both harmless, but they shouldn't be here."

"Would either of them have crossed the Fold on their own?"

"Perhaps out of curiosity, but it wasn't easy for me to cross. I don't know why they would bother trying now if they never had before."

"It's not like we don't have stories about weird creatures," Sunny said.

"True. But it's been a long time since the Fold was doubled to keep the realms separate. It shouldn't let small creatures like that through anymore."

"Unless something is weakening it."

"There would have to be a steady flow of magic passing through it for that to happen."

"Like a mind-to-mind connection between two dragons hatched in the same nest." Sunny didn't ask, but rather made the statement, and Emile gasped.

Because of course he was right. Hakko's determination to remain connected was exactly the kind of low-level magical stream that could point a finger right at the weak spot in the Fold. It was an invitation for a curious pixie or pixie-dragon to fly through simply because they could. Both species were easily intelligent enough to figure out how to do it safely, unlike tatzels or salamanders, who would just ram through even the most uncomfortable of barriers if given the right incentive.

"Then you just have to sever that connection."

Emile studied Sunny's freckled, open face. "It's not that simple. It isn't something we decide to have or not have. It just is. I don't know what it would do to either one of us if it was cut off."

"So you have the same thing with Ananth? And all your other— what do you call each other?"

"Broodmates. But no, not nearly as strong, because, as is proper, all the other eggs came from different stock. The strength of the magic between me and Hakko comes, in part, from our similarities. We have each other's power as well as our own. I had hoped to weaken his by coming here, but I don't know that it worked."

"Then if you sever the connection, you weaken your magic?"

"I can't see how that would not be the case."

"How much?"

"I have no idea. I may lose my shift. I may not be able to cross the Fold."

"You'd be stuck here forever."

"If I were to sever this connection, Sunny, I would have to go back. I would have to confront him, and I would have to do it in dragon form. He would never meet me skin to skin. Not when he can be dragon and have the upper hand. So we would have to meet scale to scale."

Sunny swallowed hard, his face going pale under the yellow light of the lamp bulb. "You'd have to fight him."

"Confront him, at least."

"In dragon form, over there. And even if you win, you might end up stuck in scales on that side of the Fold forever."

Emile cupped his cheek, soothed by the texture of the wiry short hairs on Sunny's jaw and that reminder that Sunny was so very real and vibrant and different. "Coming here was a risk. I always knew it might not work, but when all I had to lose was my own freedom and happiness, it was worth trying. If he followed me here, even just up here"—he touched the side of his head—"I always had the option of going back and doing it the hard way. It wouldn't have been the end of the world for me to be trapped in my scales if it meant I could be free of him. I'd rather have the shift. That's why I tried this first. But I could have lived without it."

"Could have." Sunny stared at him, eyes bright.

"I didn't know you then."

Sunny lunged at him, rolling Emile onto his back as he kissed him with a relentless need that almost distracted Emile from the problem.

"Sunny." He stroked the sides of Sunny's face, tried to kiss him back to calm. "Sunny, please."

"We don't have to talk about this any more right now," Sunny insisted, fumbling with the string on Emile's pants. He got the string loose, pushed the pants down, and flung back the covers so he had access to Emile's rapidly responding cock.

Emile threw his head back as Sunny began his descent, kissing and nipping along his throat, chest, and stomach on his way to his goal. He touched every part of Emile he could reach, hands moving with feverish speed, fumbling, shaking slightly, in his haste to push Emile into the abyss with him.

It didn't take a lot of persuading. Emile stroked fingers into Sunny's hair, letting the wild curls wrap around his fingers, spreading his legs so Sunny could nestle between them and take Emile's cock into his mouth. Sunny's warm, wet finger at his entrance was a new sensation between them, but Emile welcomed the invasion, then welcomed Sunny, the magic between them swelling bigger than ever as his body opened to let Sunny inside.

This time, he had no doubt that Sunny noticed the splashing of light and the wild whip of power between them as they joined. The room flashed with the sparks as the magic ignited and spit energy into the air around them. It twined deep into Emile's being, interlocking with his own, creating something new, stronger, fixing his dragon to the flow of magic that was Sunny, the land, everything in this place.

He could feel the oil-slick that was Hakko's connection to him, the way Sunny's bright magic slid away from that unhealthy energy only to meld more firmly with Emile's. Sunny's eyes shone brilliant and golden as he stared into Emile. His lips parted, Emile's dragon name whispering out of the magic and off his tongue as he came.

"Emikku." Sunny savoured the sound, repeating it like a mantra, winding his magic up in the name, in the form that came with it, in the deepest part of Emile that only magic and true connection could reach. He made *Emikku* into a spell that could never be undone, and that bound them together as surely as Emile—in any form—was bound to Hakko.

The magic that splashed up between them as Sunny came pushed Emile over the edge too. He cried out, gripping Sunny to him as his orgasm racked his body. Magic tightened around them, made them glow for a moment, then snaked like roots from where they lay down through the house, the ground beneath, out into the world, the forest, the trees and the creeks and the very air.

His dragon licked at the energy, tasting the new power, smelling the tang of flux and considering the magic as it flowed from Sunny into Emile and out to the world, then back again. There was a deep shudder that made Emile's bones creak and the house around them tremble. A sharp sizzle ran down his body, intense where his shoulder was damaged, and he felt his scales ripple just under his skin.

"Green?" Sunny whispered, stroking fingers over his chest and throat. "I thought you were pink."

Emile shivered and held Sunny close. "Pink would stand out here."

"So you just changed them?"

"Eh." Emile drew in a deep breath and let it out slowly. "More like the magic chose this." He raised a hand over Sunny's shoulder to where he could see the shimmer of green and gold under his skin. It was odd, in a beautiful way, to see his own scales in this new light. Even as he thought that, the scales shimmered, colour rippling through them until they were the familiar pink.

"Wow." Sunny kissed the side of his jaw. "That's so cool."

"I've never known a dragon who could be two colours."

"Have you ever met a dragon who crossed the Fold before?"

"No."

"Well then." Sunny rolled and snuggled into Emile's side with a yawn. "Go you for being awesome." He yawned again, and even as Emile thought about what the twining of their magic could mean, he felt Sunny's weight sink into him. Heard his breathing even out and, in his heart, felt the quiet contentment of his sleep.

This was definitely going to complicate things.

EMILE WOKE with a start. Sunny slept on in the still-dark room. Outside, the very edge of the sun tipped the horizon, bringing on that peculiar time of day when darkness peeled back but light hadn't yet arrived. The witching hour tingled in Emile's bones.

Careful not to wake his lover, Emile slid out of bed. The soft susurration of scales against hardwood, as his tail slithered across the floor, offered the only sound in the room. There was no indication of what had awakened him, only an unsettled expectation nagging at the back of his mind and his magic poking at his dragon.

He had a sense that something approached their haven, but no idea what it could be. He hadn't had any indication before now. Not when Glimmerleaf had appeared, and not when the tatzel rattled the bushes and drew them into the forest.

Something stronger tugged at his awareness, but he couldn't figure out what, or where it was coming from.

He made his way to the main floor, found no sign of Fernforest, then snuck out the door, not bothering with his clothes. If there was danger, he was better off in his dragon form anyway. Once on the front lawn, he felt the tug more strongly, pulling from many different directions: towards the stream and the willow, and off down the drive as well.

Maybe it was just the oddness in the air at dawn poking at the magical beings they knew lived in the area. Dryads waking. Water sprites teasing at his awareness. Glimmerleaf poking in the underbrush.

When the distinct sound of a salamander braying in fear and distress echoed through the trees, though, he began to run. If Glimmerleaf was in trouble, it was up to Emile to soothe him before he made others aware of his existence. He'd just crossed the bridge and entered the cool shadow of the overhanging trees when an unfamiliar vehicle pulled into Sunny's drive.

Emile stopped, torn between going back and finding Glimmerleaf. But then the salamander called again and there was no choice. Whoever this newcomer was, they could not know about the magical creature hidden in Sunny's woods. Emile had to find and quiet him before he made his presence known.

Emile dropped to all six legs and scrambled along the path deeper into the forest. He kept his form light and agile, soft scales giving him manoeuvrability and silence his harder, heavier body would not. Sunny's yard and the first rays of sunshine glowing down over the treetops were soon left behind.

By the time Emile found Glimmerleaf and the edge of the stream near the Fold, he was too far invested in his course to turn back, and too much occupied with the plight of the salamander lying in the mud near the edge of the stream, to notice his mistake.

Out of the shadows from under the weeping willow, a huge, almost night-black dragon emerged, a toothy grin on its face.

"Well. Hello, little jester. So nice to see you come when I call."

"Hakko!" Emile skidded to a stop, glaring up at his Sire.

"Of course, Emikku." Hakko reached a front arm forward, drawing one sharp claw along the ridge of Emile's lower jaw. "Who did you expect?"

A breeze blew up, heavy and hot, scented with a cloying fog of maleness and desire that went straight to Emile's head. He blinked, swayed, and leaned his jaw against Hakko's clawed hand. "You, of course, Sire," he whispered.

CHAPTER 27

"SUNNY!" THE sound of a car door slamming made Sunny jump and sit up straight in an empty bed. The sheets were cool and the house quiet.

"Sunny! You home?" Daisy called from the driveway, then closer as she approached the house and opened the front door. "Hello?"

"Yeah." Sunny blinked in the morning light. "Be right down." He didn't really wonder why she was there. He'd put off going into the city to see her for so long, he wasn't at all surprised she'd brought the meeting out to him.

Quickly, he found a pair of pants—happily, they were the ones he'd stripped off Emile last night, and they still held his forest-y scent. Below, the jingle of keys and the thunk of a bag hitting the floor told him Daisy was making herself at home.

"Holy crap. Sunny, what did you do to your coffee maker?"

He stumbled down the stairs to find her holding the coffee carafe in one hand and what looked like the water tank off the back of the machine in the other.

"Oh. Um." He huffed out a breath. He probably should have shown Emile how to make coffee a long time ago, but he'd not gotten around to it, and then Emile had tried to make some coffee for him a few mornings ago, and. Well. Now he needed to buy a new one. "That. I need a new one." He took the parts from her and dropped them into the sink. "Sorry. Did you need coffee? I might have instant. Or I have tea. Probably."

"No." She waved a hand at the bits of coffee maker, then waved him closer. "I need a hug from my big brother. Come here."

"Bossy much?" But he did shuffle forwards and accepted the embrace, holding her tight the instant her familiar smell wafted over him. "Hey."

"Hey to you too."

For a few minutes they stood like that, and Sunny found himself sniffling, wondering why he'd waited so long to see her.

"Don't worry about it," she whispered.

"I missed you."

"Never mind." She pulled away. "Show me around. Then I want to hear all about this new guy."

"What new guy?" Although he did look around and noticed how very unlike him the house appeared, with the books and blankets nested on the couch and pairs of dirty dishes—two mugs, two bowls, two water glasses—on the counter left from yesterday. Daisy knew him well enough to know he was too much of a neatnik to not clean up after himself.

"Whatever, Sunshine." She grinned at him and held him at arm's length. "You look like you've been spending a fair amount of time outside, and working hard, even." She squeezed a bicep. "Gardening?"

"Some, yeah. Just small stuff for now." He glanced out the kitchen window at the front yard, but there was still no sign of Emile or his dog. Had he heard Daisy's car and left the house so as not to be noticed?

"Well. Come show me, then." She took his hand and pulled him out of the house. "This is all this year?" She fingered a basil leaf, then smelled her fingertips. "Nice."

Sunny grinned and nodded. "Yup. Put up the boxes in the first few weeks I was here and planted soon as I could. It worked out. The plants are doing a lot better than I expected."

"No shit. Sunny, this is, like, impossible." She ran her fingers over the leaves of a tomato plant he'd started indoors and moved to the beds as soon as he'd had them ready. "They shouldn't be this far along considering the amount of time you've had to grow them. You started so late."

"What can I say? This place is magical."

"It must be." She smiled as she turned to him and took his hands. "And so are you. Like Mom." She bussed his cheek. "She'd be so proud of all this."

"Not worried that I basically ran away?"

Daisy shrugged. "She'd understand that if anyone would, I think."

"Do you?" Sunny asked, suddenly, irrationally worried his sister wouldn't be able to forgive him for leaving her with the company and all the work.

"I know you deal in your own way, yeah. So don't worry. We're good."

Fernforest startled them out of the serious talk, dashing from around the side of the house to greet them with frantic yips. He danced around their feet, licking fingers, feet in constant motion.

Daisy laughed. "What is the matter with your dog?"

"I don't know." Sunny glanced around the clearing with a frown. "Where is he?" He looked to the dog, who jumped up to put both paws on his chest.

"Show me," he demanded, refusing to let worry gnaw at his shattered calm.

Fernforest rocketed down the yard the instant his front feet hit the dirt.

"Ferny!" Sunny called after him, took a few jogging steps, then remembered Daisy. He turned. "Wait here, Daisychain."

"Like hell." She minced down the yard in her wedge-heeled slides. "Besides, you know what he's like. He'll run all the way to wherever he's trying to take us and all the way back a thousand times while we try to keep up. Let him wear himself out, I say."

Normally Sunny would agree with her, but the reminder of their parents, of the wreck his life had become in one instant, and not knowing where Emile had gone or why he'd gone had put him on edge. The rain-fresh, idyllic golden morning was too—idyllic. It felt off.

"You can show me the rest of the property," Daisy said. "I'm sure your guy is just out enjoying a morning walk. We'll find him."

"Sure." Sunny led the way down the path to the end of the drive, where the rose bush rustled.

"Sunshine, there is something in your rosebush," Daisy muttered, picking her way amidst the lumps and divots in the turf. "It has a lot of flowers for this time of ye—oh shit!" She tripped back as the bush shuddered violently and the dryad rose. She backed right out of one of her heels as she scrabbled and took position behind Sunny.

"Sunny!" Her shriek near deafened him. "Sunny, what—Sunny!" She dug her fingers into his shoulders.

"Daisy, stop!" Clapping one hand over his ear, Sunny held out the other to the shivering dryad. "Shh. Wait. Please. She wasn't expecting you." He patted Daisy's hand in hopes of saving his skin before her nails pierced it. "She's… excitable."

Daisy slapped his arm. "I am not!" Her other grip didn't abate, but she leaned against him to peer over his shoulder. "What is it?"

"A dryad. They belong to trees. Or—"

"I know what a dryad is, silly." She slapped him again, and her pinching grip eased. "You… have a dryad?"

"No. It's—he's—not mine. He lives in my bush. *Is* my bush? I'm not really sure how it works."

"I think he's wanting to tell you something." She pointed over his shoulder at the dryad.

When Sunny followed her finger, the dryad was staring intently at him, pink eyes aglitter in the slant of morning sunlight. "I'm looking for Emile," Sunny told him. "Do you know where he went?"

Giving a leafy shudder, the dryad looked from Sunny to the bridge at the head of the path, then slowly back again.

"He went into the woods?"

That got him a tilt of the dryad's head.

"There." Sunny pointed, indicating the bridge. "He went over the bridge? Into the forest?"

The slow nod was excruciating.

"When?"

Another head tilt as the dryad considered the question, and Sunny realised a nonspeaking creature, intelligent or not, might not be able to answer him.

Finally the dryad raised an arm with all the hurry of molasses running in January and pointed directly at the sun. Equally as slowly, he lowered his arm until his finger indicated a spot just above the eastern horizon.

Sunny followed his progress, then squinted. "I don't get it."

"What time was sunrise?" Daisy asked.

"What?" The non sequitur made Sunny turn and blink at her.

She was thumbing through her phone and made an "a-ha!" sound when she found what she was looking for. "5:58 a.m." She glanced behind her at the horizon, then up at the sun. "It's, what?" Another glance at her phone. "6:16. So…." She considered. "I'd say your man wandered into the woods a few minutes ago, judging by where your dryad said the sun was when he left."

"That's what he said?" Sunny returned his attention to the dryad, the sky, back to the dryad. "Really?"

That earned him a laugh from Daisy and another light slap. "Think about it."

"You're taking this all very… calmly."

"It's—he's—right there, sweetie. I had my moment, but what else is there to do? Pretend I'm imagining this? Obviously not. That's not practical."

And Daisy, bless her, was nothing if not practical.

"Okay. So. You go on inside." He picked up her shoe to hand it to her. "I'll go find Emile. Maybe you can make some coffee or—"

She snorted as she lifted a foot and removed her other shoe, grabbed the one Sunny held out to her, then tossed them in the open window of her car. "Not likely. I'm coming with you."

"Daisy."

"Shush."

"You should stay here."

"And miss what? More dryads? What else? Water sprites? Elves? Dragons? No way!"

She was animated and glowing, and what the hell? Wasn't his plan to introduce her to a dragon anyway? "Fine. I will take you to the end of the property, at least, and maybe we'll run into him."

"What is he doing? Why is he out in the forest? Does he just wander it at random?"

"He's probably looking for Glimmerleaf."

"Who? Did you get another dog?" The tease in her voice was unmistakable. "A stray? You're such a softie."

"Um. Not exactly." He had to smile at the memory of Glimmerleaf curled around his legs. "Come on." Taking her hand, he led her towards the bridge and the edge of the trees. He noted as he passed that the nightshade had reached the end of the bridge. Soon it would be crawling across his lawn. He ran a finger over one spade-shaped leaf. The plant already sported a wealth of purple-and-yellow flowers that would soon give way to the green globes of tiny berries.

"So pretty for something that'll tie your guts into knots, isn't it?" Daisy asked.

"At least it's not the kind that will kill you," he replied. "Come on."

The forest shivered as they passed under the trees' branches. Despite the sunshine breaking through the clouds, under the rustling leaves, it was cool and darker than expected.

"Weird," Daisy muttered. "What's the deal?"

"No idea. Can we just keep our ears and eyes open?"

"Will we see more dryads?"

Sunny scowled into the gloom. "No idea about that, either. The rose bush is the only one I've ever seen." He didn't mention how much more sense some of his recent experiences made now he knew there might be live, sentient beings in the forest to make noises, shake the trees, and who knew what else.

"It's really pretty here." Daisy trailed a hand over the bark of a tall red pine. Above them, the branches trembled, raining a gentle shower of long, rusty needles into their hair. "I think your tree likes me," she whispered.

Sunny glanced up into the branches. It looked like any other pine tree. Except he got the feeling it was looking back at him. He also got the impression no tatzel would dare lurk in the branches of that particular tree, which eased his growing nerves.

"Do you know where Emile is?" he asked and then felt like an idiot. Because he was asking a tree a question, but worse, expecting an answer. "Shit."

"Shh." Daisy touched his arm. "Listen."

In the sudden stillness that followed her order, they could hear the splashing laugh of water tumbling over rocks.

"The stream is loud," he mused.

Even as Sunny glanced towards the water, the aspen trees drew back, affording him a view in the direction of the clearing and the willow tree, as well as Fernforest, standing there watching them, as if waiting for his dense, slow humans to get with the program and catch up. Sunny couldn't see the actual tree or its mossy yard, but there was no mistaking the hint. That was the direction they needed to go.

"I'm gonna go with more dryads," Daisy whispered.

"You should go back to the house."

Her only reply was a soft snort.

After a heartbeat, Sunny followed Fernforest's disappearing behind along the familiar path. Daisy stayed close at his back. He wanted to worry about her being there but was too busy taking comfort in her presence.

The silence under the forest roof buzzed in Sunny's ears, conspicuous because he could feel a light breeze lifting the hairs on his arms. The aspen leaves should be rustling, but the trees held themselves motionless. Sunshine flashing along the upper reaches of the trees didn't penetrate, despite the breaks in the cover. A pall hung over the forest, dampening the sounds of their footfalls and making it difficult to see very far ahead.

"This isn't normal," Daisy observed.

Sunny returned her earlier snort. "You think?"

"What's causing it?"

Sunny remembered Glimmerleaf's cloud of ash and smoke with a shudder. Surely a single salamander, even one as sick as theirs, couldn't cause this thick a blanket of gloom. "I'm not sure," he said at last, not liking any of the scenarios in which this was caused by a single salamander, or worse, an army of them. But then, if it wasn't that, what could it be? It wasn't a natural phenomenon, which left magic, and anything that could affect this wide an environment had to be powerful.

If Sunny were to believe Emile that he had any magic at all, it certainly wasn't enough to combat this. "Stay close." He took Daisy's hand again. "I don't like this."

"Sunny?" She spread her free hand over his back as he walked ahead of her. "Your Emile. He's not…."

"Not?"

"Is he a dryad? Is that why he hasn't come to the city? Does he have to stay near his tree?"

"He's not a dryad. And I don't know if they have to stay close to their trees. He hasn't come to the city because I don't go to the city. Maybe. I guess." He huffed. "He wouldn't fit in there."

"Then what is he?"

Nothing got past his sister. Sunny bit his lip. "Just—" He squeezed her fingers. "Meet him, okay? I want you to meet him before anything else."

But first they had to find him.

CHAPTER 28

WHEN THEY reached the spot where the path branched, one leg heading in the direction of the willow and its clearing, the other towards the old shack where Sunny had first found Emile, Sunny hesitated. Fernforest had vanished a few minutes ago, and Sunny didn't know which way the dog had gone.

"Let's check the shack first," he decided and took a few steps down the narrow path. Trees crowded close, brushing their shoulders, dropping yellowed leaves into their hair. A root lifted, snagged Sunny's toes, and he cursed. He swatted at a branch, irritated by the scratching and grabbing. He didn't remember the path being so overgrown, but then, he hadn't been this way in a while. He'd have to remember to trim it back later.

The branch shifted out of his way, but only for the barest instant before it swung back and smacked him in the face.

"Really?"

Another branch hit him in the chest, and as he watched, a thick root lifted, dripping soil as it bent upwards to almost knee height, then stopped, right across the path.

"Honey, I think they don't want us to go this way."

"But why?" Sunny glared at the offending tree. "Is it because that's where Emile is? He's mine." He slapped his palm hard against the bole of the tree. "You can't have him."

"Sunny."

"Get out of my way!" He hit the tree again, and it shuddered, but the root remained, and a few more branches shifted to push against his torso.

"Sunny!" Daisy grabbed his arm and yanked.

"What?" He whirled on her but stopped when she pointed.

Behind them on the path stood a dryad, branchy arms crossed, a feral look on its face. This one had sparkling eyes of palest green, diamond-bright and glaring. A thin mouth with rough bark lips pressed in a frown that marred an otherwise human-looking face. Its skin was the pale silver-green of aspen bark and glowed in the gloom.

"Sorry," Sunny muttered. "This your tree?"

The dryad's lips twitched.

Sunny petted the thick tree trunk. "Sorry," he repeated.

The dryad gave a sharp rustle of its leafy mane, then stilled.

"I need to find my friend. Emile." They stared at one another. "Do you know him?"

Nothing.

"Please. I need your help." What good was a magical creature if all it did was stand there and stare?

"Honey, let me." Daisy moved him gently aside and held out her hand. "Hi. I'm his"—she pointed a thumb over her shoulder—"sister. He's upset right now. Normally he's very kind."

"Daisy, we don't have time—"

She laid a hand over his mouth. "He's impatient," she said to the dryad, "which I know you probably don't understand." She grinned. "Hasty, you might say. But in this case, it may be warranted. We want to find his friend and make sure he's okay. Can you help us?"

The dryad reached out with one long leaf-tipped branch finger and stroked the side of Daisy's face. It tilted its head, curling its lips to form a slightly terrifying rugged smile before offering one slow nod. The branch finger curled around the back of Daisy's neck and pulled.

"Oh!" Daisy stumbled forward. "Okay. Careful." She gripped the dryad's enormous hand. "You're very strong."

The dryad picked her up by both shoulders, wrapped another branch around her waist, turned, and began a slow shuffle back down the path to the fork.

"Um." Daisy squealed and wriggled. "I can actually walk if—okay." She squeaked again as a branch cupped her butt, giving her a place to sit, and the branch around her waist shifted. "Not so tight. You can carry me."

The dryad's shuffling strides weren't very fast, but they covered a lot of ground, and Sunny had to hurry to keep up.

"Daisychain?" He pushed past more branches until he'd made it out onto the wider, clearer path. "Daisy, are you okay?"

She grinned down at him. "Fine, brother. I told you your trees like me."

"A little too much, maybe."

The dryad shifted Daisy to its other side, farther from Sunny.

"It's okay," Daisy told it, patting its face. "I like you too." She settled back in her makeshift seat and winked at Sunny. "Let's just see where this leads, okay?"

What could he do but nod? He couldn't leave her now. Not until the dryad released her. He only hoped the creature was also bringing them to Emile.

The rest of the trees parted in the same way the trees had blocked their path earlier, making the walk to the willow smooth and quick. As they approached the clearing, a deep gold glow—much too deep to be the morning sunshine—speared through the trees to strike the path. The dryad slowed and so did Sunny.

"What's out there?"

The dryad curled a branch around Daisy's middle and watched the path, expression troubled.

"Did Emile go this way?"

Gently, the dryad set Daisy down, then lifted a long finger to point off to one side, along the bank of the river. Sunny followed the motion to see a dark hump lying half in the pool of water where he'd bathed Emile the day they had….

"Shit. Glimmerleaf." After rushing past Daisy and her escort, Sunny skidded through the slick mud to collapse at the salamander's side. "Glimmerleaf?" He touched the animal's scaled side, relief flooding him when it rose and fell under his palm. "What happened to him?"

The salamander sluggishly lifted his head enough to peer over his shoulder at Sunny. His eyes glittered with fury, but Sunny didn't feel it directed at him. "Who did this?"

The dryad knelt next to Sunny and caressed the salamander's neck, its touch tender, its face sad. Tree roots slithered out of the soil to lie across Glimmerleaf's body. A soft radiance pulsed through the threadlike roots, bathing them in the greenish glow.

"What's happening?" Daisy's voice was soft. Her hand shook slightly as she ran it over Glimmerleaf's scales. "Is this a dragon?"

"No. A salamander. Glimmerleaf. Maybe Emile came looking for him."

"What's wrong with him?"

"I don't know exactly, but I think it amounts to someone poisoned him. He wasn't this bad the last time I saw him." He clenched a fist. "I wish I could *talk* to someone!"

"You have to be patient," Daisy admonished. Her hand was steadier now, gliding smoothly over Glimmerleaf's scales. "Poison needs an antidote." She looked at the dryad. "Is that what you're doing? Curing him?"

The dryad looked sad and turned its head to look at the water. It sparkled even though very little light reached its surface through the trees. The creek boiled over its banks, tumbling along the bed with abandon. If he squinted, he could see the sprites splashing water over the prone salamander.

The tree roots draped over Glimmerleaf thrummed, the light pulsing, a soft hum emanating from them. They were thin and threadlike, crisscrossing his hide in a network of soft light.

"What is this?" Sunny touched a root with a fingertip. A zap of energy sparked and tingled up his arm to his elbow, like a particularly strong zing of static electricity. "Daisy, I don't know if they're hurting him or helping him." The flakiness to Glimmerleaf's scales that he had noticed before was more pronounced now.

"Would he have brought us here if he was trying to hurt your pet?" she asked.

"I doubt it."

"Then wait here. Watch." She rose from where she had been crouching and moved

After a long moment, the dryad pointed across the water. It rustled its leafy hair, covered Glimmerleaf's neck with a gentle palm, and continued to look sad.

Sunny peered over the running creek, which had risen even as they lingered on its bank. He was pretty sure that now, in its deepest part in the middle, it reached at least to his chest. If it kept rising at this rate, it would be over his head in less than an hour.

From the other side, a number of glittering points peered back at him—eyes like sunshine on a forest stream: dark depths with brilliant sparkle in tan, smooth faces, much like the colour of sanded cedar. Beards and hair of flat, scalelike cedar leaves covered heads and faces fixed in serious, worried expressions.

"He has to get across the water," Sunny guessed. "Whatever type of flux he was fed is what's hurting him, and you can't help him." He looked up at the dryad. "Can you keep him alive?"

The dryad frowned more deeply, and one shoulder came up in a slow gesture of uncertainty.

"But they can. Do the cedar trees give off the flux he needs?"

For once the dryad's face brightened, but only for a heartbeat. Glimmerleaf was clearly too weak to cross the wildly flowing creek, and Sunny guessed the cedar dryads could not cross the water away from their trees. Nor could the poplar dryad leave his side of the creek.

Surely if Emile was here, he would know what to do. He was a dragon. Maybe his magic could have helped Glimmerleaf. Alone, Sunny was at a loss. And if Emile had sensed Glimmerleaf's trouble, where was he now? Why wasn't he here, helping?

"So." Daisy petted Sunny's hair as she spoke. "How do we get him over there? We need something as strong as a dryad to lift him, but not bound to one side of the creek or the other."

"Like a dragon," Sunny muttered.

Daisy giggled, and the sound was only slightly hysterical. "Do we have one of those?"

"The only one I know of is afraid of the water." He glanced around the woods with growing worry. *And nowhere to be found.*

"Okay, I have to admit, I'm freaking out a little bit that you're serious right now." Daisy plopped into the mud next to him, where she could lift Glimmerleaf's head and put it in her lap.

Sunny stood so he could pace. "Emile hates the water because his scales are thick and heavy. He'd have to soften them so he didn't sink if he wanted to cross the water."

"Emile. Is that…?" She pursed her lips and stared at him. "Is Emile your guy or the dragon?"

Sunny gulped but turned to meet her gaze. He didn't have to actually answer her. A sharp, short laugh escaped before she covered her mouth with one hand. "Sorry," she whispered from behind her fingers. "Don't answer that."

"He's both," Sunny said dryly. "And I wish I knew where he was and why he's not here. If we found Glimmerleaf this easily, he had to know the poor guy is in trouble. So." He sniffed and pushed his fingers into his hair.

"They can do that? Change their scales? How much they weigh?"

"I think so. But he wouldn't use his soft scales. He doesn't feel safe that way." And yet… *he would.* If Glimmerleaf needed that kind of help, Emile would do it. Sunny knew he would.

"Why not?"

"It makes him vulnerable to the one thing he ran from in the first place." Sunny had the impression Emile could protect himself as a male dragon. As an Egg-bearer, maybe not so much. "They never sent Glimmer here to hurt us. He was bait."

Sunny spun in place to face the path leading towards the willow. "All Hakko needed him to do was make himself vulnerable." Which didn't explain why Hakko hadn't come after him in his most vulnerable form of all—his human one. But that didn't matter. It only mattered that if he was right and Emile did change his dragon form, and Hakko had come for him, Sunny had to go get him back.

"Stay with Glimmer, Daisy."

"No, Sunny." She started to shift Glimmerleaf's head from her lap, but both Sunny and the dryad put a hand on her shoulder.

"Please, Daisy. I need you to stay with him. If we can't save him, I don't want him to be alone."

"Where are you going?"

Sunny grinned at her, aware the expression was a little on the feral side. "To get my dragon back."

He turned without another word and dashed down the path towards the willow clearing. This time not a single twig or leaf barred his way.

CHAPTER 29

THE WILLOW tree stood, as majestic as always, at the far end of the clearing. Scrambling noisily past its feet, the stream ran over its toes without a care, swamping the bed of moss Sunny and Emile had lain on. Sunshine flooded the area, its light cool next to the blazing gold that streamed between the weeping leaves of the tree.

Magic thrummed, hitting Sunny in the chest and slowing his headlong rush towards the source of the glow. He had made the middle of the clearing before he finally saw the willow's dryad.

The creature was tall, soaring nearly twice Sunny's height. Long furls of moss tangled in its leafy flow of hair. Crags as deep as the tree's bark lined her face. Her eyes glowed yellow as a flame, ever-changing in the shimmering light under the tree.

You seek passage, human.

The statement ground into Sunny's being, and he slowed even more.

"What?" Was the dryad talking to him? Her lips didn't move, but she stared at him as though weighing his reply.

You seek passage to the other side of the Fold. She tilted her head, a rustle of leaves accompanying the movement. She indicated the fall of branches veiling the far side of the clearing and the other side of the creek.

"If that's where Emile is, then yes." He picked up his pace again, crossing the rest of the distance to the imposing dryad in a few heartbeats. "If that's where Hakko has taken him, then that's where I'm going to get him back."

He does not belong to you.

"He doesn't belong to Hakko either."

You think he belongs here? With you? Away from his kin? His kind?

"He came here on his own. Hakko has no right to force him back."

What makes you think he did?

Sunny scowled. "I won't believe Emile went back on his own until he tells me so himself. If the only way for that to happen is for me to cross to his side of the Fold and ask him, then that's what I'll do."

Relentless.

"You're a tree. I suppose you would know something about relentlessness."

She inclined her head, a small smile turning her lips.

He frowned as he reached the dryad. "Why can you talk to me, but the others can't?"

They are young.

"So they'll learn someday?"

Do the young ever learn? The dryad shuffled sideways and lifted the veil of branches to reveal the source of the golden light flooding the secluded area.

Sunny blinked into the brightness. The gold was shot through with every colour, the magic sparking lightning in his soul and heat in his veins. He could *feel* Emile on the other side.

"Wish me luck."

The dryad remained stoic.

Heat and chill passed over Sunny's skin as he pushed through the thickened air beyond the tree. He breathed in fire and exhaled ice. Tiny sparkling jewels of his frosted breath fell and shattered at his feet, only to melt into a river of molten light that flowed over his toes, sending tendrils of fire up his legs. Burning cold gripped his heart, constricted his lungs, froze the moisture on his eyelashes as flaming breezes fluttered and frizzled the tiny flyaway hairs that escaped his curls.

Then he was through and standing just under the eaves of enormous cedar trees. The boles of the trees, as thick around as that old dilapidated shed, marched back into the ancient gloom of a forest that had stood for centuries. Branches moved in the windless interior. Deep green eyes stared at him from the depths of mossy faces that vanished just out of sight as soon as he turned to look at them head-on.

At his back the glow remained, veiled once more by the branches of the willow. The creek flowed behind him, laughing and sparkling in the light of the magic, and his feet sank into moss that petered out as he stepped under the trees.

A thick pall of unfriendliness pushed against his will to enter the forest.

"Emile?" The sound was swallowed in the damp and dark, muffled by the weight of the years that hung from the branches and dripped from the flat leaves of the trees. He cleared his throat and tried again.

"Emile!"

Branches creaked. Magic thrummed through the air and clogged his lungs. He swallowed.

"I'm not here to hurt anyone," he whispered. "I only want Emile back." He peered into the shadows. Nothing met his gaze directly, and yet the shimmer of movement teased his peripheral vision. The glitter of eyes flashed but disappeared when he tried to find the source.

Roots groaned. The ground shifted under his feet.

The will of the forest urged him not to enter, to take a step back out from under the canopy and into the light of the mossy verge behind him. He breathed in the resistance, and it clogged his lungs. He had a feeling that if he turned away, he'd be back through the Fold and the way would not open for him again. He couldn't take that chance.

Something hard butted up against the sole of his foot, and he looked down to find roots pushing up out of the dirt. He kicked off his flip-flops to stand barefoot in the loamy earth. The cool soil grounded him, and he took another breath, clearer this time.

"You think I don't belong here." He studied the forest, searching out the smooth, tan faces under the mossy beards. "You think I have no magic, or that I'm here to hurt you." Crouching, he dug his fingers into the rich soil. "I'm a gardener. I nurture things from seed to fruit."

Around his hands, tiny roots tickled and searched like they were sniffing out the truth of his words. "I would never take what wasn't given freely. Nor should anyone ever do that. A friend of mine was brought through here recently." He waved over his shoulder at the junction between worlds and the fluctuation of magic that throbbed at his back. "I think he was brought here against his will, and I want to find him. That's all."

Leaves shimmied against each other, like the softest susurration of voices he couldn't be sure were real.

"His name is Emile. At least, that's the name he told me."

The shifting of sound grew.

"He's a dragon."

Twigs snapped and tree trunks moaned and creaked. Branches screeched; wood tore. A dryad whistled like a gust of wind whipping through the branches of a tired, brittle tree, and went silent. The woods emptied as a majestic cedar tree shuddered, leaned, then toppled, shaking the ground and sending Sunny sprawling.

A dragon roughly the size of Sunny's house and deeper green than the forest gloom crawled up over the trunk of the fallen giant. It slithered on its belly, its enormous snakelike body helped along by four thickly muscled legs near the rear. Two more limbs, longer and lither, emerged from broad shoulders, and a long, sinuous neck snaked down so the dragon could peer closely at Sunny. Yellow eyes glared at him from under bushy grey-green brows.

"This, brother?" The dragon's voice was as overwhelming as its size. "This is what you fled to?" It—he—laughed, and Sunny's bones creaked under the derision.

"Leave him, Hakko." A smaller dragon, glowing with all the colours of the most brilliant sunset, slipped out from behind the huge one. Pink and yellow feathers adorned this dragon's ruff, forearms, and shins. A row of spikes, perhaps made from stiff hair, swayed along its back and tail. Its sides glowed in the light emanating from the Fold, and it moved with all the speed and agility of a dragon *not* sporting hard, heavy scales.

"Emile," Sunny breathed. His dragon was breathtaking.

There was no mistaking the connection that jolted Sunny when Emile met his gaze. Nor could he ignore the shrouded light in those normally brilliant blue eyes. "Go home, Sssunny." The soft hiss of resignation shrivelled Sunny's momentary relief.

He scrambled to his feet, ignoring the mud and moss that stuck to him. He took a few steps closer to Emile, but Emile reared back, lips curled.

Hakko moved his head to intercept Sunny. His eyes had a fire deep within their amber depths. "He came back to *me*, human. He belongs to me."

"He fled you." Sunny took another step, then another. When Hakko didn't move out of his way, Sunny sidestepped so he could get a better look at Emile. "Come home."

"Thiss iss… my… home." The words dripped with uncertainty. Emile gazed at him a long time.

"You know that's not really true," Sunny argued.

Something rippled on the air that Sunny didn't quite see or hear, but he felt it, like the graze of static over his skin, lifting the hairs on his arms and the back of his neck.

Emile's eyes lit with all the fire of the brightest summer sky. His nostrils flared and he took another step back, away from Sunny.

"No." Sunny reached for him.

Hakko growled. The sound rattled the trees and shook Sunny to his core.

"You crossed the Fold to escape this life, remember?" Sunny pleaded with Emile as his dragon shuffled back another step, claws gouging the soil, as though he was trying to hold his ground but couldn't find purchase.

"I am dragon." Emile lifted his head, straightening like he was bracing himself. "This is my place." He glanced at Hakko, then back at Sunny. "Hakko is my Sire." Even as he said that, he looked to Hakko again, and his eyes hooded. His tongue, long and forked, came out to taste the air. He shivered, and the momentary resistance in his limbs slackened. He crouched, hunkering down and making himself small in Hakko's shadow.

"You see?" Hakko preened, using his head and neck to tuck Emile against his side. "Emik-kik has made his decision."

Emile shivered again, crowding Hakko's side and staring at Sunny, confusion in his eyes.

Was he under some kind of spell? Sunny had to believe that was the case, but even so, what could he do to stop it? He closed his eyes to feel the air, wiggled his toes to feel the earth. He could sense the trees watching, the dryads, hidden but listening, waiting… *hoping*? For what? If Hakko was using magic against his lover, Sunny couldn't feel it. Not like he could feel the flux of the trees and plants rising like mist all around him or the distant waves of converted magic that meant somewhere, salamanders thrived. And if he couldn't identify it, how could he counter it? How did he fight something he didn't understand and couldn't see or feel?

"Come, Emik-kik." Hakko shifted and swung his body around. "We have eggs to collect. A new generation to nurture, yes?"

"Of course." Emile shook himself. A flutter of feathers drifted down around him as he turned and, stuck to Hakko's side, retreated into the woods with his Sire.

"Emile!" Sunny started after them, but Hakko swung his tail, catching Sunny in the side and lifting him off his feet. He sailed across the clearing to land on his back in the cushioning moss and dirt.

"Fuck that," he wheezed, staggering to his feet. "Emile. Wait!"

Both dragons stopped. Hakko remained motionless, but Emile turned, crept back a few paces, and crouched, side still pressed to Hakko. "What?"

"What are you doing? You fled this. Don't you remember?"

"I wass… wrong." His nostrils flared. He breathed in a deep breath, flicked his tongue out. Once more his eyelids fluttered almost closed. "I have a purpose here." If dragons could smile, that was what he did, though it appeared dreamy and far-off. "I should never have left. I should never have taken my human form for so long and forgotten what it was to be scaled and true."

"Your human side is true too."

"His human side is flawed. It interferes with who he is. Stops him feeling his true self," Hakko rumbled. "*This* is who he truly is. Go home, human. He isn't for you." Hakko began walking again, and Emile slowly turned to follow.

He paused once to glance back over his shoulder. "I am dragon, Sunny."

"You're human too!"

"Come, Emik-kik." Hakko swished his tail, a forceful swipe that snicked the sharply spined tip against Sunny's cheek, drawing blood, while the thick of it thudded into Emile's side hard enough to echo between the tree trunks. Emile grunted, then turned back to the forest and walked away.

"His name is Emikku," Sunny called after them. "Your name is Emikku. Your choice is yours to make! You don't have to stay here. It is *your* choice, Emikku. Never forget that." The dragons were gone. "Never forget who you are," Sunny whispered as he sank back down into the moss.

He'd been so sure Emile had been dragged back here against his will. To see him calmly walk off with Hakko broke his heart. He had to believe this was somehow Hakko's doing. To believe anything else meant there was nothing for him here.

And yet he knew. If he went back to his own side of the Fold now, he would spend the rest of his life regretting it. He would die trying to find his way back to Emile, knowing Emile had refused him, but never really being sure it *had* been Emile's will and not Hakko's.

Long after the damp of the mud on his legs had dried and the scratch of the moss should have driven him to his feet, he remained. His eyes burned, his jaw ached from clenching it around the pain of realising he'd only been a convenient place for Emile to hide for a while. That the lure of magic and his home, of opening up to Hakko again, was more than Sunny could fight.

"Will you come home?"

The voice floated on a wave of light and energy, and Sunny took a long time to place it. The instant he did, the willow dryad stepped out of the light of the Fold and settled next to him.

"You don't belong here," she reminded him.

"Do you have a name?"

The creature considered this a long time. *"There are so many,"* she sighed at last, her voice sounding like wind through silvery leaves. *"In your tongues, such mundane ones. Willow. Salix."*

"What about your own language?"

"What language do trees speak?"

"Huh." Sunny pursed his lips. "Good point." He settled with his back against the dryad's sturdy torso. "Which side of the Fold do you belong on?"

"Neither." After a moment she amended, *"Both."*

"So dryads can cross the Fold whenever they want?"

"Anyone—anything—can cross. Where you belong is where you decide to stay."

"Are there humans here? On this side?"

"Is a dragon a human when he wears no scales?"

"I thought—" Sunny gulped and fell silent.

"My tree straddles the Fold," the dryad said after a while. *"Therefore I am never far from it, no matter which side I step into. Other dryads do not have that luxury. Your dryads are sweet and young and much more like their trees than the dryads here.*

"But even here, the magic of their life is tied to the life of their tree. It grows with the tree, diminishes if the tree falls ill or is felled." The dryad gazed sadly at the downed tree whose top branches, already beginning to wilt, fluttered at the very edges of the light cast by the Fold. *"The flux is thinned when such a mighty tree falls. The dryad will diminish. Perhaps it will find an offspring of the tree to share its magic and knowledge before it fades completely. The salamanders who live here will suffer for the blow dealt to this forest today. Some may die. The magic they produce will falter for a time.*

"Eventually the forest will find a new balance. Your salamander came from those woods." It pointed to the darkness that had settled across the clearing and dipped the trees there into inky shadows. *"He thrived on the flux those ancient trees produce. He was strong. Happy."*

"Until Hakko drove him across the Fold into a poplar grove where the flux poisoned him. I figured that out. I need to get him across the river to the cedar grove."

The dryad hummed.

"What?"

"You want to help him, though he isn't part of your world."

"Hakko made him part of my world. Glimmerleaf didn't do anything to deserve that. He was just following his instincts—either obeying his master or fleeing a threat, I don't know. But just because it wasn't his choice doesn't mean I can ignore that it happened. He doesn't deserve to suffer because someone else used him. Once he's better I'll figure out how to get him back here. Or how to keep him. Whatever he wants. He'll know he's safe and he can make up his own mind."

"He is an animal."

"More instinctual than dragons, but not unintelligent. That's what Emile said."

"And just how instinctual are dragons?"

"They're not instinctual. They're people." Sunny sat up straight. "Except when they aren't." He turned to the dryad. "But he spoke to me. As a dragon, he spoke to me."

"And do you not speak when you are in the throes of mating? Of pairing? Of courting?"

"Of course." But everyone knew what hormones and lust did to a person's brain. "But that doesn't always mean we make the best choices. Sometimes we act on instinct, and that isn't always great." He hadn't always been as thoughtful as he could have been about decisions made in the heat of the moment, and none of the men he'd ever been with had the advantage of enticing Sunny to transform into a creature who acted more on instinct than intellect to get their way.

"I'm an idiot."

"You are in love," the dryad helpfully pointed out. *"Emikku is not the only one letting instinct drive his decisions."*

Sunny rose. "I have to go after them."

"You will not get through the woods at night, human."

"But—"

"You will be no good to anyone lost in the magic or torn under a wild tatzel's claws. Wait."

She was probably right. Sunny gazed at the black void where he knew the forest stood, hidden by the night he was sure had crept on faster than it would have at home. Lights appeared among the tree trunks— glittering pinprick brightness, foggy globes of blue iridescence, wisps of pink and orange that trailed in sinewy drifts close to the ground, and steady, staring pairs of green or purple high in the trees.

As his eyes adjusted to the strange night and his ears to the sounds he didn't recognise, he realised that in a world of magic, he was the odd one out. No one here was like him, and no one would understand him. Was it so surprising Emile had come back to the place where he was family? The place he was understood? Of course it wasn't. And maybe Sunny shouldn't be quite so determined to rip him away from that.

CHAPTER 30

THE SMELLS of home still overwhelmed him. More than the huge dragon at his side or the soothing wash of magic over his skin, more than the cool shade of the trees under which they travelled or the sounds of wildlife that didn't exist anywhere else, the scent of it all went straight to his head.

He'd first noticed it in the glade near… near…. He shook himself, trying to think back. On the other side of the Fold, this heady scent had been all but absent. He hadn't even realised he missed it until he'd smelled it again. He'd been in the woods, close to the stream. The water sprites had been angry about… something.

Emik-kik shivered. They had been rising ever higher. Something had riled them, though now he didn't remember if he'd ever known what that something had been. And *this* had hit him, the smell going straight to his brain. He'd already been in his scales by then, soft and light, but now he didn't remember why.

"Are you chilled?" Next to him, Hakko puffed his sides. A warmth emanated from him, heating his near-black shimmering scales and transferring the warmth to Emik-kik. He leaned closer. The scrape of sharp, hard scales against his softer flank drew his attention.

Gently, he flicked his tongue over the hurt. The soft scales felt wrong. He was too exposed. Too weak.

No, not weak. But vulnerable.

"You will get used to the change, Emik-kik. There is much to be enjoyed in these scales that you never could have before." As if demonstrating, Hakko ran one of his talons along the mane of stiff hair on Emik-kik's nape. Under the touch, Emik-kik's scales flittered up. His feathers ruffled and his skin undulated, causing him to gasp. It did feel good, that touch, that sensitivity absent when he had harder, more protective scales.

Was that all he'd been doing, refusing to try this form? Protecting himself? Putting on armour against the chance he could be happy like this?

"Perhaps you will learn to swim…."

Emik-kik shivered once more—not from cold this time, just the thought of water. But he had enjoyed it once. Not in this form. A dragon was not built to swim, not even in soft scales. But his human form—that, he remembered—immersed in the stream, the heat and security of a body supporting him. Of… a human?

"We are almost home, Emik-kik." The rumble of Hakko's voice vibrated through him. It was reassuring, the bulk of him so close, protection against the cool early-morning air and the dangers that dwelt in a forest this ancient.

He'd never felt this vulnerable. Had he?

The foggy remembrance of skin with no scales at all drifted at the periphery of his thoughts. He remembered cold nights, an empty belly. He remembered scratchy blankets. Soft bread, grilled meat. Gentle hands. Hot, wonderful lips….

"And here we are." Hakko moved aside, depriving Emik-kik of his comfort and whisking him out of his memories—or dreams?

They stepped out from under the eaves of the forest onto a prominence of stone worn smooth from generations of dragons climbing to this point—in scale and skin—to look down on the majesty of one of the greatest remaining dragon achievements. The area where they stood had been cultivated with flowering gardens and stone shelters near the edges of the forest to accommodate mating ceremonies, celebrations, and gatherings of all kinds.

Revealed in the valley at the foot of the sandstone cliffs, the spires of their home rose, pulled from the bones of the earth with magic and will. Rays of sunshine turned the pale rock spires gold with their first caress, while the homes nestled at the foot of the grander castles still slumbered in the last shadows of night.

Far in the past, many generations before their own eggs had hatched, their ancestors had controlled the will of thousands of salamanders who could render such vast amounts of flux into pure magical energy that allowed the dragons to achieve anything. They had forced the land to their own desires. They had built this with nothing more than their will, the borrowed magic, and the bones of the earth. No force could shake the castle whose roots were the backbone of the world itself.

There were no dragons left alive, that Emik-kik knew of, who could harness such power now. The salamanders had evolved from that time and had learned to be wary of dragons in any form. They were harder to

control and better protected by their own cunning and the loyalty of the
dryads and nymphs who fed them. No such gathering had happened since
the Dispersal that had broken the dragon civilisation into the Enclaves
and Houses.

Emik-kik was not the dragon to challenge Hakko, so he had fled.
He'd torn himself from his home, from everything he knew, to find
refuge in a strange, empty land.

And he'd found… what? Solace? Acceptance?

"Is it all you remember, little mate?" Hakko asked. "Is our home
everything you've dreamed of since you left me?"

"Little mate?" A new voice, one half-remembered from the nest,
caught Emik-kik's attention. "Have you given in, then, my wild one?
Are you to give up all your hard-won freedom for a false Sire's desires?
Have you forgotten everything our Bearer taught us about pride? About
history? About the dangers of too much power in too few hands?"

Emik-kik turned to face the sinuous, winged form of one he had
never expected to see again in this life. "Ananth."

"You've returned." Ananth's soft body slinked up next to his,
sandwiching him once more against Hakko's hard, abrasive scales. Their
golden hide sent a frisson of happiness exploding right through him. He
hadn't realised how much he missed Ananth until they were pressing up
against each other like they hadn't since they were hatchlings.

"I—" He had returned. It had been for the best.

A waft of clearer air lifted the downy feathers along his ruff as
Ananth swept wings in an arc over them all. Only slightly bigger than
Emik-kik, that wingspan was still enormous, and finding a comfortable
position for them stirred up dust motes and pushed away the heavily
aromatic air that surrounded Hakko.

Emik-kik sneezed at the dust and blinked as though a veil had lifted
from his eyes.

"Playing with his senses, Hakko. Now is that really fair?"

"Silence, Ananth."

Ananth grinned, showing rows of sharpened teeth, but said nothing.

"Come, Emik-ki—"

"*Emikku.*" The correction passed his lips before he could think
better of it. "My name is Emikku." He curled his claws into the rocky
ground, rustled his much smaller wings. Nothing grew this close to the
cliff's edge, the land's magic and life having dried up centuries ago.

Gravel scraped the pads of his feet. The satisfying sound of brittle stone cracking under the pressure of his grip steeled his nerves.

"What our Bearer named you out of the shell is of no matter. Everything changes as soon as we return to the roost. You know that." Hakko puffed himself up, heat rising from him in visible waves. A heady scent of hormones and desire rose with it, clouding Emikku's thoughts.

"You do no one any service by appealing to his baser instincts, Hakko," Ananth scolded. The tone was light, but the underlying warning was not. "Bearing our future is a lofty post—one best entered into with a clear head and a resolve that will carry him through the decades of confinement that it requires. It is not for the faint of heart or the wild of spirit. Let him make up his mind without your scent-fog clouding his judgement." Ananth nudged Emikku. "Remember our travels, wild one? How we roamed the woods and danced through the prairie grasses? Do you remember the hours we spent reading the stories and histories, and the days—years even—when we travelled to find the source of the myths?"

Of course he did, now that his head was clear. He and Ananth had spent years away from the castle roaming the lands to find the truth behind the stories etched on the thin parchment pages of their House histories. Something had always drawn Ananth home. Though Emikku had been content to follow them back to the broodnest from time to time, he had never wanted to stay. He thought Ananth hadn't either, and the last time they'd left without him, he'd believed he would never see them again. He'd believed that he would have to find his own way out of the castle and Hakko's plans, and he had.

He'd run to the Fold. He'd found Sunny.

"Sunny." His own voice sounded a little strangled in his ears, like there was an injunction against saying the name at all. He had to struggle to remember Sunny's face or recall his scent. Every time he almost had it, Hakko's pheromones overtook him, and he had to shake the mist away again.

With a mighty heave and a blast of air, Ananth rose to hover above them, letting out a screech as only a dragon could. Heavy wingbeats stirred up a gale around them.

Hakko's scent blew away, and with it, the fog over Emikku's senses. The heat Hakko produced wafted past him, hot blasts with every beat of Ananth's wings.

Emikku shook himself and scuttled sideways, distancing himself from Hakko. He stared at his fellow hatchling, huge against the glow of the eastern horizon. The sun was rising, bringing a fresh light and new clarity.

He had allowed his dragon's instincts to overpower his good sense. "I should not have come." He backed a few more steps away from Hakko, sliding into the shadow Ananth created.

"You should never have *left*!" Hakko's roar was furious, and he rose onto his back legs, snapping at Ananth's tail, whipping his own tail up to score a gouge through one of the beautiful membranous wings.

Ananth screamed, faltered, tipping sideways in the sky and dipping below the edge of the cliff.

"Ananth!" Emikku lunged for his falling nest-mate, even as the ground shuddered and the scrape of claws on the stone of the mountainside rent the morning.

"Is this what we come to, brother?" Ananth asked, clawing up to level ground. "You would pull me out of the sky, destroy your own broodmate, to get your way?"

"This isn't about getting my way. It never has been. It's about restoring what is rightfully ours. What should never have been taken from us in the first place." He waved a forelimb, indicating the brightening city, the palace with golden light glittering off its highest windows, the indestructability of the ancient home their forefathers had built and their House had inherited.

"We had power once," he spat. "We should have that power again."

"Did you not read the stories?" Ananth asked, voice breaking over old heartache. "Do you forget what once stood there?" A wave of the bloodied wing out over the cliff drew Emikku's attention to the view again. "Our ancestors tore a portion of the world's skeleton up out of the depths to claim it as their own. But what did they destroy in the making of what we call home?"

"What does it matter? The world moved on."

"Do you know why brownies live underground?"

"They're brownies."

"Because the forest they lived in was ploughed under to create our stony, cold haven. Miles and miles of succulent farmland and ancient groves were torn apart so we could build out of rock and stone something that could never be torn down by our rivals. They went underground to try to nurture the last ragged roots of *their* home. *Their* world. Do you even know what it looks like now?"

Hakko's jaw clacked, and he gazed out over his city as the sun rose over the eastern peaks to pour light down the slopes.

"They live in the faintest echo of what they once had. It's beautiful, don't mistake me. The hills are hollowed out in places to let in the light, and the water sprites enticed to travel miles out of their way to send rills and trickles through the cracks of stone to feed their underground gardens. Trees knee-high to our human forms that are centuries old, dryads no bigger than the brownies themselves, salamanders the size of our big toes." Ananth smiled. "They have survived, but it never had to be that way. The land dispersed us for a reason."

"The world was jealous of our power."

"And rightly so!" Ananth took a step towards him. "We destroyed entire civilisations to best our own kin. Because we *could*."

Hakko turned his attention on his golden nest-mate in a searing glare, but Ananth rose up, meeting his eye, unafraid. "So everything our Sire and his Sire before him have done to strengthen our House, you would throw that away?"

"I would ask you why. Why do we need to strengthen our bloodline so much? Why do we need more power than the others?"

"Every generation they pull back, refuse to mingle their blood with ours. Every Sire has more difficulty convincing the other Houses to hold to the Dispersal agreements and allow us to nurture their eggs."

"Did you ever think that perhaps they held back not out of jealousy, but out of fear? That amassing so much magic in our small valley might be making them nervous? Did it never occur to you that multiplying the power you hold might be the reason they refuse to hold to old agreements that would make them even weaker?"

"Ananth is right." Emikku stepped forward. "They all know the same things you do about how our magic multiplies. The rules about egg sharing and honouring the Egg-bearers were created for a reason."

"It was a flawed law." Hakko's voice took on a threatening snarl.

"Was it?" Emikku edged himself between Ananth and Hakko. "We protect the Egg-bearers of all Houses, all the Enclaves, because we will never know which Bearer holds our own offspring. That is how it should be. Our Grand-Sire was the jealous one, not telling his Bearer the truth, trying to manipulate the outcome. What he did was wrong."

"A lot of good it did." Hakko's face twisted with anger as he turned to Emikku. "I will never produce the egg he hoped for if you refuse to cooperate, Emik-kik."

"If I agree to this, the magic our offspring bears will be double yours. Our offspring would be so strong none of the other Houses could stand against them. *You* would not stand against them."

"Why is that a bad thing?" Hakko's words roared out over the valley. "We have been the smallest, the weakest for so long. Why can't we be the ones with the power for a change?"

"Because look what we do with it." Emikku backed a few paces away from his Sire, keeping his voice low and Ananth out of Hakko's reach. "Manipulation. Harm." He nosed at Ananth's wing. "A dryad older than any dragon living—dead so you could prove to a nonmagic human how strong you are. It was our own hubris, our own shortcomings that brought on the Dispersal, and we have yet to learn the lesson we were meant to learn from that, even hundreds and hundreds of years later.

"Yes, the brownies have moved on, the forests have regrown, the water sprites have forgiven, if not forgotten, what we did to their sacred pools and clear rivers. *We* are the ones who still need to learn."

"Listen to him, Hakko," Ananth said, voice a soft, gravelly purr. "Step back before it's too late."

Hakko swung his head around to stare at Emikku. "And if I agree that everything you two have said is true, then what? I let you go? Become a Sire with no offspring? Our House dies here."

"Perhaps that is the penalty we were always meant to pay for the damage we did, the harm we caused to so many others."

"I won't let our House die with me," Hakko vowed, moving towards Emikku. "You will give me the egg I need, and if I can't convince you to carry it and care for the hatchling, I'll take it." He rose, claws sharp and glinting in the morning sunshine, fangs dripping acid that steamed when it hit the ground, crumbling the smooth rock into pockmarked, treacherous terrain.

"I won't." Emikku lowered his head. "That is one thing even your most persuasive manipulations cannot force me to do. You will have to kill me. Even an egg will feel the violence of such a beginning. Would you scar the hatchling in such a way, risk so much damage to an innocent, just to get your way?"

CHAPTER 31

SUNNY'S STOMACH grumbled, forcing him out of a fog of unsettled sleep he couldn't remember falling into. He shifted, straightening cramped back and leg muscles, to find himself surrounded by tiny, wrinkled little creatures with huge moon-coloured eyes and skin like spun silver but streaked with dirt and clumps of soil.

"Uh." He sat up and scrambled back, expecting to fetch up against the willow dryad's thick body, but he was alone. Well. Alone except for the curious—fairies?

"Hi." He waved one hand, keeping his arms close to his body.

The creatures crouched and mimicked him.

"I don't suppose you speak English?"

Some of them tilted their heads to one side, while others giggled. An exceptionally wizened one rose on legs far longer than human-proportioned to a pot-bellied, stout torso, and took a few steps towards Sunny.

"Human?" the creature asked.

"Um. Yes. I am." Sunny tried a smile. Most of the creatures around him mimicked the expression, revealing mouths full of wide, flat teeth and thick red tongues that a few of the younger creatures stuck out to waggle around like they were sensing the air.

"No magic," the old creature said.

"No. Not really. Not like you would call magic, anyway."

"You do here?" One gnarled finger pointed to the ground.

Sunny assumed the little creature was asking why he was on the wrong side of the Fold for a human. "I'm looking for my friend. He's a dragon—"

A horrified gasp went up among his watchers, the smallest of them vanishing, some literally, others by ducking behind older, bigger members of the group.

So. They didn't like dragons. This might be a problem.

"He's kind," Sunny hastened to assure them. "Gentle."

"Dragons raze." He swept his hand out in a horizontal sweep, like he was wiping away everything in its path. "Old man know." He thudded a palm on his chest, then propped his hands on his narrow hips and scowled. "All dragons."

"Not this one, I promise. He ran away from the other dragons." Sunny pointed back towards what, in the morning glow, looked like an unassuming, perfectly unmagical willow tree. "He crossed the Fold. That's where I met him."

"Dragons kill," the little man insisted.

"I am afraid other dragons might hurt—or kill—my dragon. Please. All I want is to know where they might have gone. Can you help me?"

"Help dragon?" His fierce scowl deepened, turning his face into a scrunched study of stubbornness with bushy brows. "Help human." He shook his head. "No help brownies."

"Brownies? Is that what you are? A brownie?"

The man looked at him like he was an idiot, then huffed and slapped his own chest. "Root and tree and seed and care and back and back and back." He waved a hand, indicating the passage of time.

"You take care of tree roots?" That seemed an odd occupation, but what did Sunny know of brownies?

"Trees. Roots. Time. Better trees. Back and back and back. Best to better to always."

Like he could hear Daisy's voice in his head, he finally made sense of what the little man was trying to say. "You're a tree biologist."

The man's eyes got huge and he gaped.

"You improve tree stock. You make trees better by planting the best ones and keeping them safe."

This time the wide, round-eyed look was accompanied by an equally wide smile and a vigorous nod that sprayed small chunks of soil from the man's beard and hair across the ground at his feet. "Yes, yes, yes. Human thinks."

"I try," Sunny muttered. He smiled at the little man. "Okay. So what do I call you?"

The man tipped his head to one side, shuttering the pale glow of his eyes behind narrowed lids.

Sunny touched his chest. "I'm Sunny." He fingered his hair, pointed at the sky, then tapped his chest again. "Sunny."

The man nodded, touched his chest, and a long exhalation of sound, like roots digging into earth, pebbles tumbling over one another, and water running and dripping through echoing stone caverns came out of his mouth all at once. He nodded, grinned at Sunny, and once more tapped his own chest.

"Um. O… kay." Sunny sighed but shook his head. "I'm not going to be able to repeat that. Mind if I call you Rootstock?"

Rootstock nodded and tapped his own chest. "Rootstock." He shuffled over to an elderly female brownie and laid a loving arm over her shoulders. "Rootstock's best and other." He waved behind him. "Rootstock's more Rootstocks."

Sunny grunted. If he was claiming this entire large group as his progeny, then the man was well and truly living up to his name.

But it was something Sunny could work with. He spread out his arm as though draping it lovingly over someone's shoulders, as Rootstock had done to his wife, and indicated the empty air under his arm. "The dragon I'm looking for, Emile—Emikku—is Sunny's best and other." He laid his hand over his heart. "Please. I need your help."

CHAPTER 32

IN THE end, the brownies were only willing to go so far. They did guide Sunny safely through the huge cedar grove, each one filing past the fallen giant to run hands mournfully over its bark as they passed.

Following their lead, Sunny did the same. He could feel the eyes of many dryads on him, though none showed their faces. He wished he could do something for the fallen cedar and its dryad, but he could hardly replant such a behemoth. All he could do was vow to himself he would confront Hakko and do his best to make sure the dragon couldn't take anything, or anyone, from anyone else.

He knew it was a tall order when the brownies began to slow. Dawn sent shafts of pale light between the tree trunks, and Sunny began to notice their party dwindling as the forest thinned. He didn't see anyone leave, and yet by the time he could see sky and open space between the boles of the trees, he was alone with Rootstock and his wife, whom he'd begun to call Mamaroot in his head.

When the wizened little couple stopped, Sunny stopped next to them.

Rootstock pointed ahead. "Dragon waste." He thumbed back over his shoulder. "Home safe."

Sunny nodded. "You don't have to go any farther. But I have to keep going. I have to see Emikku one more time. I have to be sure."

Rootstock nodded to him. "Best and other." He patted Sunny's calf. "Sunny." He smiled up at Sunny, teeth white against gunmetal lips and skin smudged with forest shadows and earth. "Luck and light."

"Thanks." Sunny smiled back at him, then took a few steps forward. When he glanced back, the brownies were gone. "Perfect."

As he neared the last trees, he realised the forest ran almost to the very edge of a cliff, and that the space beyond was occupied. The voices he heard were gravelly and very much not human.

He recognised Hakko's angered words as he raised his voice, and Sunny dashed forward to see three dragons perched on the edge of the world, sunshine rising topaz and mauve and pink behind them.

Hakko stood out bleak and dangerous against the delicate light. "I won't let our House die with me." He moved towards Emikku, who all but blended into the shining light, his colours echoing the rising sun that glinted from his scales like it was bouncing off polished metal.

"You will give me the egg I need," Hakko bellowed, "and if I can't convince you to carry it and care for the hatchling, I'll take it." He rose, claws flashing, fangs dripping something that steamed when it hit the ground. Bubbling rock sizzled where the drops landed.

"I won't." Emikku lowered his head. "That is one thing even your most persuasive manipulations cannot force me to do. You will have to kill me. Even an egg will feel the violence of such a beginning. Would you scar the hatchling in such a way, risk so much damage to an innocent, just to get your way?"

Sunny gasped in horror as he took in the scene.

The third dragon, all soft golds and shimmering, pale peach, turned to him. They moved to put their body between Sunny and the imminent violence.

"No!" Sunny dashed forward, shoving at a surprisingly soft hide. "Don't. Hakko!"

"Stop!" It wasn't Hakko's booming voice that halted Sunny, frozen in stride. Emikku rose up to his hind legs. His hide crackled and popped as his scales sizzled and reformed, even more brilliantly coloured and reflective than before.

"Emikku." The golden dragon keened loudly but kept the bulk of their body between Sunny and Emikku.

Sunny could feel the heat wafting off Emikku as he puffed out his chest. Cracks began to show between the soft sections along his belly, chest, and throat, glowing with a light so white-hot Sunny had to shield his eyes. The stench of singed hair and feathers sank heavily over the plateau, and Emikku screeched in obvious pain.

"What are you doing?" Hakko's furious roar was barely discernible as words, and he rushed forward as though he intended to batter himself against Emikku's body, but the golden dragon once more intervened, stepping between the two males.

Hakko drew up short, rearing back as he glared, eyes wild with fury, maw gaping wide.

"Kill me and you truly do kill our future, Hakko," the golden dragon said, voice so soft they shouldn't have been able to hear.

Hakko's nostrils flared. "Why are you doing this?"

Freed from the small dragon's guard, Sunny rushed forward, reaching for Emikku. He had to battle through such intense heat he thought his skin would blister up and fall off, but he forced himself forward until his hands came into contact with Emikku's scales.

They were hard as glass, sharp enough to draw blood, and scalding to the touch. Sunny refused to pull back, expecting to smell his own flesh burning, but in the instant before he screamed in pain, a flush of cold like liquid ice infused the spot where he and his lover connected.

Emikku ground out a moan, shivered outward from where Sunny touched him, and settled back to all six legs. His weight landing on the stone made the earth shudder and a cloud of dust rise around them.

He sagged, drooping until he all but lay on the ground, but his tail curled around to pull Sunny close to his side. "That was foolish," he whispered.

"You looked like you were going to explode. I couldn't—" Sunny gulped. What had he thought he was going to do, other than burn right alongside Emikku?

Emikku sighed.

"He might have burned himself alive from the inside out if you hadn't stopped him." Hakko sounded coldly furious, but his deep voice shook, and his eyes held a wild, frantic look.

"Why would you do that?" Sunny asked.

"The alternative was to let him have his way, either manipulate me with his pheromones or force me with violence, perhaps cut me open and take any eggs I might have had. Better I burn off my own magic than let him become something so ugly." He laid his head on the ground, a slight lean to his body that brought him closer to Sunny. "No eggs hatched from such an unfavourable start would have produced any light."

Hakko's nostrils flared. "I have only ever wanted what our House deserves."

"No, my broodmate." Emikku lifted his head to glare at Hakko. "You wanted something that is long past and should never return. Too many have been hurt by what you call power. Better we have nothing than that we harm innocents."

"And now we will have nothing," Hakko said, bitterness edging his words.

"No eggs of our line," Emikku agreed. "I've turned them all to ash and glass." He turned to look at the third dragon. "I'm sorry, Ananth."

"I'm not." Ananth nuzzled his cheek. "It was the right thing to do." Yet she looked sad. "You've done something that can't be undone, though." Her tongue flickered over his scales.

"It will be fine. This was always the form I was meant to take. I don't expect anyone else to understand that."

Sunny gasped. What had he done that was so irreversible? "Emile?"

His dragon slowly shifted, swinging his head around to peer at Sunny. His neck drooped, and his eyes were half-lidded, but even through the burning blue and despite the slitted pupils, he saw his Emile in the eyes of Emikku the dragon. "Sssunny," he whispered, drawing out the *s* and sighing away the last syllable. He shuddered, laid his head on the ground, and went still.

"Emile!" Sunny pushed at his bulk, but he didn't move, gave no sign that he heard or felt Sunny's touch, even when Sunny threw his entire weight against Emile's side.

"Stop." Ananth pulled him away with their tail, nudged him with remarkable gentleness with the side of their face until he was a few feet from Emile. "There is nothing any of us can do now but wait. He generated a lot of heat that he didn't release. There was no place for it to go but inward. All we can do now is hope he didn't burn up all his magic along with his eggs and his egg pouch."

"He did that to kill his own offspring?" Sunny asked.

"It isn't exactly that simple," the dragon said. "Our eggs are not life, exactly, until we will them to be, and he never did. Instead, he petrified the tiny buds that might have become eggs, had he so chosen. And in doing it how he did, he may also have hardened his physical form permanently. He might always be a hard-scale now. Hard-scales don't have eggs. Not in the same sense that a soft-scale does."

Sunny turned to Ananth. "You have eggs?"

That got him a smile. "I do."

"Ananth?" Hakko shuffled a step closer.

Ananth swung to face the Sire, gaze flat. "I would have told you first, Sire, if you had taken a moment to listen."

"You told us long ago you had no eggs of your own."

"Because I don't. I carry three eggs from three other Houses who agreed to take a chance on us. They allowed me to take their already fertilised eggs on the understanding that *I* would carry them, not Emikku."

"Only three?"

"Three is more than none. You will never be allowed to raise them. Come your Reckoning Day, you will be replaced. A new Sire has already been chosen. There can be no Corcaird tie to these eggs. That was their stipulation, and now I cannot refute them." Ananth cast a sad glance to Emikku's still form. "What happened here can never be forgiven." Straightening to the full height of golden scale and feather, Ananth lifted both wings, gave a single, voluminous beat that raised a cloud of dust around them. "You are cast out."

"You can't—"

Behind Hakko, a huge midnight blue dragon rose over the edge of the cliff. It crawled up to level ground, opened its huge maw, and let out a deafening roar. Hakko cringed, but Ananth puffed out their chest, ruffling scales and feathers in a ripple of welcome.

Sunny stood next to them. "You should go," Sunny suggested to Hakko.

"I should listen to a human?"

The blue dragon lifted one clawed front foot and brought it down on Hakko's switching tail. "Take the human's advice. While you can."

Hakko curled a lip, glanced to Emikku, and snarled softly. "Fool thing," he rumbled. Then, with a snort and blast of wings that sent sand and grit into Sunny's eyes and slicing at his shins and arms, Hakko scrambled nimbly over the edge to disappear but for the scraping sound of his claws below on the cliff face.

"Where will he go?"

Ananth sighed. "Who's to say? What he did—or threatened to do—to his own broodmate…."

The huge blue dragon snorted. "He is a fool." With a much gentler flourish, the blue dragon slipped away over the edge of the cliff.

"Is he your new Sire?" Sunny asked.

Ananth nodded. "Rokkan. He will be a good Sire. He is kind. He is a handsome dragon and fierce fighter, but his magic is not strong, so while he will be the one to enhance them, we will have to rely on the magic of the hatchlings themselves to carry on our House. Rokkan will raise the hatchlings with care and compassion and wisdom. If it is meant to be, our House will remain, small, yes, but intact. If not?" She shrugged. "If not, the nine remaining Houses will carry on without us."

"Maybe Emikku would have...." Sunny shrugged awkwardly. "For Rokkan."

"Rokkan would never have asked him, Sunny. And *that* is why he is a worthy Sire."

"I can't believe this was the only way to stop Hakko." Sunny ran a hand down a spike on Emikku's shoulder.

"He did what he thought he must," Ananth said softly. "Now we hope it didn't cost him everything."

"Tell me how to help him."

"You already did all you can do," Ananth said. "You stopped him killing himself. That is more than any dragon could have done. Now all we can do is wait to see if his magic remains strong enough to pull him through."

"Will he turn back? To human?"

"Who knows?" Ananth petted Emikku's long neck, clawed fingers floating around the base of a line of sharp spikes that marched down the back of his neck. "If his magic hasn't all burned away, perhaps."

Sunny gulped. What would he do if Emile was gone forever, and only Emikku remained? He stared at his dragon, willing him to open his eyes.

"You can do nothing more for him."

"I won't leave him," Sunny blurted, realising that whatever the outcome, he wasn't leaving, at least until he knew.

"It could be years before he recovers," Ananth said.

"Then I will wait." He moved to Emikku's side, folded his legs under him, and sat, back pressed to Emikku's rigid scales. He crossed his arms over his chest and ignored the loud rumble of his belly.

"You love him that much?" Ananth asked.

"I guess I do." Sunny flattened a palm against Emikku's neck. He felt a warm, steady pulse under his hand and smiled. "I love him enough to wait."

After some time, Ananth spoke. "I have to go."

"Then you should go."

Ananth sighed, folded their good wing, but held the other out awkwardly, then turned to follow after where Rokkan had disappeared. At the top of the path, they looked back at Sunny. "You aren't what I thought humans would be like."

Sunny shrugged, not really caring what this dragon thought of him or his kind.

"Emikku is lucky to have someone who cares so much."

"I am lucky to have him too."

"Love can be powerful magic."

Looking up, Sunny smiled again. "I hope so, because it's all the magic I have."

CHAPTER 33

HOT SUN on Sunny's face woke him. Or maybe it was the weight on his chest, like a small cat perched there and plucking at his lower lip.

A string of noises like rustling leaves and the hard-scrabble sound of rocks rolling over rocks brought Sunny fully awake. He blinked into the light—and into a pair of huge moon eyes with filigree black lashes blinking back at him above a pert, round nose and broad mouth. The mouth smiled, revealing wide-spaced, flat teeth just breaking through the gums, and then the body attached to that interesting face shook under a gale of giggles.

Sunny startled straighter, fully awake now. The movement dislodged the small body from his chest. It toppled backwards, and he scrambled to catch the young brownie before she tumbled end over end to the ground.

"Easy!" He cupped her small frame as he sat upright and lowered her to her feet. "Who are you?"

Rootstock peered from the edge of the trees, his face set in a furious glare, his arms waving madly at the child Sunny had addressed. He was saying something to her in a language that sounded more like a stick dragged through pebbles than words Sunny could understand, but the older brownie's intent was clear.

He wanted the girl back in the woods. Pronto.

"Go on." Sunny gently turned her around and nudged her towards her father. "You're scaring him to death, little root."

She glanced over her shoulder at him, patted her chest proudly, and declared, "Ittaroot."

"Okay. Sure. Ittaroot." He had to stop naming things. What if he was unleashing some kind of naming magic he didn't know about? He waved again, and her gap-toothed baby grin widened. "Go on now. Before his head explodes." He made a shooing motion, and she toddled back to her father, who gathered her up in a tight hug, then promptly smacked her bottom before handing her off to an older boy and pointing back into the woods.

Other brownies peered past their patriarch at Sunny, and even past Sunny to the dragon he'd been dozing against. He'd been there, to the best he could figure out, about three days. Emikku breathed steadily at his back, but there was no other sign of life. Just the slight warmth emanating from his body and the even, if shallow, rise and fall of his back. Sunny had found a spot, safe from the deadly spikes that had taken the place of the hairy mane along his spine, to lean and wait.

From the shadows of the trees, his audience, about the same size it had been for the past two days, though the faces constantly changed, watched them. Only Mamaroot had remained for the entire vigil, watching him, singing lullabies to babies Sunny thought might be grandchildren or even great-grandchildren, weaving vines into the many necklaces and bracelets her clan wore, and twining roots, pinecones, and other small forest items into the longer hair of the older children.

Rootstock came and went, watching, saying nothing. Sunny wasn't sure if any of the other brownies spoke English, but Rootstock hadn't answered any of his questions.

Ananth had come once to leave a huge basket filled with leather water bladders and some cheese and what he thought was probably smoked fish. The dragon had guaranteed him the stories about eating and drinking on this side of the Fold were so much "salamander sludge" and assured him that keeping himself hydrated would not affect his ability to go home when it was time.

Sadly, Ananth hadn't stayed long or answered any of his questions about Hakko other than to tell him Hakko was gone and that many of the Houses had sent their best hunters out after him. She hadn't been able to tell him any more about Emikku.

As for Emikku, there was no way to tell if he would ever wake up or if he would ever have enough magic to change to his human form. Or, Sunny had to admit to himself, if he would want to return to his weaker human form.

"Stay with him," Ananth had encouraged. "At least for a little while longer. If I know my wild one, then I know he feels you here, and that's good for him."

"Why are you helping me?"

"Because. Love is strong magic." Ananth smiled at him in that unnerving, sharp-toothed dragon way, and stretched out delicate wings to flap them about a bit. The gash was nothing more than a thin gold line twisting through the membrane now. When Sunny asked, he got a shrug. "I will fly again. Someday."

Sunny wondered if perhaps this would be one of those Bearers who went feral in the end. He hoped not. A little while after that, Ananth walked off along the clifftop to the path and disappeared over the edge, not even saying goodbye.

That was the last he'd seen of any of the dragons other than Emikku.

The brownies, though. They were curious. Sunny figured they were also afraid of the dragon he was leaning on. Or at least the older ones were. The younger ones seemed inquisitive more than anything.

"You can come out, you know," Sunny said, watching Rootstock, who crouched just in the shadows of the trees. "Even if he wakes, he wouldn't hurt you."

Rootstock pointed past Sunny and Emikku. "Dragon waste."

"Yeah, I get it. They did some pretty terrible things. But not Emikku." He didn't know exactly what they had done, but he'd ask Emikku. Eventually. He stroked his dragon's thick neck, still amazed at the glassy hardness of scales that shimmered with every colour of the sunrise. They should have felt cold to the touch but didn't. "In fact, none of the dragons alive now did the things that hurt your people," he guessed. He didn't know, but he got the feeling that all things considered, the dragons were young and foolish when compared with the dryads or even the brownies. He wondered if humans must seem like children to the old brownie.

"Waste," Rootstock said, a stubborn set to his jaw.

"They laid waste to your homes?"

Rootstock nodded.

"Emikku told me stories of captive salamanders. He said that was a long time ago. Before his time. That the dragons—most dragons—didn't keep them captive anymore. Wouldn't that limit the magic they can use?"

That got him a *harrumph* from Rootstock.

"I looked into their valley." Sunny waved at the cliff edge. "It's all stone. No green things." He tilted his head to one side. "I think maybe dragons can't grow plants very well."

"Burn and flame and dragon... short sight." Rootstock waved his arms. His chest heaved, and his moon eyes flashed. "Rock heads." He pounded his fist on the ground, making a few tiny pebbles jump. "No future think."

Sunny took a moment to parse that, but Rootstock went on before he could comment.

"Life-sucking hot. Water steamed. Rootstock—" He thumped his chest, then waved his arm behind him at his enthralled family. "—all Rootstocks fled. Under earth, under root. Start new and tree seeds and trickles. Small life." He plopped down on the earth, dug strong fingers into the hard, dry soil so it cracked and turned to powder under his touch. "Strong Rootstocks. Small life is big. Trees grow. Trickle to flood."

Sunny had to grin at that, watching as more and more brownies appeared from the trees behind the wrinkled, passionate little man. A flood of strong Rootstocks indeed.

"Dragon fools have land top. Brownies have earth. Life. Safe. Let dragons turn husk." But he lost some of his fire at that and looked troubled.

"You don't really mean that," Sunny said. "You don't want the dragons to die out and turn to husks. Not really."

Rootstock huffed, nostrils flaring. His wife folded herself cross-legged beside him and took his hand in hers. He said something to her in their rapid-fire pebble-and-leaf speech, and she frowned, glanced at Sunny, then turned back to her husband.

Her reply was equally rapid, gentler, more leaf-and-grass, but vehement.

He shook his head.

She thumped his arm and looked fierce.

He sighed.

"Best and other," Rootstock said, resigned. But he leaned over and kissed her cheek, patted her shoulder as he rose, then plodded out of the forest towards Sunny.

He didn't do much of anything, really. Just prodded Sunny to one side so he could grab hold of one of Emikku's spikes to pull himself up onto his shoulder. From there, he lay on his stomach, reached down, and slipped a hand under one of the plates of Emikku's armour. He grimaced, muttered "hot hell," and pushed farther.

"Ah!" He smiled grimly and reached back to Sunny, wagging his hand until Sunny realised he wanted Sunny to take it, then drew Sunny close to lean awkwardly between Emikku's spikes.

"Here," Rootstock said and shoved Sunny's hand under the armour guarding Emikku's chest.

The heat was excruciating. Sunny yelped and sweat broke out over his back. He tried to pull away, but Rootstock was a strong creature, and he pushed Sunny's hand deeper.

Then he felt it: a cool spot deep in Emikku's chest. It pulsed in time with his breaths, slow, steady, but not strong. It was like a void. There was nothing to touch. Like Emikku had emptied himself of something in order to change into this impenetrable—or nearly impenetrable—being.

"What is that?" Sunny wiggled his fingers but felt only that palpable nothing.

"Dragon-heart," Rootstock murmured.

"There's nothing there."

"Love. And magic."

Sunny's heart cracked. Emikku had done this, sacrificed his own magic, his own love, to save his brothernest-mate from going down a road that would have destroyed him. "Well, then."

Sunny reached deeper as Rootstock withdrew. He curled his fingers around the nothing and squeezed, as though force of will could keep it from getting any bigger.

"Take my heart, Emikku." He snorted at himself. Like he hadn't already given the dragon his heart. "Keep it. It's not a lot of magic, but it's all the magic I have."

He took a moment to imagine that cold void he'd closed in his fist transforming into golden light even brighter than the Fold itself, and hotter than the sunshine they had played with after their first time together. He remembered what he'd said to Emile that day. *"...Alive like this. Like if you reached out you could touch the sunshine. Cup it and hold it and form it into dreams that you can make come true. You know?"*

He'd thought then that Emile would think he was nuts, or a hopeless romantic. "You're my dream come true, Emile," he whispered. "I'm not ready for it to end." He imagined all that light leaking out between his fingers to fill the void he couldn't see. As insubstantial as hope, as intangible and as ruthless, it bled into Emikku's chest to simmer and heat him from the inside out.

Beneath him, Emikku gave a great shudder, then went still again.

Sunny withdrew, sliding his hand down the hard scales, a last, lingering touch. "You know where to find me when you can," Sunny told his dragon. "I can't leave Daisy behind. She's not ready." After moving to Emikku's head, Sunny kissed his muzzle. "Under the willow," he whispered.

When he straightened, the sun was slanting towards setting. The brownies stood on the cliff, watching the dragon. Emikku glowed as though the full light of the noon sun still bathed him. His scales held jealously to that light, though this body remained nearly motionless.

"You have to help them, Rootstock." Sunny turned to the eldest brownie. "I know they don't understand what they did. They don't know everything. But Ananth and Emikku, they aren't bad. They need teachers, and I bet brownies know more, are older and much wiser than the oldest, wisest dragon."

Rootstock huffed, his expression declaring that the obvious truth.

"I know. It's scary. So is leaving him here."

Rootstock reached for Sunny's hand and led him towards the trees. When he was under the branches, he looked back. Emikku's scales blended with the sunset until he was nearly invisible, just a shimmer on the very edge of the world. Like a dream that had almost come true.

AT THE far side of the ancient cedar grove, Sunny stopped by the fallen tree. He searched until he found a handful of viable seeds. The Rootstock clan watched in silence as Sunny knelt, poked a finger-sized hole in the soft earth near the torn ground at the tree's ripped roots, then dropped a seed into the hole. He pushed the dirt back over the seed, wishing with all that was left of his heart that it would be enough for the dryad to cling to until a new tree was born.

"I know it's not a lot."

Rootstock patted his shoulder. "Seed and Tree. Trickle to flood." He nodded sagely, laid a hand over the pocket of hope, then motioned to the willow tree across the clearing.

"Yeah. Time for me to go home." His smile was hard to force and quick to slide away. "Thank you for your help."

Another pat from Rootstock, and then Sunny was wading through the little rill at the edge of the clearing, blinded by the light and heat and chill of the void, then stepping through to soft, dry moss on the other side.

If he'd expected dryads and water sprites to greet him, he was disappointed. But only partly, because he found Daisy lying under the tree, her head propped on Glimmerleaf's side, Fernforest curled against her ribs. She was reading a book, tipping the pages towards the fading light.

"Hey," Sunny whispered.

All three of them tackled him, and for a short time, it was enough to stave off his heartbreak.

CHAPTER 34

A CONSTANT patter of pebbles fell to earth, leaves rustled, breezes wafted through tall grasses. It had been going on for a while now, even though no breeze rustled his feathers. Although sunk in an inky darkness, the feeling of warmth brushed over him occasionally, and the sense of light wound through the black voids deep inside. The weave of light and dark followed no discernible pattern, but even when it seemed the light was distant, cold, it never truly left.

Weight pressed down on every breath, forcing the air into a thin stream. Sometimes he thought it might almost be easier not to take the next breath. Then that light, like a thousand pricks of energy, would make him gasp, air would rush into his chest, and he was *he* again.

He jerked upright, forcing weakened forelegs to push upward, to fight through the sharp agony of pins and needles as blood rushed back into his extremities.

Around him came the hard clatter of stones on granite and the shrill whistle of wind through treetops, the rush of hurricanes through grass… and the distinctive patter of feet and *pop* of displaced magic.

Then silence.

A hushed, held breath.

He heaved, but he had no strength. The scales were too much, too heavy for weakened limbs, and he shuddered, curled his shoulders, *willed* them away, even as he tried again to force his feet under him.

His heart thundered. Magic flooded, uncontrolled, the lash of a sharpened whip through his being. Scales fell away, glass and steel raining down around him, and then he was standing in the midst of their brittle remains. Brilliant yellow feathers fluttered down to tangle in his aubergine, lemon-tipped hair. The flicker of iridescent pink and purple shimmered just under his skin. His nails glinted black and sharp in the morning light.

As he stood and gazed out across a valley at a brilliant blue horizon, streaks of fuzzy peach morning softened the glare, lightened the shadows to a silvery gossamer veil, then burned off the night to reveal his city glowing in the very first and best light of day.

A shuffle behind him caught his attention. Afraid if he moved to quickly or too far he might collapse, he swivelled his head to look.

A brownie, freckled face lined with years and wisdom, stared up at him. His expression was determined and fierce. He pointed an almost accusing finger up at him. "Sunny. Best and other."

Emikku tipped his head, feeling the soft fall of his hair over bare skin. "Sunny," he repeated, touching his chest where a thin line of gold bisected his body from navel to collarbone.

"Best and other," the brownie repeated, poking his finger through the air again. "Gave magic. Dragon live." He stomped a foot. "Rootstock help Sunny. Dragon…." He narrowed his eyes as though he'd just asked a question and wanted an answer.

"Sunny." That word—no, the name—meant something important. He ran his fingertips down the delicate line of gold, remembered the touch of other fingers, felt the magic of *other* reaching deep into his soul, drawing him back, filling the void within.

"Sunny saved me." The brownie—Rootstock, apparently— grunted. "I didn't know brownies had names."

The brownie rattled at him like stones down a dry riverbank, huge eyebrows drawing down over his furious eyes. It took a moment for Emikku to recognise that he was being soundly rebuked, only in a language he hadn't even understood *was* a language until that moment.

"We have a lot to answer for." He frowned as the memories of an entire race paraded, dim, half-understood shadows, through his mind. Dragons had so much to answer for.

Rootstock crossed his arms over his chest with a little huff and flare of his nostrils.

"We do have much to answer for, my wild one." The new voice, accompanied by a soft susurration of delicate scale and clink of claw on stone, brought sharper, more vibrant memories to the fore.

He turned to face the golden dragon gliding up over the lip of the cliff. The deep rainbow glow of growing eggs illuminated their abdomen, and they gazed warmly at him for a moment before turning their attention to the brownie. "Your human has opened a door for us we should never have closed." They bowed slightly. "Good morning, Rootstock."

"My human." He studied the pretty dragon, trying to focus on the bright memories of other places, smaller cities, wild ocean, stretches of sand…. He recalled the whirring, comforting sound of wings overhead, the flash of light and dark as a dragon whirled in the sky, racing him as he sped along the ground, his own small wings not up to the task of lifting his heavily scaled form into the sky. "Ananth," he said finally.

Ananth's smile was toothy but relieved. "Yes."

More memories flooded him then, of Hakko's strong will, his determination, and yes, his pride. He had never been gentle. For an instant, Emikku felt the bulk of his own dragon self—scales, feathers, spikes, and claws—settle on his shoulders. He shrugged it off. Emikku was painful right now. Lost. Cast from the protection of a Sire he hadn't trusted.

He gazed at Ananth. "Hakko?"

"Gone."

He pulled a breath in through his nose, the scent of his home flooding his senses. There was… something missing. Something necessary that he had to dig deep to remember.

"Emile," he whispered. And his skin snugged around him, a velvet softness of longing as he remembered Sunny, Sunny's touch, his voice, his soft sighs and his strong, sweet hands. Emile looked up at Ananth. "I have to go."

AN ENTOURAGE of silver-skinned, big-eyed brownie children followed him through the watching cedar forest. He felt the dryads in the shadows of their trees, but none of them showed their faces. When he reached the far side and the giant trunk of the fallen tree, he slowed.

Near the roots, a sapling, spindly but vibrantly green, reached upward to the sun filtering through the hole in the canopy. A wisp of a presence crouched in the cavern of the old root system of the downed tree. A tentative connection between the ephemeral dryad and the new tree made the air shimmer. As he neared it, Emile felt the same connection, like the magic that had filled his empty spaces had encouraged this tree to break through the soil and reach out to the dryad.

"Sunny," he whispered and picked up his pace.

He was over the tiny creek and through the fabric of the Fold in another instant, emerging, as he had once before, into a land that felt a little colder, a little plainer, a little duller than the one he was used to.

This time, though, the faintest of golden threads stretched between his heart and the central glow of the magic that had brought him—the dryad, this *place*—back to life. He sped once more, ignoring the sharp stab of rock and root at his feet, the careless slap of branches against bare skin, the chill drops of old rain that splashed off the wet leaves into his face.

As he neared the creek that ran along the far edge of the poplar grove, he smelled something so familiar, so like home, it slowed his pace. Along the bank of the creek, in a ragged row, were a dozed knee-high cedar trees. They were different than the ones he had first sheltered under when he'd arrived. They were obviously younger, but they had the scent of magic in every cell.

They didn't have dryads, but as Emile ran the flat leaves through his fingers, he could feel the stirrings of sentience, the first burgeoning of *self* deep in the trees' hearts. It might be years before the trees grew strong enough to support that kind of life outside their own rough skins, but he thought eventually they would become aware of their own potential.

Curled protectively around the thin trunks of the tiny grove, Glimmerleaf slept peacefully. His colour had returned to the shimmering depths of green and teal it was meant to be, and the flakiness around his eyes and nose was less. Thin white curls of smoke rose from his nostrils with every exhale, and a light blanket of soft white ash dotted the land around him.

"Of course." Emile had changed to his dragon form to try to carry Glimmerleaf across the creek to the cedars, hoping that would help him recover. That had been his undoing, when Hakko had appeared, his pheromones magically enhanced to snare him. "But Sunny came for me." He ran a hand down the salamander's neck. "Just like he came back for you."

Glimmerleaf grunted in his sleep. His tongue flicked out to lick at his lips, but he remained quiet. The air of peace in the grove calmed Emile's racing heart, reminded him that this place, everything about it, belonged to Sunny. That included Glimmerleaf, magical creature that he was. He was safe here because he had accepted Sunny's touch.

The thought made Emile grin. He could still feel Sunny's touch deep in his being. Sunny had thought he was giving up his magic—his heart—to save Emile.

Only that wasn't how magic worked.

Like so many other things that were hard to define, impossible to explain, it worked much better, grew exponentially stronger, when given freely. That was why Glimmerleaf stayed, why the dryads had awakened, and why Fernforest trusted Sunny so completely.

Sunny had touched them all. He loved them all.

Emile heard Fernforest barking and padding along the path long before he saw him. As soon as the dog spied him, his tail waved so ferociously his entire body waggled in a merrily drunken line towards Emile. A wave of relief washed over him.

"I'm coming," he half laughed as Fernforest jogged up to him, butted his head against his shin, then shimmied around behind him to herd him the rest of the way towards the creek and the little bridge spanning it into Sunny's yard.

The instant he stepped foot onto the bridge, the door to the little house at the top of the slope burst open. Before he'd reached the other side, Sunny had him in his arms.

"You woke up," Sunny whispered against his skin. "You woke up."

Any reply seemed too obvious to utter, so Emile simply held on to his lover and revelled in the way his magic fluttered, flared, then settled, linked to Sunny's in a way he would never have thought possible.

"Come inside," Sunny said after a moment. "Please. You don't have to stay, but—"

Emile gripped Sunny's chin, turning his face so he could cover his mouth in a kiss that promised much more than simply staying. The circuit of magic between them melded and flared once more, burning brighter than anything Emile had ever felt on his own side of the Fold.

It ignited a heat that was far more immediate than just magic, so when Sunny stepped back and took his hand, Emile followed willingly into the house and up to Sunny's bed.

THEIR LOVEMAKING burned fast and hot and died out quickly, leaving them both sweaty and sated and tangled in the sheets.

"I guess lying in the sun regenerating your magical core kind of takes it out of a guy, huh?" Sunny said as they lay in his bed, both naked, with sun streaking across their bodies and a light breeze floating the scents of late summer through the room. He was so overwhelmed to have Emile back, he didn't want to jinx it with too many questions or by bringing up all his worries. But there were so many questions. So many worries.

"I suppose it does." Emile stroked Sunny's face, pulling his thumb repeatedly along his eyebrow as if he was trying to smooth out the tiny wrinkles.

"I thought maybe…." Sunny frowned, and Emile leaned in to kiss the spot between his eyebrows. His hand was warm on the side of Sunny's jaw, his breath sweet wafting down over his face. "You were so still. I didn't know if—"

"I'm here now." The blankets behind him rustled. His scales glinted in the sunlight, a swath of darker pink glimmer just under the milky skin along his hip.

Sunny reached over to caress the spot. Heat warmed his fingertips, and he sighed. He couldn't feel the pattern of scales under his palm. None of the rigid, glass-like sharpness of when Emile was fully dragon translated, even though Sunny could clearly see the outline of each delicate plate.

"Can you transform?" he asked. "Or, change? Shift? Whatever you call it?"

Emile chuckled and the blankets shifted once more. The very tip of Emile's tail stroked the back of Sunny's hand, and Emile leaned in to kiss him again.

A lot of kissing and touching later, after the sun had moved to throw shadows on the far wall and Sunny was feeling languid and relaxed despite his semihard dick, he found himself staring up into eyes too brilliant blue to be human, too intense to look away.

"Can you stay?" Because of all the questions and worries he had, that was the only one that mattered.

"You don't mind that I have scales?"

"I think they're pretty."

Emile raised one elegant eyebrow, and Sunny's face heated.

"Thank you." He kissed Sunny's forehead, then snuggled down until his head was on Sunny's shoulder and his arm, a leg, and his tail wrapped around Sunny. "There's no reason for me to go back, Sunny."

"You'll have to bring Glimmerleaf back. Eventually. He can't stay here."

"He likes it here."

"He's... hard to explain. I mean, if anyone were to see him."

Emile chuckled. "Fortunately you're a recluse, so no one will come calling who will need an explanation."

"And Daisy already knows about him."

"Hmm. Daisy. I'll get to meet her soon, yes?"

Sunny chuckled. Daisy had called more than a few times, demanding to know what was happening and why she hadn't been invited back. She was obviously as curious about Emile as she was worried about Sunny. But she had sworn to him that she would never spill their secrets, just as long as she got to see Glimmerleaf again. She was that kind of awesome.

"She's coming for a visit on the weekend. She's been worried ever since I got back. I mean. Of course, she has. I thought I'd never see you again." Even with Emile curled around him with all the possessiveness of a dragon curled around his hoard, the cold pit of that possibility that had opened in Sunny's gut the instant he had stepped home through the Fold still hadn't closed.

"I'm here, Sunny. Hakko has vanished. Ananth will be busy with their eggs and the hatchlings when they come. Rokkan's rule will go easier without me there to remind the other Houses what the Sires of Corcaird tried to do." He smiled sadly but kissed Sunny's temple. "There is no other place for me to be than here with you. No other place I want to be."

"And so you'll be here when Daisy comes this weekend." For some reason saying it out loud made it more substantial.

"How long is that?"

"I'll show you a calendar tomorrow."

"A what?"

Sunny leaned his cheek against the top of Emile's head and closed his eyes. "Everything, Emile. I'll show you everything. Later." For now he was content to have his dragon back in his bed, and his dog and his salamander curled cozily together out in the cedar grove. And there was a dryad at the end of his driveway pushing blooms out of his rose bush any time Sunny smiled at it, and water sprites splashing in the creek at the end of his lawn. Beyond that, he caught occasional glimpses of the poplar dryad, and he was sure there were smaller, more timid pine spirits as well. He hadn't dared approach the willow tree, but he had no doubt she was still there, waiting and guarding the passage between worlds.

The matters of his unnaturally robust garden and the nightshade that had well and truly taken over his bridge were interesting. He suspected it was more than his love for the land that encouraged the plants to grow so happily. Later he would have to ask Emile if it was possible that brownies had tunnelled under the Fold to set up house with his front yard as their roof. It would explain why everything was thriving so wonderfully.

As he sank towards a contented sleep of his own, it occurred to him that he'd come a long way from the city to find his solitude. Instead he was surrounded by more life than anyone would ever believe. He chuckled to himself. Hadn't Mom always told him there was magic in the natural world and all he had to do was believe it was there?

He held Emile close. If believing in magic had brought him all of this, made the dream of the home he'd wanted come true, then believing in love had brought Emile back to him.

"Are you all right?" Emile asked.

"I am now," Sunny whispered. He felt the bond between them heat and knew he didn't have to say the words of love for Emile to feel it and know the truth.

JAIME SAMMS has been published since the fall of 2008, although she's been writing for herself far longer. Often asked what's so fascinating about stories where men fall in love with other men, she's never come up with a clear answer. Just that these are the stories that she loves to read, so makes sense they are also be the stories she loves to write.

These days, you can find plenty of free reading on her website in addition to her stories scattered across several publishers.

Spare time—when it can be found rolled into a ball at the back of the dryer or cavorting with the dust bunnies in the corners—is probably spent crocheting, drawing, or watching movies. She also loves to garden, weather permitting, since she is Canadian! She has a day job, which she loves, and two kids, but thankfully she also has a wonderful husband who keeps her fed and caffeinated.

She graduated some time ago from college with a Fine Arts diploma and a major in textile arts, which basically qualifies her to draw pictures and create things with string and fabric. One always needs an official slip of paper to fall back on, after all….

Website: jaime-samms.com
Facebook: www.facebook.com/profile.
php?id=100000982219151&ref=tn_tnmn
Deviantart: dontkickmycane.deviantart.com
Twitter: @JaimeSamms
Amazon Author page: www.amazon.com/author/jaimesamms

JAIME SAMMS

LIKE NO ONE IS
WATCHING

DANCE, LOVE, LIVE

Dance, Love, Live: Book One

Dusty has finally landed a job he thinks he'll be able to keep long-term, even with his broken brain and bum knee. He didn't anticipate that cleaning a dance studio would reawaken his yearning to dance—even though he is no longer capable—or that meeting the studio's director would rouse his dormant libido. Or his sleeping heart.

Conrad thinks his life is finally complete with his successful dance studio and a steady stream of students. When Dusty arrives, he rediscovers his thirst for a man who will let him hand over control and give him the undivided attention he's never had. The trouble is, Dusty isn't sure he's worthy of the studio director's submission.

To make their relationship work, Dusty will have to trust his ability to dominate the powerful and beautiful dancer, and Conrad will have to stop talking long enough to hear Dusty's promises.

www.dreamspinnerpress.com

PERMANENT
INK

JAIME SAMMS

Beauty is only skin deep, but some marks—and what they represent—are impossible to escape.

Eric resents his comfortable college life and the restrictions his family's expectations put on him. Dwayne, his best friend Angel's cousin, is a pierced and tattooed ex-con trying to rebuild his life. Eric sees only the tattoos and the way Dwayne's upbringing have dictated his future. It takes a surprising revelation from Angel to force Eric to see past Dwayne's defenses to the generous heart beneath and to realize it's time for him to break free of his own instilled beliefs. The men can't keep apart, and they gradually learn that everything they thought they knew about each other might be wrong.

Opposites attract as two men from very different backgrounds move from enemies to lovers in a story of understanding, compassion, and redemption.

www.dreamspinnerpress.com

www.ingramcontent.com/pod-product-compliance
Lightning Source LLC
Chambersburg PA
CBHW071005280626
47160CB00015B/1399